Task
Force
Nightshade

A J Huston

AJ Huston

Task Force Nightshade

Copyright A J Huston 2013

First Published by MTM Group

ISBN 978-0-9576696-1-1

Cover design © Matthew Sergison-Main

www.taskforcenightshade.com

Eleven and Three Quarters

And a Dot.

CHAPTER ONE

Present Day

Will Richards was staring out of his office window straightening a paperclip when the telephone rang. He glanced at it and looked away, uninterested and indifferent, preferring to study the highly prominent ridges in most of his fingernails. He looked back at the paperclip and threw it on his desk, an unpleasant memory prompting him to frown. From his desk he could see two mounted soldiers of the Household Cavalry on guard in Whitehall, outside Horseguards Parade. It was raining and they were wearing their capes. Even so, there were still enough tourists to block the pavement for people who wanted to pass by. Will watched as a blonde girl wrote her mobile number on a page in her diary, tore it out and tucked it in the Trooper's riding boot. The soldier made a spirited effort to keep staring forwards but eventually buckled and glanced at her. He smiled, and so did she as she walked away arm-in-arm with her girlfriend. From his vantage point in the Old War Office Building, Will smiled too, knowing exactly what would happen that evening. Doubtless something much more exciting than he would be getting up to.

The phone was still ringing. The ringtone was the double ring of an outside line, but the digital display showed the number was blocked. Will looked at it again, put the straightened paperclip on his bin and blew air through his lips. He would have waited for the call to go through to voicemail except he had only had his desk at the Defence Intelligence Staff for three days, and hadn't bothered to set it up yet. Will had done very little in his first three days at the DIS; he was bored and didn't want to be there. Boxes of pencils, pens, writing pads and other assorted office paraphernalia remained unopened on his desk.

The phone continued to ring. It was beginning to irritate him more than actually having to speak to someone might do, so he lifted the receiver.

"Hello," he said, knowing it was an external number and deliberately not identifying himself or his office.

"Who's this?" came the response.

Will put the phone straight back down. If people didn't know who they were calling he was singularly uninterested in speaking to them. He spun around in his chair and looked out of the window again. It was a late afternoon in December and the light was already beginning to fade. The rainclouds didn't help. The civil servants of Whitehall were already heading home, rushing for the London Underground under their collective tent of umbrellas. Will's phone rang again, and this time he didn't even bother to look at it. He stared at the rain-soaked pavement of Whitehall, and made the executive decision to go to the toilet.

He actually enjoyed the walk, almost because it gave him something to do other than sit in his office not answering his phone, and not responding to asinine emails about human resources policy issues or mission statements. Shit like that bored and angered Will in equal measure. As he walked along the marble-floored and wooden-panelled corridor at least half a dozen civil servants came out of their offices, umbrellas in hand, raincoats folded over their arms. Four of them failed to make eye-contact, one did and smiled, almost apologetically, one actually came out with, "Goodnight".

Will glanced at his watch, it was just past four o'clock, and he hated them for it. But then he saw a mental image of his own desk, the unopened correspondence and the stationery still in its cellophane wrapping. Perhaps he should not be so quick to judge. Perhaps these people who were rushing home to their families or to the pub to meet with friends for a drink had as much interest in sitting in the Defence Intelligence Staff as he did. Which was not very much.

Will returned from the toilet to find an exceptionally composed man standing in his office, although he clearly had something he wished to talk about. Will had no idea who this man was.

"Major Richards?" the man asked quietly.

Will regarded him, noting that he was not wearing any identification at all, which was unusual for the DIS. That said, neither was Will, but he preferred not to on purpose because he enjoyed being deliberately wayward.

Will stood still, put his hands in his pockets and simply asked, "Who are you?"

"Sir," came the gently voiced response.

"Okay, not clichéd at all. Alright then, I'll try that again. Who are you?" Will asked, deliberately avoiding the term of address.

"I'm the Security Service Liaison Officer, Major Richards. The one who only found out about your organisation this morning and the one who's been trying to get hold of you for most of the afternoon." The man looked over Will's desk, making a show of picking up some of the un-opened stationery and tossing it aside peremptorily. "You just back from some sort of top secret mission Richards?"

"No Sir, I've just been to the toilet."

"And what country was this particular toilet in? Albania?" The voice remained studiously calm.

"No Sir, just down the corridor, right out of this office and it's the first door after the water-cooler." Will's voice was as unwavering as a child answering an obvious question. His hands remained resolutely in his pockets.

"Two bloody hours the Security Service has been trying to get hold of you Major Richards."

"Would you like to sit down?" asked Will as his visitor began to lose the measured calm he had exhibited to begin with. "I really think you should sit down, and until you tell me your name, and what this is about, I shall be genuinely thinking about getting my coat and heading home."

The man took his wallet out and handed over a business card. The white card with embossed gold lettering read, "Lieutenant Colonel C R York, Adjutant General's Corps, Military Liaison Officer to the Security Service."

"Thank you Sir. How can I help?"

"Someone, apparently connected to your organisation, whatever that actually is, has caused a stir at the Chinese Embassy."

"Okay, well that's interesting." Will took his hands out of his pockets and sat down on the incredibly uncomfortable government issue sofa in his office. Then he stood up again and carefully closed the door. "How do you know he's connected to my organisation," he asked.

"She," Lieutenant Colonel York corrected him. "Five are unimpressed," he said, referring to one of the Security Service's many unofficial monikers. "They received a call from the Chinese Embassy earlier today saying if the British Government wants to stitch them up could they possibly try to do it with a bit more style. The Chinese were actually affronted by the amateurishness of what happened."

"Sir, I'm afraid I still don't know what you're talking about."

"Are you trying some sort of entrapment operation? Because if you are, you don't have the authorisation to do so, and we will shut you down." The Colonel said with a hint of threat in his tone.

"Hang on a second. We?" Will's forehead creased with confusion.

"The Security Service."

Will looked again at the business card. "But you're in the army aren't you Sir? You're not actually in the Security Service."

"I am attached to the Security Service Major, and as such I speak for them." Colonel York emphasised the word 'attached' as if it meant he had passed some sort of elite selection process. Will knew better.

"Right. Okay. Well, do you want to tell me what's actually happened and I'll see if it's anything to do with us or if this is all a big misunderstanding. Why don't we take a walk to Thames House eh?" he asked, referring to the London headquarters of the organisation. And you can take me through it all." Will got up from the sofa, grabbed his jacket from the hook on the back of the door and walked to his desk. He took a key from his inside jacket pocket, unlocked the hard-drive from his computer and put it in the wall-mounted safe. Then he took a key out of the side of his encrypted telephone and put that in the safe too. Finally, he put the key he'd used to unlock the hard drive in the safe, along with the unopened correspondence that sat in his in-tray. Then he closed it and spun the electronic lock. "Can't be too sure," he said to the Colonel, before adding, "and security really get their knickers in a twist if they find anything left out".

Will indicated the door. "Shall we?" he asked the Colonel and they left the office. As he closed the door, Will took a card from his wallet, swiped the reader, and entered a code on the digital pad. The distinct sound of electronic locking bolts sliding into position could be heard.

"Well, they really have looked after you, haven't they?" the Colonel asked.

"I insisted on it. You never know who might walk in," Will replied, with a wink.

The green LED on the reader turned red. The sign on the door next to it simply stated, "Room 304 - Contingency Planning Group".

As they walked down the corridor Will could almost feel the Colonel's desire to tell him what had happened. He was clearly feeling very important, something he probably didn't feel very often while walking the corridors of Thames House. How on earth this man was the military liaison officer to the Security Service was a mystery to Will. He could only assume it was because his own people didn't want him anywhere near them and got him the posting. And precisely what background and experience qualified an Adjutant General's Corps officer for the post of liaison officer between the Security Service and Military Intelligence was also an enigma. But Colonel York's presence was not what concerned Will at that point, it was why MI5 had sent him rather than contacting Will directly, and how on earth the Contingency Planning Group had come up in whatever this affair was, because Will knew his organisation wasn't running any operations against the Chinese.

Colonel York turned left at a junction in the corridor as if to go down the main stairs. "Sorry, I don't go that way," was Will's response. "If you'll follow me Sir?" he asked.

"Where are you going Richards?"

"Back door Sir."

"What back door? There is no back door."

Will kept walking and York followed, clearly irritated by the lack of further explanation. They arrived at a service lift and Will called it. It was old and filthy, but also had a swipe-card reader by the buttons. Clearly no-one was going anywhere without clearance. Will put his card through it and pressed

'Basement 2'. "Where on earth are we going Richards? For crying out loud."

"Department of Health Sir."

"Department of Health? What is going on Richards?"

The lift opened in one of the basements of the Defence Intelligence Staff and Will walked out directly and turned left. The corridor was slightly dank and had a myriad of ducts, cabling and pipework following the walls and ceiling. "Mind your head, there are a couple of low bits," said Will. From time to time there were reinforced steel doors off the side of the corridor. None gave any indication of what was behind them. They simply had alpha-numeric denominators such as C-1134 or J-1354 stencilled on the middle of the door.

"Richards? Richards? What the hell is going on?" The Colonel was getting agitated. "Where the hell are we and where are you going?"

"Thames House Sir, as I said, it's just that I've got a bit of an aversion to walking out the front door of this place." Will skipped over a piece of pipework on the floor. "You'll want to watch that," he advised, without looking back or pointing at the obstruction.

In the dim light ahead of them, Will could make out the figure of a man with a torchlight coming towards him. "Hello Billy," he called.

"Hello Will, how you doing?" came the response.

"Not too bad mate. Just glad I'm not up there in the rain."

"Fair one. Me too. No doubt see you later," said the torch-carrying Billy as he squeezed past in what had now clearly become a service passage. "Evening," he nodded to Colonel York, and disappeared into the gloomily lit tunnel where Will and the Colonel had come from.

York's voice raised a little. "Who the hell was that?"

"Billy, I think."

"What does he do?" asked the Colonel.

"I have absolutely no bloody idea," Will replied.

"Well how do you know his name?"

"I asked him," came the simple response. "Come on Sir, time and tide and all that. The passages under Whitehall are deceptively longer than you might expect."

The Colonel was beginning to lose patience, Will could tell even in the low light. "You've been in this job for less than a week, and you're wondering around in tunnels under Whitehall speaking to complete strangers and not actually asking what they do!"

"Yes Sir." Will kept walking.

"How did you get this job? And what kind of security risks do you think are acceptable Major?" The Colonel's earlier measured calm was becoming replaced with frustration and indignation.

"Sir, you're the Military Liaison Officer to the Security Service?"

"Yes."

"Do you think there's a reason why Billy and I know about these tunnels and you don't." Will stopped and turned to what looked like a cleaner's cupboard, took out a triangular shaped key and opened the door. "Shall we?" he asked again.

The lift took them up to one of the back corridors of the Department of Health, some distance down Whitehall from the Defence Intelligence Staff in the Old War Office Building. There was a small CCTV monitor next to the lift buttons. Will waited while two women walked past and then opened the inner door. Using the same triangular key he opened the outer door and pulled the Colonel clear of the lift before locking both doors quickly. "Off we go," he chirped.

Following Will's lead, the two men headed for the main entrance on Whitehall. "I don't understand," York stammered. "What's going on?"

"Well, I hate surprises, you're a surprise and I'm not a big fan of the front door of the Defence Intelligence Staff either. There's a bus stop opposite and lots of people take photographs. Although, to be honest, it's the ones who sit there and don't take photographs who concern me the most. And there's quite a few of them. I like to keep things nice and simple. No-one in the press or foreign intelligence communities really gives a toss about this place."

As they crossed the reception lobby a civilian security guard nodded at Will. "Evening Mr. Will, have a great night." The Caribbean accent was strong.

"You too Clement. Take care." The sentiment was genuine.

As Will and Colonel York left the Department of Health they were bathed in a sea of television camera lighting and a plethora of paparazzi camera flashes. They had walked straight into the background of a press conference that a junior Health Minister was holding on the steps.

"Brilliant work Major Richards," said York as he shoved his hands into his coat pockets and lowered his head, quite conspicuously. Will walked on regardless.

"Thank you Sir. Takes years of practice to stuff things up quite this impressively. Let's just keep walking shall we?" Will put his arm around Colonel York's back and artfully guided him to the roadway. No-one paid any attention to them.

They walked the short distance to MI5's London base in total silence. As they entered the lobby the Colonel approached the security reception desk, producing his ID card and asking for Will to be allowed through.

"No need," said Will chirpily as he pulled his own card out and swiped himself through one of the revolving plastic security doors. The Colonel followed, clearly slightly put out that Will had access to the building. "So who was it exactly that asked you to come looking for me?" he asked. He had nearly used the word 'sent' but knew this would have irritated the Colonel, and his brain was now trying to compute whatever it was that was going on, rather than prepare for verbal sparring.

"The Director General herself," came the sober reply.

Will grinned broadly. "Oooh!" he said, "this should be exciting," masking his own concerns.They stepped out of the lift on the third floor and walked to Anne Tremaine's office. The pretty young PA in the outer room recognised Will immediately and stood up as he entered, smiling warmly. "Will! I haven't seen you for ages, where have you been?"

"Hiding," he responded playfully while shaking her hand. "What you been up to?"

"Oh, nothing much, it's all a bit dull around here. Spies, spies, terrorists, spies. You know, usual thing."

Will indicated the door. "Can we go in Sue?"

"Yes, she interrupted her last call when your card came up on the reader."

"Now, that is cool, isn't it?" Will said to the Colonel, turning to the door.

"Except," Sue rushed out, and looking apologetically at the Colonel added, "just you Will."

The Colonel wore the same expression of disappointment he had had in reception, reluctantly taking a seat in the outer office. "I should be getting used to this by now," he added, finally smiling. "Twenty-five years of service just to be an errand boy."

Will walked into the Director General's office and shut the door behind him. "Anne, what the hell is going on?" he asked incredulously. "What's all this sending a military liaison officer to get me about? Why didn't you just pick up the damn phone? That one there," he added, pointing at Anne's large mahogany desk, "you know, the red one, the one that Inspector Gordon uses in Batman. I've got one too, I'd have picked it up."

Anne Tremaine was not in the mood for humour. "Sit down Will. We've got a problem."

"I'm so glad my name isn't Houston," he quipped.

"Yes, you're funny," she said, "but what happened today isn't".

"York said something about the Chinese Embassy."

"Indeed." Tremaine took half a dozen A4 sized CCTV stills from her desk and handed them to Will. "You recognise her?" she asked. The images were just outside the entrance to the rather grand Chinese Embassy in Portland Place.

Will paused. "Are you kidding me? These are black and white traffic camera images, she's wearing a hoody and a baseball cap and the camera's got to be at least twenty feet up a pole. I can't recognise the top of a girl's head that I can't even see anyway. That's even if she is a girl." Will looked up, his face clearly indicating confusion.

"I know she's a girl because the Chinese Ambassador rang me up himself and told me she was."

"Fair enough," said Will, "I think it's fair to say we can go with that then. So what's she done and what are the Chinese so upset about?"

"You see that satchel she's carrying?"

"Yes," said Will, sounding like he was being patronised, "of course". He raised his hands in the air, as if to ask, "And?"

"Well in it are more than a dozen pages of a highly classified British government document outlining a five year business development strategy with, guess who, China's best friend in the world, Taiwan."

"Ooh," said Will, serious now as he rested back in his seat.

"Precisely. Ooh," Anne replied.

"You want me to find her?" asked Will.

"Yes. But there's more. Significantly more. The reason why I didn't shine a big light in the sky with your face on it is because we are now in a non-comms environment. I couldn't call you Will. This isn't just about a breach of national security," Anne looked grave. "It's now become about the Contingency Planning Group itself."

"I'm still confused," said Will, adding offhandedly, "actually, I've been a bit like that all day." He waved his hand, "it happens. But what did she actually do?" he asked.

"According to the Chinese Ambassador, she walked through the door, took the papers out of her satchel and spread them out on the receptionist's desk. Then she said she wanted to sell them for twenty thousand pounds."

"I think I know what's coming next," Will said, putting his head in his hands.

"Yes, I think you do. The receptionist, Yu-Jin Wong, who we know is actually employed by the Ministry of State Security and not the Chinese Foreign Office, immediately picked up the phone to her Head of Station, who promptly turned up in the lobby and looked at the documents without even touching them."

"Good skills," said Will, remembering his own training and the dangers of leaving fingerprints on things he shouldn't really be touching.

"Indeed. The HoS then used the same phone to call the Ambassador, who arrived shortly afterwards."

"Not a busy man then?" asked Will, sarcastically.

Anne was straightfaced, "I'm just getting to that," she said. "After they sent her away he called me and berated me for twenty minutes that he had been pulled out of an exceptionally important meeting with the Russian Defence Attache to respond to the clumsiest entrapment operation the Security Service had ever attempted."

"Was it?" asked Will directly.

Anne gave him the look she gave her seven year old daughter when she was pushing the limits of her patience. "Sorry," he said meekly. Then his face scrunched up again as he processed all the information, something he was particularly quick at. "Okay, I get all that," he said, "but I don't get the connection with the CPG," he added. "What am I missing?"

"Her name," Anne replied, meeting his gaze.

"I'm all anticipation here Anne..."

"Rebecca Taylor."

Will felt his pulse increase and his mouth went a little dry. "You have got to be shitting me," he said.

"It's late. I want to go home to my family, cook dinner and watch a film. Why would I make this up?" She paused. "As Miss Taylor left," she added, emphasising the name, "she said that if anyone wanted to get in contact with her they should use the personal ads in the Daily Herald."

"You have got to be shitting me," he repeated. "This is not a coincidence. Can't be."

"Nope. This is someone who wants to get the attention of the CPG. She is obviously smart, she knew what the Chinese response would be and she knows something about the organisation. Find her Will. Find her and find out what she wants. This is supposed to be the most covert capability this country has ever had, and this is precisely why we put this structure in place. You have become an incredibly expensive man in the last six months Will, now's the time to make it pay off."

"I've got to make a trip to Wapping haven't I?"

"Yes, you have. Don't use the name though, the Chinese will be looking for it."

Will looked aggrieved. "Oh please," he said, "I do crosswords, I'll figure something out." Anne looked at her watch, pointedly. "Okay, I'm going," he said as he stood up and left the office.

He waved goodbye to Sue, "Say hello to the cat for me."

Colonel York stood up and started walking with him. "Well?" he asked.

"Well thank you very much, Sir," Will replied. "I'm afraid I don't have much time, so have to fly."

York caught his shoulder. "Richards, how come you're unhappy to walk out of the Defence Intelligence Staff but quite happy to walk in the front doors of MI5?"

"Oh, I'm quite happy walking into these buildings Sir. It's the leaving bit when you tend to get caught on camera. I'm quite happy for people to take pictures of the back of my head." With that Will walked down the corridor, leaving York in a state of mild confusion as he slowly figured out what Will had said.

Will went subterranean again and emerged from a cleaner's cupboard in London Underground's Westminster station to catch a train to Tower Hill, the nearest station to Wapping. "This could be interesting," he thought to himself, as he approached the offices of the Daily Herald.

CHAPTER TWO

Earlier that day…

Hannah Roberts' alarm went off at six a.m., as it did every day except Sunday, when she allowed herself the indulgence of a lie-in until seven. She grabbed her dressing gown from the back of the bedroom door and walked the four paces to her tiny kitchen in her tiny rented flat in east London. At least it was convenient for work. She put the kettle on and stared out of the tiny window at the industrial wasteland that was being re-developed outside. This was not the way it was supposed to have turned-out.

Hannah was originally from Washington, but a summer tour of Europe when she was reading English at Harvard had captured her heart. London was the obvious place for her; she didn't speak any other European languages, but the thought of spending stolen weekends in Paris, Berlin and Rome was bewitching. The shelves in Hannah's flat were smothered in travel books, and the pinboard in her bedroom was covered with postcards she'd sent herself from around the continent. She hated herself for not having the self-discipline to learn French or German, Spanish or Italian, but secretly delighted in the fact that almost everyone she'd met on the continent spoke English.

The kettle had boiled and she made herself a cup of coffee. She put some pancakes in the microwave and got the maple syrup out of one of the two cupboards in the kitchenette. There were certain bits of America she just couldn't leave behind. Much as she loved London and, almost, all of its people, she could never reconcile herself to the tininess of the way the British lived. Yes, the holiday cottages were quaint and the traditional pubs were fun, but there just didn't seem any requirement to live like Hobbits.

After breakfast she changed into her running gear and ran the three miles to her desk at The Daily Herald in Wapping. She enjoyed running, especially at that time of the morning because there was so little traffic about. She loved the East-End. It was the old wharves and docks and the Victorian hospitals and schools and everything she didn't have back home. She supposed it was the contrast which she found so attractive.

Arriving at the newspaper offices, she showered and changed and walked up to her desk. While her career path as a Pullitzer prize winning journalist hadn't quite worked out, she did have the benefit of having the corner desk in the open plan offices of the fifth floor, meaning no-one could look over her shoulder and she could stare out over the Thames when she got bored. Which was often.

Hannah spent the first two hours of her day reading the morning papers and wishing she was the Berlin correspondent of The Times or Europe Today. She spent the next two hours going through an avalanche of emails which accumulated as fast they were taken care of. Then she went for lunch. Hannah always bought lunch at Franco's. There were two reasons for this. Franco made the best chicken wraps in St Katherine's Dock and he was also an outrageous flirt. Franco was old enough to be Hannah's father, but he was funny, and because he would often not charge her for the salad pot he put in the bag, or throw in a free drink that he hadn't mentioned, Hannah felt a strong sense of loyalty to him.

"Hello Signorina. You have a smile for me today?" he asked.

"Of course Franco," and Hannah put her hands together, cocked her head and smiled like a cherub.

"It not funny to tease an old man like that you know," Franco responded. "Okay, so chicken wrap yes?" He was already putting the ingredients together.

"You got any plans for the weekend Franco?" she asked.

"Yeah, shut down this bloody van, no deal with any bloody rude customer who take the piss and then I fancy running off with some eighteen year old girl."

"Oh Franco, you'll break my heart."

"You want this chicken wrap or not? I thought it was just English who were sarcastic. Now bloody Americans too? You been here too long."

Hannah looked out across the river and back to The Daily Herald offices. "You could be right there," she agreed.

Franco was finishing up with Hannah's lunch. "So, how many dead today?"

"Guess," she responded immediately, this time smiling naturally.

"Okay, it winter, winter normally quite good for dead people, I'd say twenty."

"Higher," she replied.

"Thirty?" he asked.

"Lower."

"Okay, okay, it not bloody TV show. Twenty three."

"Exactly right," she beamed at him.

"What else you got today?" he asked.

"Well we've got God again."

"Every day. I tell you, you so predictable. But because I win the lottery with twenty-three, you get free soda." Franco handed over the paper bag and winked at her. "So you got plans for the week-end? You going anywhere? Doing anything? Off with boyfriend?"

Hannah laughed. "Franco, you know I don't have a boyfriend. I'm saving myself for you. When you have the courage to ask me out..."

"You terrible. One day Missy, one day I'm gonna do it." He paused. "And then you'll learn about romance Italian style eh?"

"Take care Franco." And Hannah went back to her desk, smiling. Very little else of interest happened for much of that afternoon. She answered some more emails, took a few phone calls and watched, unusually, a Royal Navy destroyer sail down the Thames.

"Don't see that every day do you?" asked Ben, who had the desk opposite Hannah's. "What's that about?"

"Don't know," Hannah replied absent-mindedly. At the time she was checking to see what the weather for the week-end was going to be. She had seen adverts for the new open-air ice rink off The Strand and thought it looked fun, but only if it wasn't absolutely freezing. She had memories of ice-skating in

Washington as a teenager that had left her almost crying with the cold.

At half past five Hannah started packing her bag, ready to leave work. Then her desk-phone rang. This irritated her, because she was heading for drinks with her neighbour in a nearby pub and it had been a long week already and she really could just do with a Jack Daniels and Coke and a gossip. All the phones at the Herald had number recognition, and had it been any name she had recognised she would probably have ignored it. But it was Reception. Hannah could never remember ever being called by Reception. She lifted the handset.

"Miss Roberts?"

"Speaking," she replied.

"It's Jan from the front desk. There's a gentleman here asking to talk with you."

"What about?" Hannah asked.

"He won't say," answered the receptionist. "But he is quite insistent. I wouldn't let him up to the offices so he's just sitting in reception, waiting for you. There are three guys from security down here at the moment so there's nothing to worry about."

"Does this happen a lot?" Hannah asked.

"We're a newspaper honey, it happens about ten times a day."

"I'll come down," Hannah said, and replaced the phone. She left her bag where it was but kept her coat on. The lift stopped at a mezzanine floor above the lobby, with escalators running to it. She had a good look at the only man sitting in the lobby, wearing a long black coat over a smart suit. He was reading today's issue of the Herald and frowning.

Hannah walked down the escalator and towards him. He stood up as she approached.

"Hello. Hannah Roberts. How can I help you, Mr....?" she let it hang.

"Richards. Will Richards," he responded warmly, extending his hand, which she took. He showed her a business card with no contact details at all. It simply said "William Richards, Contingency Planning Group, Ministry of Defence", and he was clearly just showing it to her, it was not for keeps.

"I'm not sure what this is about but I think you may have the wrong person Mr Richards. I compile the Births, Deaths and Marriages for the Herald. If you want our defence correspondent...?"

"No, Miss Roberts. It's you I need to speak to. I'd like to make an announcement about a death."

"Oh. Oh, I see. I'm so very sorry. I misunderstood," she stammered.

"Oh no. Please. No need to be sorry. No-one's dead." He rolled his eyes at the ceiling, "At least not yet."

"What?"

"Complicated. I need to speak to you in person because I know you need to see a death certificate before you can publish. We don't have a death certificate and it takes a while to make one and we're in a dreadful hurry. We need to get this in tonight's edition."

"What are you talking about?" Hannah was, to say the least, very confused.

"I can understand that. Fair one. Look." Will took a phone out of his coat pocket and pulled up a number. "You see that name?" he asked.

"Yes."

"You recognise it?"

"Yes. It's Andrew Telfer, he owns the paper." Hannah stared at the phone. "Jesus Christ," she said slowly.

"We need this done tonight Hannah. It's very important. One button and you can call him. It's his private phone, not his work one. Give him my name and ask him what to do."

Hannah took the phone and stared Will straight in the eyes. Then she glanced across at the reception desk where Jan nodded to her. This was not something she was used to.

She called the number.

Andrew Telfer was being driven to a debate at the Oxford Union that evening when his phone rang. "Hello Will," he answered. "What the devil can I do for you? Has something exploded?" he asked, leaning back into the uncomfortably slidey seat of the London minicab which was the limit of the Union's travel budget.

Hannah recognised the voice immediately. "Umm, sorry, this might sound odd. My name is Hannah Roberts and I work the births, deaths and marriages announcements at the Daily Herald. A man called William Richards has just walked in to our reception and wants me to add an announcement of a death for tomorrow's paper. But he says that no-one's actually dead and there's no death certificate."

"Splendid. Well, if you've got Will Richards stood in front of you, please do whatever you can to assist him. He's a thoroughly good chap. Very important stuff."

Hannah ended the call and returned the phone. "That's not your real name is it? I'm not even a British citizen. I could get arrested for this. This is massively screwed up."

"More than you know. Please Hannah, help us out here." Hannah shook her head and turned away.

"I have no idea why I'm doing this, come on," she said as she walked back to the escalator. Will followed. "And if you think it's just because you've got pretty eyes you're wrong Mister, I'm still holding out for the Italian guy twice your age who owns the sandwich stall."

The open plan office was practically deserted as Hannah returned to her desk. "Is this some secret British spy stuff or are you a reporter doing something you shouldn't?" she asked.

"What do you think?" asked Will.

"I have no idea. This is a first for me." She logged into her computer and then looked at him, "So, anyway, what am I writing here? You have a maximum of 600 characters."

Will had been racking his brain all the way from Whitehall about the best way to phrase the announcement. "Okay, this is what I've got," he said, closing his eyes as he recalled the fiction he had constructed during the journey. "Becky Sower, that's Becky with a cee kay, not two cee's, 'Sower' as in person who sows seeds."

Hannah gave him a withering look.

"Peacefully in her sleep, today's date, blah, blah, blah, no flowers, donations to the Worshipful Company of Merchant Tailors. Funeral details on request."

"Maiden name?" she asked stonily, without looking up from the keyboard.

Will was caught on the back foot. "Umm, hadn't thought of that actually." He pondered for a moment, "Portland", he answered.

"Okay, that's all done. It'll make tomorrow's edition. Anything else you want me to do?" she asked.

"I expect you'll get a call tomorrow, asking for the details of the funeral. I would like you to hand me the phone when that happens."

"Weird," said Hannah, "I kinda expected you to be wired into it or something. You're gonna be here?" she asked.

"I'm staying with my sister tonight and she lives quite close, so it seems sensible. And I like the view," he said, looking out at the Thames. "Well, I think our business here is done Miss Roberts, thank you very much for your assistance, it's greatly appreciated. I'll see you tomorrow." He stopped and turned as he was leaving, "I'd be grateful if you didn't talk to anyone about this," he said.

And with that he left, leaving Hannah staring after him as he left the office. "Weirdsville," she said to herself, shutting her computer down and grabbing her bag. "I really do need a drink now."

CHAPTER THREE

Eight Months Earlier...

Miranda Stevens heard voices. Powerful, persuasive voices. She had never told anyone about them but she believed them and she acted on their instructions. They first started when she was fourteen, after the death of her parents in a coach crash. They were returning from a skiing holiday in Austria when the coach was hit from behind by a heavily loaded truck driven by an alcoholic. The coach hit the tunnel wall and flipped over, blocking both carriageways, and was then promptly hit by another truck coming the other way. Of the forty-eight passengers, only Miranda and one other survived. If Miranda had not been sitting right next to the emergency exit door she would have perished in the flames that later engulfed the tunnel, killing just over another two hundred people. As she ran for her life to the tunnel entrance, she saw the decapitated body of the driver, still held in place by his seatbelt.

But that felt like a long time ago now. Miranda was halfway through her second year studying Chemistry at King's College, London University. She was the standout student of her intake, although her tutors thought that she found it difficult to interact socially, both with them and her fellow students. The special project she was working on this year was pesticides. She had explained to Professor Traynor, her Director of Studies, that she wanted to make a real difference to crop yields in Africa. The year before had seen a horrendous decrease as a result of locust infestation, and Miranda was adamant that she could do something to help.

So it was that Miranda spent as much time in the College Library in Chancery Lane as she did in the laboratories in College. She felt compelled to understand the history of chemical science in the development of agriculture. Her compulsion was instigated by the voices she heard. There were three altogether, two female and one male. The male voice sounded similar to her father's, and one of the females' to her mother's. The third voice was almost identical to her own.

Not long after the accident Miranda had been in a history class and was learning about the development of chemical warfare from the mustard gas of World War One through to the supposed Weapons of Mass Destruction of the Second Gulf War. It was shortly afterwards that the voices started. Miranda had never come to terms with, and had never forgiven herself, for scrambling out of that coach in the Austrian tunnel. Neither of her parents were moving when she ran, but others were, and they were screaming. And then came the explosion and the fireball. And then the whole tunnel felt like a volcano in a tube as vehicle after vehicle smashed into each other and there was no way out. The image of the headless driver haunted her dreams regularly. Miranda cried herself to sleep most nights. And she had come to realise that she deserved to die, and so did as many other people as possible, because they DID NOT KNOW. Only when other people really knew would they understand, and Miranda was going to teach them, because she had been told to, by her mother, her father and herself.

Because of her studies on pesticides Miranda had a special pass to the restricted area of the library; the places where the criminal psychology students and various other assorted specialist researchers had access. There was no door but there was a librarian gate-keeper, who recognised her and waved her through an airport-style metal detector which would alarm if any of the electronically-tagged books was taken through it. These books were considered too dangerous to be liberated by students. The occult, abortion, pornography, child abuse – this really was the secret library of the seventh level of hell. And Miranda knew about that. She'd been there.

Just past the section on DNA reproduction and chemical and biological weapons Miranda found what she was looking for. The voices had told her that she should be careful about what she was seen taking from the shelves. Even if she couldn't take the books outside the building, people would be watching. She had noted the hemi-spheric plastic domes dotted all over the ceilings – the cameras were everywhere, and you never knew who was watching the screens in tiny air-conditioned security control rooms.

So Miranda studied the agricultural scientific development of the Germans in the 1930s. And that is where she first learned about sarin. If Miranda entered a quiz with the specialist subject being nerve, chemical or blood agent poisons, she would have won every time. But the nerve agent sarin was her favourite. She knew the signs and symptoms of every biological or chemical weapon known to mankind, the voices repeated them to her quite often. The thing was, of all the versions she'd looked at, sarin was the only one she could make in her bedroom.

And she had.

Miranda's sarin production was limited, and she knew it had a very short shelf-life. None of her flatmates in the west-London district of Hammersmith had ever been, or seen, inside her bedroom. In addition to the standard lock she'd put a hasp and padlock on her door. Whenever any of them knocked she would only open the door with the chain on, and she almost always had the light off and the curtains drawn when she did.

Miranda's bedroom looked like a chemical factory. And that's because it was, albeit on a small scale. She had managed to distil almost 500ml of liquid sarin. It had been quite some undertaking and had taken just over six months, a lot of careful theft from the labs at the college and many sleepless nights. Miranda wasn't afraid of dying, but she was afraid of not making the point. Dying in her bed alone was not the plan, so the carefully prepared nerve agent was poured into a flower sprayer and placed on a pillow in the middle of her bedroom floor. Her parents had both been professional historians, with a strongly left-wing interpretation of history and often-repeated distaste of the collections of the British Museum. Miranda had done some research and knew that the British Museum was busiest on Saturday mornings.

Miranda walked the short distance from her flat to Shepherd's Bush tube station and boarded the train to Tottenham Court Road. She was slightly nervous to begin with, knowing what she had in her backpack. She remembered what it was like after the bombings in 2005, when everyone looked at each other suspiciously. Then she composed herself, the male voice in her head telling her to look at how many other people were carrying bags and reminding her that she looked white and middle class – not like a mass murderer.

Miranda walked into the British Museum un-accosted. She admired the vast Great Court and its astonishing glass roof before slowly walking up the stairs to the restaurant, where she sat down and had the last pot of tea of her life. She knew that this was the right thing to do. She had been told to do this.

After finishing her tea Miranda took the flower sprayer out of her bag and sprayed her table. No-one seemed to notice, although if they had, they may have thought she was a waitress cleaning up. Then she walked down the steps, spraying a de-humidifier in the Great Court lobby. Miranda went to a lot of the galleries that day, many of which she had never been to before. She spent a lot of time in the Greek areas; the Cycladic Islands, the Minoans and Mycenaeans, the Bassai Sculptures and the Mausoleum of Halikarnassos. After that she spent some time in the Assyrian galleries, an area where both her parents had specialised. Then she went to the Upper Floor and had a look around the Egyptian exhibits and the European and Roman Britain galleries.

And then she threw herself off the balcony.

Miranda died instantly. Her victims did not. Miranda had been spraying her liquid sarin in every ventilator and on every surface she could find, without attracting the attention of the museum security guards or room monitors. She had been into several toilets, sprayed every door handle she could find and even the triple-folded pamphlets advertising other London attractions in the reception area.

No-one was really paying attention when Miranda threw herself off the balcony. When her body hit the floor in the Great Court with a deadening thump, no more than two feet from Stacey Jordan, she thought someone had dropped their bags. Before she had time to turn around one of the girls in her class started screaming. And pointing. As Stacey turned she saw the body of a young woman, her skull cracked open and blood pouring out like red wine from a dropped bottle. In her right hand was a flower sprayer. Empty.

Stacey didn't know whether to get the children away first or see if she could help. It only took a few seconds for her to realise what had happened and that the girl was dead. As she turned back to the primary school class, who had finished their trip to the museum and were on their way home, she noticed the look of shock. Runny noses were part and parcel of any primary school teacher's day but she had never seen all the children suffer at the same time. Their pupils were constricted. Miss Jordan had been on courses to recognise when pupils had ingested toxins but this was unlike anything she'd ever encountered. Then the children started to cry and the tell-tale signs of dark wet patches in the boys' trousers and the girls' tights started to appear. Then Stacey felt her own nose start to run. She felt sick; really, really sick. Her stomach cramped and she doubled over, unable to stand, but desperately wanting to help the children. She vomited on the marble floor and as she did so her bowels gave way and she soiled herself. Primary school teacher Stacey Jordan only had to endure the embarrassment for another sixty seconds. The spasms which followed broke her neck. Had they not, she probably would have only lasted another minute.

Between the hospital and the undertakers she was cleaned up before her fiancé saw her in her casket. So were the other twenty-eight children from Miss Jordan's class and the five hundred and thirty eight other people who perished in the British Museum attack.

The sarin gas, as it vapourised, spread through the building quickly. The requirement to keep the galleries dry and ventilated, particularly considering the height of the ceilings, meant that Miranda's chemistry homework spread like magic dust. Hundreds of people found it difficult to breathe and to see. They started dribbling. Then they started being sick. Many people thought they were vomiting because they were watching other people being sick. This was not the case. When they started urinating and defecating involuntarily a small number, mostly with a medical background, really knew that something was wrong.

Not a single one of the first paramedic, ambulance or police staff who attended lived. They all rushed in, anxious to help the public. It took over two hours with specialist teams to cordon off the building and get the few survivors out. None of them were visitors, the only survivors were the backroom staff who had hurried to the security control room once they were aware of the tragedy occurring on the other side of the doors.

CHAPTER FOUR

One week after the British Museum attack...

A lot of people thought it odd when David Johnson was appointed Chairman of the Intelligence and Security Committee. He had been appointed to the House of Lords only six months earlier, after a career spent almost exclusively as a trade union official, culminating in the leadership of a small but powerful union representing transport workers. His appointment was doubly surprising because it was Prime Minister David Marshall who made it, and the two had clashed on a number of occasions.

What most people didn't know was that the Prime Minister and the union leader had become firm friends, despite their political differences. Both men respected each other's clear commitment to the country and its people, even while they had distinctly separate ideas about how to improve things. Johnson recognised the intelligence and incisive thought process of the Prime Minister; the Prime Minister saw a man of integrity and ability, and with a streetwise common-sense approach to problem solving which he recognised he lacked. David Marshall accepted that he could over-complicate things, his wife had told him often enough for him to accept that. When he appointed Johnson to the House of Lords, (as much a surprise to Johnson as it was to the media and public), he waited only a day before asking him to 10 Downing Street for a drink. The Prime Minister had a sherry, Johnson had a pint of stout. Despite the previous warmth of their relationship, Johnson felt uneasy. Having a drink with the Prime Minister as a peer of the realm was very different from discussing fuel taxes as the leader of a trade union.

The two smiled uneasily after the housekeeper had brought them their drinks.

"Well, this is different," said Johnson.

"Isn't it?" replied the Prime Minister. "Would you like a seat?" he asked, indicating one of two leather chairs by the fireplace.

"No thank you Prime Minister. Didn't you know it's against the law for a Yorkshireman to drink sitting down?"

The Prime Minister laughed, "Fair enough". He seemed thoughtful and looked out on to the garden behind Number Ten.

"If I've got you figured right, and we've known each other a few years now, you're about to ask me something, aren't you?"

The Prime Minister turned around quite quickly. "You're absolutely right, I am. So no point buggering about eh?"

Johnson smiled. "No. None."

"I'd like to appoint you as Chairman of the Intelligence and Security Committee. What do you think?"

Johnson's eyebrows raised. "What the bloody hell's that?" he asked.

"Clue's in the name David."

"Well I don't know anything about that kind of stuff. That's for spies and spooks and God knows who."

"You know and understand people David. And you know when they're bluffing you and you know how and when to bluff other people. You've pretty much been playing poker your whole life."

"And who would I report to?" he asked slowly.

"I think you know the answer to that one," came the reply, and the Prime Minister smiled warmly. "Just me."

"Can I think about it?"

"You have until you finish that pint," said the Prime Minister.

"Is it all secrets and undercover missions and SAS stuff?" Johnson asked.

"Not for you. You just get paperwork and committees."

Johnson beamed. "Committees, now I know about committees," he said and downed his pint, thumping the empty glass on the mantlepiece. The Prime Minister had ensured that it was a traditional jug-handled one.

* * *

Johnson took his role seriously, and quickly made contact with the Secretary of the Joint Intelligence Committee. Ffion James was a bright and ambitious civil servant, who had been spotted by the Director General of MI5 while she was working at the Home Office. Anne Tremaine had personally championed Ffion's appointment, and it proved to be a good decision. Rarely, if ever, had the JIC been administrated so effectively.

Johnson remembered the first time he met her. "Ffi", as she liked to be called, spent two whole days explaining the difference between MI5 and MI6, what exactly it was that GCHQ could and could not do, and describing how the SAS were not actually bulletproof supermen but highly trained and capable soldiers. He received a crash course in satellite technology and precisely what carnage a nuclear armed submarine could actually do. It was a steep learning curve. She also had the decency to show him the Security Service's file on him from 1976, when it was assessed he might have been a communist agent.

At the end of the week Johnson thought his head was going to explode. He had just finished reading another briefing note, this one was about the strategic implications of contracting out international phone interception capabilities to a Norwegian company, when his patience finally broke.

"That's it!" he shouted, slapping the desk.

Ffi's head poked around the door from her adjoining office. "Everything alright?" she smiled.

Johnson stared at her. "Yes. Just peachy". Ffi frowned at him. "Don't look at me like that," he said, and then sighed. "This is too hard Ffi. I'm not clever enough for this. I used to shout at men in suits, confident they didn't know what they were talking about. And now look at me. I'm the man in the suit and I don't know what I'm talking about."

"Shush," scolded Ffi, walking into the office. "The PM did not put you here by accident. Anyway," she said, pausing, "long week. What does it take for a grumpy northerner to buy a Welsh girl a drink?"

Ffi took him to her favourite pub in Pimlico, and Johnson thanked her for everything she'd done. Over time Ffi became a surrogate daughter to him and he rarely made a decision without talking to her first.

* * *

Two weeks after the British museum attack Johnson was staring out of his office window in Portcullis House, overlooking the River Thames, remembering the day he'd been asked to take on the job. The scale of the tragedy had hit him hard, and he felt a deep personal responsibility to make sure something like it never happened again.

At that moment, Ffi knocked on his open door, rousing him from his thoughts.

"Minutes of the last Joint Intelligence Committee meeting," she said. "The one where the Chief of the Naval Staff got all stroppy. Need you to sign them off please."

"How did we miss it Ffi?" Johnson asked, still pre-occupied with the sarin attack.

"Sorry," Ffi replied, "you've lost me there".

"That girl in the British Museum," he said. "All this capability we have, the thousands of bloody cameras, GCHQ monitoring websites and email, students recruited by MI5 to pass information about extremists. Well, I don't need to tell you. How did she slip through the net? What's the point of us if we can't stop that?"

"Well, the conventional wisdom is that if you've got a lone nut there's not much you can do. She did all her research in the university library, none of it online, she didn't have any accomplices to email or call. You're not suggesting we bring in psychics or fortune tellers are you?"

"Okay, fair point. But look at the response. Almost as many people died afterwards as during the attack. We just weren't prepared for it – no-one had thought of it, no-one had planned for it. Everyone, albeit with the best of intentions, just charged in there."

Ffi put the kettle on. "Tea, I think," she said, "you're about to get thoughtful again."

"Am I?"

"Yes, you do it about once a month. I recognise the symptoms."

Johnson leaned back in his chair and took a jelly baby from the bowl on his desk. He put his fingers together and stared at the ceiling as he tried to focus his thoughts. "Now, you said to me that after 9/11, you lot all started looking at the tall buildings, Canary Wharf, the London Eye, all that kind of stuff."

"Yep." Ffi was adding the milk and the three spoons of sugar which her sweet-toothed boss insisted on.

"But you also told me, I remember this, someone said something about submarines in the Thames."

Ffi handed him his tea. "Yes. It's a military thing, they're pretty ruthless about critiquing themselves. One of their constant fears is what they call 'fighting the last war'." Johnson looked confused. "You'll know this from your union days. If you use the same tactics and think the same way you did from your last campaign then management and government are ahead of you. It's not difficult David."

"What was the submarine thing again?" he asked.

Ffi put her own tea down on a table. "A very clever army officer pointed out that while we were looking at the tops of tall buildings and putting anti-aircraft guns on them, some madman could come down the Thames in a submarine or a speedboat, or even fly in on a microlight and blow the Houses of Parliament to pieces. He said we had to think the unthinkable."

"Who was he?"

"At the time he was the Operations Officer for the SAS. As of two months ago he's the Director of Special Forces. You've met him, Major General Jim Green."

Johnson rocked back in his chair. "I remember him! Lovely chap. I thought he was going to be all aggressive and mental. We actually had a game of darts in a pub in Kent."

"I know David, I was there. You won, and he was very gracious about it."

"I thought he was going to stick a dart in my head."

"Well, he didn't. Anyway, what do you want with General Green?"

"I'd like to talk to him." He paused. "Can we get him on the phone? I've had an idea."

Ten minutes later Johnson and Ffi were sitting in one of the secure communications rooms in Portcullis House on a video conference with the Director of Special Forces, who was dressed in a suit and talking to them from another secure room in the Pentagon.

"Good afternoon Sir," said General Green.

"And good morning to you General, hope we haven't messed up your schedule today," said Johnson.

The General laughed. "Sir, there are cleaning staff out here with more medals than me. I'm about as important as an email from a Nigerian princess. What can I do for you?" he asked.

"Can you come and work for me?"

The General smiled. "No. But I think you already know that."

"Are you guys really, really busy, I mean all the time?" Johnson asked.

"We're busy a lot, and when we're not busy we're practicing for when we're going to be busy. Can I ask where you're going with this?"

Johnson decided straight talking was the best strategy – it had always worked in pay negotiations. "I need one person, just one person, man or woman, old or young, fat or thin, I don't care. I need someone with imagination. I've just been talking with Ffi and she told me about your comments after 9/11. Now if I can't have you, who are you going to recommend to me? I need someone who can talk to everyone, politicians, media, security service, secret intelligence service, GCHQ, the police, the weather people, all of it. And I need someone who can think like you did."

Ffi stared at him wide eyed as Johnson took the lid off his pen and held it, hovering, over his notebook. As they watched him on the plasma screen General Green could be seen looking around the room.

"Come on General. Whose your suggestion?" Johnson asked.

The General looked uncomfortable. "Sir, you do realise we're using a secure link provided by our wonderful, but very suspicious cousins."

"Of course I do," came the response. "I don't care if they're listening."

The General clasped his hands and looked at the desk. "You said Ffi was there. I can't see her on this screen."

Ffi jumped in quickly, leaning into the microphone on the desk. "I'm here General," she said.

General Green smiled, "Good to hear your voice Ffi. How are the saxophone lessons going?" he asked.

"Rubbish," came the answer. "I was better at playing 'London's Burning' on the recorder when I was nine than I am after six months of bloody lessons."

"Ffi, I have a suggestion for you and the Chairman."

Johnson looked across at Ffi who shook her head as if to say, "Quiet."

General Green leaned against the table, peering into the webcam. "Ffi, Mr Chairman, I can only guess at what you're putting together here. One man stands out – you should put him in front of every stakeholder there is, preferably at the same time, really put the pressure on, he'll need to be able to handle it. Ffi, would you turn that bloody camera so I can see more than your left arm?"

Ffi adjusted the camera.

"Thank you. Mr Chairman you don't know him, but Ffi does. Ffi, get the Milk Tray Man in."

Ffi looked concerned, "He's still in hospital General," she said.

"Then get him out." As he finished his sentence a uniformed US Army Officer came into the room and handed General Green a folded piece of paper. Green opened and read it. His eyebrows raised. "I have to go Sir," he said. Nodding, he added simply, "Ffi, he's your man," and left the room.

Johnson looked at her. There was a momentary silence. "I'm assuming this is not the guy from the chocolate adverts."

"No David."

"Why's he in hospital?"

"He needs fixing. Got a bit broken a while back."

CHAPTER FIVE

Earlier

Will was sitting on the balcony of his hotel in Cyprus when he felt the familiar pain in his back. He had never figured out, and nor had any of the medical professionals he'd consulted, quite what it was. He could best describe it as a self-generated electric shock; he felt that if it could be seen it would look like an electric arc, starting from his right ear and finishing at the right hand side base of his neck. Will was also convinced that if this arc of electricity could be seen it would be blue. His standard response when it happened was to clasp his hand to his neck and swear. On several occasions the pain had caused him to fall off his chair.

He decided to make use of the hotel's spa facilities. His legs were tired from the five hour hike he had made to a secluded beach the previous day and he felt like indulging himself. He sipped his glass of white wine and smiled. Sarah would have said it was a waste of money, but Sarah wasn't there and he was, and he knew that a professional massage from someone who was paid to make him feel good was worth ten sessions from the military physiotherapists who seemed to take delight in causing him pain.

Will closed his eyes as he lay on the massage bench and sank his face into the towel. Gentle music played in the background while he inhaled the scents of the aromatic candles around the room.

"Do you have any pain in your back?" asked Katerina, the Greek masseuse who was gently placing a towel over his legs.

"Every day," he replied with a smile.

"Okay then Mr Will, if anything hurts you let me know, yes?"

"Deal," said Will, knowing that it always hurt and he never said anything, but that this version was infinitely more pleasurable than the medical centre on camp.

Katerina had spent seven years learning her craft and was passionate about it. Her boyfriend got angry with her about the amount of time she spent on the internet reading the latest research and using him as a body dummy to try out new techniques. Sometimes it was fantastic, mostly it was ever so slightly painful.

Katerina rubbed her hands in the warm oil and started to work on Will's left shoulder. She could feel him wince and recoil from her touch.

"Sorry. You okay Mr Will?" she asked.

"Yes, yes, I'm fine," he answered.

Katerina had studied hard, and she recognised something. "Have you ever dislocated this?" she asked, gently holding his shoulder. With the low light, the scent of the candles and the soothing music he remembered back to when his body had originally been close to breaking point...

* * *

The Venezuela Incident

Will had been in the hide for three days when he finally caught sight of his target. Alberto Gomez was one of the most powerful drug lords in Venezuela and every western country wanted to see him in custody or dead. Will was cold, wet and uncomfortable, and living on the edge of his senses. He smiled as he remembered how this had all started.

Two weeks earlier he'd been sitting with James Black, the Senior Intelligence Officer from the Directorate of Special Forces, and Bill Reeves, James' opposite number at the US Joint Special Operations Forces Command. They should have been talking in a secure briefing room, swept daily for listening devices, but Bill had flown over from Washington specially and James knew that Bill loved the basement bar at the Landmark Hotel in Marylebone. When Will arrived, James and Bill were waiting for him in the high ceilinged lobby.

"Hello boys," he said. "Fancy meeting you here. Anyone would think there's some sort of half-arsed lunatic suicide mission in the offing." He smiled warmly and shook hands with Jim, both men clasping each other's shoulders. "How you been?" he asked.

Jim had worked with the British on and off for twenty years and had the wit and good humour to have picked up the idiosyncrasies of British English, and amused himself by trying to mimic them and the accent.

"Good mate," he replied. "How's yourself."

Will laughed, "It doesn't matter how hard you try Bill, you're always going to sound like Dick van Dyke in Mary Poppins."

"Really, I thought I sounded quite regal. You want me to sing the chimney song?"

"I will kill you with my bare hands." Will turned to James and the two shook hands. "So, why the hell am I here mate? It's a nice place and everything..."

James cut him off. Rolling his eyes and shrugging he pointed at Bill, "This idiot." Bill grinned infectiously.

"We've had an idea, and we'd like you to help," he said. Will was about to say something but Bill stopped him with an uplifted hand. "No. Do not tell me to piss off. This one might work. Anyway, shall we?" he asked, indicating the basement bar. The three men walked past the towering palm trees in the Winter Garden courtyard and down to the lower ground floor. "Down the apples and bears," said Bill in his best cockney accent.

"Apples and pears you muppet," laughed Will.

"I know, I know, I'm just trying to irritate you."

"Fear not my friend, I'm sure there's plenty of scope for that when you tell me your idea."

They reached the bottom of the staircase and Bill stopped in his tracks. "What the hell is that?" he asked.

James responded drily. "It's a bronze horse with a lampshade on its head."

Bill shrugged again. "Fair enough. I suppose we've got weirder back home. Either of you guys ever seen the World's Biggest Ball of Twine?" Before either man had time to answer, Bill had walked into the bar and threw his arms up. "Ah, Paula!"

The pretty Spanish manageress turned from her paperwork and smiled as she walked towards him.

"Mr Bill!" she said, embracing him and kissing him on both cheeks. "How good to see you, it's been ages."

"Work has kept me busy," he replied, with his hands now on her waist and staring straight into her dark eyes.

Paula was half his age but she wasn't stupid. She took a step back and with one hand on her hip and the other pointed at Bill told him, "I don't want to know. You want the table in the corner again?" Working in a high-end hotel had taught Paula a lot of things, she had seen and heard more than most and she knew how to read people.

"This is why I always come back Paula," Bill smiled.

"No. It is because the French waitresses always flirt with you, especially Ann-Sophie." Paula led them to a secluded corner table and Bill ordered three large scotches. Ann-Sophie arrived shortly afterwards with their drinks, smiling flirtatiously with the handsome American. "Hello Monsieur Bill, are you staying for a while?" she asked.

"Just one night I'm afraid."

"Je suis désolée," said Ann-Sophie as she left them.

The mood turned, not uncomfortably, but it was time for business. "So, here it is," said Bill. "We think we know where Gomez is."

"The drug guy?" asked Will, suspicious of the assertion.

"The very same," came the measured response.

"I thought he moved every twenty-four hours?" Will asked.

At this point James chipped in. "Yeah, mostly he does, but according to our friend here there's a possibility he's got one place he uses like a safe house.

Will was shaking his head as he sipped his drink. "Possibility?" he quoted. "And the source..."

James and Bill looked at each other. There was a pause.

"Oh for crying out loud guys, it's me. Who or what is the source?" Will asked.

James looked apologetic. "Sorry mate."

"Okay, well that's just tipped it. Human source originated isn't it? What's the grading?"

James and Bill looked at each other again, this time looking slightly more concerned. "Reliability of the source cannot be assessed, reliability of the information is assessed as possible," said Bill, now staring into his scotch and unable to make eye contact.

Will sat back in his chair and smiled knowingly, slowly shaking his head at the same time.

Bill continued. "This is a really high priority for Uncle Sam, Will. If you guys jump in with us we'll be paying for the whole thing. And you know that you guys have a capability that we don't."

"You can come and visit you know, happy to teach you," Will replied.

"That's very kind, and I'll take you up on that, but we simply don't have enough time," countered Bill. "And I know I don't have to spell it out for you Will, but the US will be very, very grateful if you go with us on this."

"Last time you said that I got shot," said Will, downing his drink.

Bill looked across at Ann-Sophie who caught his eye. He waved his finger in a helicopter motion and smiled at her, mouthing, "thank you," as he did so. Ann-Sophie returned momentarily with another three scotches. None of the three had spoken in the interim.

"So. Where is he?" asked Will.

"Venezuela," James responded. "South America."

"Thanks for the geography lesson, but that's not exactly news is it? Whereabouts in Venezuela? It's not like we have the resources to cover a country."

Bill put his glass on the table and ran his hands through his hair. "He's in a prison."

Will smiled. "Brilliant. What the hell do you want us for?" He spoke more slowly now. "If he's in prison, isn't that exactly where you want him to be?"

"I said he's in a prison. I didn't say he was a prisoner," Bill replied.

"I'm getting confused now."

"We think he's using the prison as a safe-house, living a five star lifestyle in the very place we wouldn't be looking for him. It's comfortable, he can have his family around, all the staff from the warden to the gatemen are on his payroll."

"Okay, and what do you want us to do?" asked Will.

"We want you to find out exactly where he is. In the compound that is."

Will looked across at James. "Mate, we're a reconnaissance outfit, not a snatch squad. Isn't this a job for the other lads?"

"Hereford and Poole are stretched to the limit at the moment Will," he said, referring to the bases of the SAS and SBS, "and, well, politically, our cousins want to bag him and to be seen to bag him. You won't be there to grab him, Delta will do that, but they want the expertise your guys can bring to the job to find out where he is."

Will's face scrunched up. "I don't understand," he said. "Sounds like you already know where he is. Well, according to your totally unverifiable source that is."

Bill leaned forward. "We think we know where he is, but we haven't confirmed it yet, and what we really need to know, is that if he is in there, where exactly he is. It's quite a large facility."

Suddenly the penny dropped for Will and he rather lost the measured resolve which he favoured on occasions such as these. He leaned forward, head in his hands, as he absorbed the information. After a deep breath he looked up at both men. "You want us to break into a prison?"

James nodded. "Yep."

"Are you on fucking drugs?" Will had to concentrate to control the volume of his voice. "It's a prison, it's designed to stop people getting out. How the fuck are we going to get in, and out, of a Venezuelan prison and pinpoint Gomez at the same time. This isn't an anti-drugs operation, it's a fucking spend the rest of your life in prison mission."

Bill grinned. "I knew you'd like the idea."

Will wasn't smiling and his voice rose. "No, seriously Bill. This is in-fucking-sane. Venezuela? Prison? Break in and then out? You have got to be shitting me." Paula and Ann-Sophie turned their heads, attracted by the noise. Bill ordered another round of drinks.

41

Still grinning, Bill asked, "So you're up for it then?"

Will threw his head back in despair. "Well of course we're bloody up for it, you know us, we're all idiots. Just got one request though."

"Which is?"

"When this goes wrong, which I can absolutely categorically and without fear of question guarantee you it will…" He paused and looked down to his drink. "You better send the best you've got to get us out of there. I love your country Bill, you know I do. You know how much Sarah meant to me, and you know that I know how much you guys have done for us. But this is not a one man mission. I need your promise that whoever I take in with me gets back home. Whatever state they're in."

Bill did not avoid his friend's considered gaze. "You pulled me out of a basement in Srebrenica. I think you know that promise was already made before you walked in here."

Paula approached with a tray of three glasses of champagne which they hadn't ordered. Paula's younger sister was deaf from birth and they both learned to lipread together. Paula could lipread in Spanish, Portuguese, French and English. Not a word of their quietly convened conversation had escaped her. "On the house," she said, and then stared at Will. "If you get killed, I am going to be very, very angry."

CHAPTER SIX

A Job Interview for Overseas Deployment

It had been decided that the best approach was a single two-man team and Staff-Sergeant Steve Robertson was selected for the job entirely as a result of chance. Will had returned from his meeting in the Landmark Hotel and walked straight into the Sergeants' Mess. Standing at the entrance to the bar he knocked and asked permission to enter. Will was respected by the senior non-commissioned officers and a cheer went up and a beer was handed to him before he could reach for his wallet. Being a Friday night, the Regimental Sergeant Major was also in the bar. Will spotted him and walked across.

"RSM," he said, "I need a good man, or indeed woman."

"Don't we all Sir," came the deadpan response.

"Very good," Will replied. "I need someone to come away with me on holiday for a few days. Should be a short excursion."

The RSM turned to the assembled drinkers. "Darts!" he shouted. Everyone in the bar hurried to the bowl on the table by the dart board which was filled with table-tennis balls, each one with a number written on it, and took one out. Those who were too late to the bowl and had to walk away empty-handed were clearly disappointed.

The RSM smiled. "Ladies and Gentlemen, the Operations Officer of the Special Reconnaissance Regiment is looking for a volunteer. Short holiday, overseas." He paused, handing Will a single dart. "Sir, please step up to the oche." There was another small alcohol fuelled cheer as Will stepped forward.

A shout came from the back of the room. "Hope he's better with these than he is with a pistol."

Will turned round, laughing. "You can fuck right off Mr Smith. What's your number?" he asked.

"I've got seventeen Sir," came the response.

"In which case I'm aiming top left," said Will, denying Staff Sergeant Dave Smith the opportunity to come with him. He threw his dart.

"Who's got twelve?" asked the RSM. Steve Robertson lifted his arm. "Well done Robbo, you're going on holiday with the OpsO. You lucky, lucky man."

* * *

Sixteen hours later Will and Robbo were sitting in British Airways' first class lounge enjoying a beer when Robbo turned to him. "Boss, aren't we deploying a bit light?" he asked.

"Yep," Will replied, and then continued staring out of the huge picture windows at the runway.

"Too early in the morning to be funny sir," Robbo responded, opening the fridge next to him and opening another beer. It was just before eight o' clock. "You want one?" he asked.

"Yes please," came the answer.

Robbo handed him a beer and tried again. "Where we going?"

"You'll find out when we get there," was the laconic response.

Robbo was running out of patience. "I've got a ticket to Orlando and a bag with nothing in it but Hawaiian shirts, a change of underwear and a really crap book. You've got to give me more than this. Seriously."

Will looked at him. "You've got a bottle of cheap vodka as well. No need to open it on the plane this time, which is technically illegal anyway. I'll explain on the way. The cousins are paying which is why we're sitting here drinking beer at stupid o' clock in the morning, and why you'll be sitting in the biggest airline seat of your life Robbo. They'll be picking us up at the other end."

Robbo had never flown first class before, mostly his experience had been sitting sideways on plastic rope in the back of a military heavy lift aircraft. Mostly he had then been required to throw himself out of the back door before it had landed.

Once on the plane the seasoned special forces operator behaved like a child. "This is ace," he said, pressing the buttons which turned his seat into a bed.

"Stop mucking about Robbo, I can guarantee you'll break it."

Robbo did break the seat, and spent the rest of the flight trying to watch a movie whilst horizontal. Shortly before landing, Will gave a general outline of what the plan was. He could only give a general outline because he only had a general plan.

"What about the kit though?" Robbo asked.

"Cousins are providing," came the response.

"Better than ours then?"

"Almost certainly."

They were met at the airport by Bill, who ushered them straight into a waiting limousine. "Hey, Will. Seems like only yesterday we were chatting with the girls in that cellar bar."

"That was Tuesday, and today is Saturday, so you're wrong," said Will, quietly. He was not without his concerns.

After stepping into the car Robbo looked around wide-eyed. "Has this thing got a mini-bar in it?" Bill pressed a button in the seat and the fridge door opened. "Cool," said Robbo, grinning as he opened another can of beer.

Bill turned serious. "You guys good to deploy tomorrow night?" he asked.

"Absolutely," said Will. "You got everything we asked for?"

"It's waiting for you," Bill replied. "We'll send a car to your hotel at three. Susan will be driving you."

Will smiled. "How is she? I haven't seen her for a while." he asked.

"She's still wonderful," Bill replied. "Volunteered for this when she knew it was you."

Robbo looked up, temporarily distracted from his beer. "Something I should know, Boss?"

"Nope," came the response. "You want these Bill?" Will asked as he pulled his passport out of his pocket.

"Damn, nearly forgot," said Bill, as he pulled two British passports from his own jacket, handing one to Robbo and one to Will after checking the photographs. Robbo handed over the fake passport that he'd been travelling on to Bill as well. He flicked to the second page of his new document.

"You have got to be kidding me!" he spat.

"What's wrong?" Bill asked.

"Cecil! You've called me Cecil?"

"Special request," smirked Bill, looking straight at Will, who failed to stifle a smile.

Robbo turned to him. "You Sir, are a shit of the highest order."

* * *

Robbo and Will were sitting in the hotel lobby waiting for their ride when Will stood up, surprising Robbo a little. Will walked across to a silver-haired lady and embraced her gently.

"How are you Will?" she asked.

"Ready to go," he said. He beckoned Robbo over and the two walked to the car, Robbo looking decidedly puzzled. After a short drive they arrived at a small port and Susan walked them to a mid-sized fishing boat.

"This is you," she said. "Transfer at sea, tonight."

"Thanks Susan," said Will, as she kissed him gently on the cheek.

"Yeah, thanks," said Robbo. She nodded at him, and walked back to the car. "What's going on there?" he asked.

"Potential future Mother-in-Law," Will replied as he walked up the ramp to the boat.

"Potential? I didn't know you were seeing anyone," said Robbo.

"I'm not." Will turned as Robbo stepped aboard. "I was." Will's eyes looked to the deck and then back up to Robbo, and they were not as piercing as they usually were.

Robbo was a bright man, but he was also straightforward. "Didn't work out or dead?" he asked. Will didn't answer. "Right then. Fuck this, there's got to be a galley on this hulk somewhere. And if there isn't, I've still got a bottle of vodka."

"Permission to come aboard sir?" Will asked as he shook hands with the Captain.

Captain Roland Lopez looked after his guests extremely well. Considering they were only on his vessel for a few hours, the effort he went to cooking freshly caught lobster was impressive. He shoo-ed the other crewmembers away after supper.

"Don't worry, they can drive the boat," he said. "You done this before?" he asked.

Will and Robbo looked at each other, both shaking their heads. "Nope," said Robbo.

"It can be difficult, but takes a special kind of idiot to really mess it up. Just don't get caught between my boat and his boat. That way, you go squish. Make sure you get on top."

It was just before midnight when the fishing trawler and the US Navy mini-submarine met up. It was a half moon that night which helped the illumination and the sea was calm. "Easy one this," said Lopez, as he, Will and Robbo stood on the foredeck. A hatch opened at the front of the submarine and a head popped up, followed quickly by a rifle aimed straight at them. Another hatch opened on the stern of the submarine and a man stood up with a pistol.

"Infinite?" came the shouted question from the man at the stern.

"Monkeys suck," Will shouted back. "It would be much funnier with meerkats."

"What's your favourite meerkat book then?" The questioner kept his firearm pointed at the three men on deck.

"Much Ado About Nothing," shouted Will. "How's Jean?"

"Jean's dead." The Captain of the submarine was content that the call and response codes had identified his passengers as legitimate.

"You two guys swimming it?" came the call across the water.

Robbo looked mournfully at Will. "I hate this."

"Yep, me too," he answered. Both men were wearing waterproof backpacks filled with cash, clothes, communications equipment and satellite imagery which Susan had handed them from the trunk of the car. They dived into the Caribbean. It was now midnight and not as warm as Robbo had hoped or expected. As they were dragged up the side of the submarine Robbo was swearing loudly.

As he holstered his pistol the Captain remarked drily, "Chilly, isn't it?"

"Captain?" asked Will.

"Smith," came the answer.

"Ominous," said Will, having seen yet another documentary about the Titanic only a few weeks earlier.

"I get that a lot," said the Captain, unsmiling.

"Will Richards," said Will, extending a hand.

"I am fucking freezing," came the voice from behind him.

"And this is Robbo", said Will. "Robbo is mostly unhappy."

After Robbo shook hands with the Captain all three men climbed down into the tiny belly of the submarine.

"Sorry, not a lot of room," said Captain Smith as he walked through the bulkhead. "Lucky you're only with us for a couple of hours. Hungry?" he asked.

"Swimming always makes me hungry," offered Robbo as a response.

"Kev?" shouted the captain. The man who'd popped up at the bow hatch with the rifle stuck his head around a watertight door.

"Skipper..?"

"Cheeseburgers I think."

"Done." Kev disappeared back behind the door. Ten minutes later Captain Smith, Will and Robbo were sitting at the only table in the submarine, a map table which doubled as a dining area.

"This is amazing," said Robbo, as he chewed on his midnight snack. "You know, you guys," he said, mouth full of burger, "when you get it wrong you really get it wrong, but when you get it right, you are a-bloody-mazing."

Captain Smith raised an eyebrow and looked at Will inquisitively. "Is he genuinely comparing American foreign policy with a cheeseburger?"

Will smirked. "I believe so. He's a man of great insight is our Robbo. Now then, speaking of American foreign policy, where are you going to drop us?" Smith pulled out a map and used a set of compasses to indicate the beach that Will and Robbo would have to swim to.

"We'll be about four hundred metres off-shore. You happy with that?" Will nodded acknowledgement. "There may be a few fishing boats around so watch yourselves. I am out of here the minute you boys are off my boat so you better be sure you're up for this, whatever the hell it is you're up to." For security reasons Smith had not been briefed on the mission. "Last chance to back-out."

Robbo looked blankly at Captain Smith and finished his cheeseburger. Then he turned to Will, looking confused. Will filled the silence, "We don't have to go Robbo. This is a volunteer mission."

"I know," answered Robbo, "that's why I volunteered. What's all the Jackanory about?"

Now Captain Smith looked confused and Will was beginning to think he had to explain everything to everyone. "Obscure reference. British children's programme a long time ago. It involved a lot of talking. Robbo mostly doesn't like talking unless it's swearing."

Captain Smith smiled for the first time that night. He was annoyed that he had been deployed at short notice, missing his eldest son's sixteenth birthday party, and the annoyance was heightened when he was told that he would be taking two British passengers rather than Americans. But now his mood was lightening. "So, do we all get a medal from the Queen for helping you guys out again?"

"Actually," said Will, "it's us helping you guys out."

Captain Smith took a breath. "Oh. Really?" He grinned. "In which case we won't charge you for the cheeseburgers."

CHAPTER SEVEN

Venezuela...

The exit from the submarine and the swim ashore were uneventful. Will and Robbo crawled up the beach and took up a position behind some large rocks. "I'll take first watch," said Robbo, as both men changed into the civilian clothing they had in their backpacks.

It was daylight when Will awoke. He looked around and saw Robbo wading in the sea, about twenty feet from him. Standing up and walking over to him Will asked, "Why didn't you wake me?"

"No need boss. I'm not tired and it was quite nice watching the sun come up." Robbo shrugged. "Besides, there's no threat here." Will turned around and in the bright light of the early morning sunshine saw the sleepy fishing village of Capaterida. The deployment had been so rushed that very little preliminary work had been done. "Good to go?" asked Robbo.

Robbo and Will walked up to the village, chatting as they went. "You speak Spanish don't you boss?"

"Yes. A little. Why?" asked Will.

"Because it's just over one hundred and twenty clicks to where we're going, I've checked on the map, and I'd rather take the bus than walk."

"And you can ride a motorbike can't you Robbo?" Will asked.

"Yes. Why?" came the response.

"Because I will use my Spanish and hire us a bike, and you will use your skills and ride us up to Ospino. That way, you don't have to walk and I don't have to sit in a bus with chickens and pigs."

Robbo was his usual pragmatic self. "I like that idea Boss."

Robbo liked the idea right up to the point when they found a small garage that rented second and third hand motorbikes and the only one left was a moped. "This is never going to work," he said.

"Of course it will," said Will, smiling and handing him a white helmet manufactured to the thinnest specification he had ever seen. "Now then, if you don't mind me putting my arms around you..." he added as he swung his leg over the back of the moped.

Will and Robbo waved to the owner of the garage as they began their ascent to the prison just outside Ospino. The man would never see his moped again, although the hundred dollars Will had paid as a deposit would probably buy him another three.

After several hours riding, and more than one narrow escape from the busses and trucks hurtling around the mountain roads, Robbo stopped in a narrow passing point. The roads had been mostly fine but the one they had just hit seemed more of a track. "This is going to get a bit interesting," said Robbo. The crash barriers had long since disappeared and the sheer drop off the side of the road was at least three hundred feet.

"Onwards!" shouted Will.

After less than half a mile it was obvious that the machine was never going to make the track, which had now become a boulder strewn path which only the local goat-herders used. Will and Robbo had a brief discussion about what to do next. The moped was thrown off the side of the mountain and they walked up to a high point behind Ospino Prison.

Now dressed in olive green fatigues, the two men hastily put up a small camouflage net and started preparing the hide.

* * *

"Robbo, wake up," hissed Will as he saw the car approach the prison gates. Robbo was immediately alert as Will passed him the binoculars. "That's gotta be him hasn't it?" he asked.

"Hang on," said Robbo. The black Mercedez with tinted windows had pulled into the prison courtyard with barely a questioning look from the guards. Will and Robbo had been on-target for three days now and neither had seen anything like this before. "He's a bit sloppy isn't he?" asked Robbo rhetorically, handing back the binos. Gomez was laughing and chatting in the open with some of the guards, completely unaware of the two-man surveillance team watching his every move.

"Arrogant. Confident. Lazy. Complacent," said Will.

"Christ Boss, we could take him ourselves."

Will looked quizzically across at Robbo, who shrugged. "Okay, maybe not. Once we've done this, how quick are Delta going to come in?"

"Told me they could make it in just under two hours once they get the nod. They've got a team on a ship just off the Panama Canal." Will paused. "So when do you reckon we should go in?" As he asked the question, Gomez walked through a door into what looked like the main detention block.

"I'd say we go in tonight. Let him and his goons get their heads down for a few hours. Oh-three-hundred?" Robbo suggested.

"Done."

Robbo and Will had detailed satellite imagery of the facility and had also been watching very closely during the three days they had been on target. The guards appeared to be fairly slack, conducting their patrols robotically rather than with any vigilance. The CCTV cameras were rusted, with unconnected wires hanging from them, occasionally whipping against the fence which had once been electrified, but was clearly no longer so as the prisoners routinely sat against it.

It was just before three o' clock in the morning. "Right then Robbo. Speed, stealth, in and out. No dramas," said Will.

Robbo looked up at him, "What do you think I'm gonna do boss, a fucking ballet?"

The two men left the hide and ran to the outer perimeter fence. They'd talked through the plan to the point where both were bored of questioning the other on contingencies if something were to go wrong. The outer fence was topped with razor wire so they went through it rather than over it, Robbo cutting through the thin wire with garden clippers. Having cut the fence in a single vertical line, he put his back to it and Will pushed him through. Will then turned, putting his back to the fence with his arms behind his back. Robbo grabbed him and pulled him; Will fell to the ground as he was dragged through the narrow opening. Quickly getting to his knees he cupped his hands to boost Robbo over the second fence, which was unprotected at the top, although still at least eight feet high. Robbo slung his legs over it and hung on the top like a bedsheet on a washing line. Will took a couple of steps back and ran at the fence, one boot on the metal mesh and both arms held high in the air. Robbo caught him, tipping slightly, but then regained his balance and helped Will up to the top of the fence. They dropped to the ground and ran in the shadows around the poorly lit courtyard to the door which they had seen Gomez walk in.

Robbo had already posed the question. "If there are tunnels in here, we're screwed," he had said earlier in the day. "And I bet you he hasn't got his name on the door."

As they approached the outer door of the block Will pulled a small pouch out of his belt and retrieved a solid steel L-shaped tool. The simple lock was opened in seconds. Robbo looked at Will, eyebrows raised. This was all a bit too easy. Will looked at the wooden information board on the wall in front of him, translating the Spanish and indicating to Robbo to head left up the corridor. He had seen the directions to the Warden's office and thought it might be a good place to start looking for clues to Gomez's whereabouts in the large detention block.

Will opened the Warden's office door to find sixteen of the night guards sitting around his conference table playing poker. They may not have been the world's most diligent prison officers but they moved like lightning when they saw Will, who tried to keep Robbo out of sight, but it was too late and he had already framed himself in the doorway behind Will, pistol raised. Robbo was not a man to go quietly, but there were more rifles pointed at him than he had rounds in his gun, and he recognised that, lowering it slowly. They would have to find another way out of this.

One of the guards was already on his radio and the alarm was raised. A siren wailed across the high-altitude prison and the remainder of the night-shift that had normally been comfortable with slumbering until morning parade came to life. Will and Robbo found themselves disarmed, separated, handcuffed and hooded.

Will tried desperately to cling to every bit of training he'd ever had. He knew about the shock of capture and that the most likely chance of escape was as soon as possible after initial detention. All of that made sense in a training scenario in the UK – it made little sense in a prison in Venezuela that he'd just broken into. He knew he would not be able to break out of this place – that much was obvious when he was thrown to the floor in a concrete cell and he heard the door being bolted shut from the outside. What made it worse was the fact that he knew he was not alone in the cell. He could smell the coffee on the breath of the guard commander who was in there with him.

The first kick was to his left knee, and the second to his right, both from the side. Will had been kicked before, and was expecting it, but that didn't mean it didn't hurt. Many years previously he had passed the course to be a military interrogator, and several years after that he had passed a resistance to interrogation course, a difficult, painful and often embarrassing journey to take. Both training experiences put a spotlight on human weakness, mental and physical, and Will knew now that if there was anything that could help him it was that training, some of which involved thinking of Sarah, and trying to make her proud that if he was about to die, he'd do it as best he could.

No-one asked him a question for three hours, which Will thought was odd. The beating was constant, the hood was not removed and the sadistic laughter of his captors did nothing for Will's confidence that he was going to get out of this alive. He had no bargaining position and nothing to offer. Having been asked nothing he had nowhere to go in terms of information transfer.

As they stripped him of his clothes and strapped him to a wooden pallet, Will heard Robbo scream from a neighbouring cell. Robbo hadn't spoken a word to his captors, but he couldn't stifle the sound as the car battery jump leads were attached to his teeth. Will heard the sound of a woman laughing as Robbo's fillings exploded inside his teeth. Robbo was many things to many people – he borrowed money which he never paid back, he frequently drank too much and made offensive remarks which he never apologised for and he wasn't that worried about hitting people who randomly annoyed him. He also regularly sent money to his younger sister, whose husband had run off with a

French postwoman after a camping trip to Normandy, leaving Helen to look after both of her daughters alone.

Will had worked with Robbo for a long time, and as he lay in his cell, spitting the blood from his mouth after a final kick to the sternum that evening, he vowed to himself that if he ever got out of this, he would kill the bitch that was torturing him. That said, he was not sure that he would get out of this.

He was awoken with an effortless kick in the genitals. He rolled over on the grey blanket they had given him to sleep on on the concrete floor. Will looked up to see Gomez standing above him.

"You have come to find me," he said, confidently. "I don't care who you are, I know you are a British spy, and these people will take great pleasure in killing you as slowly as they can." With that Gomez walked out the door and Will started getting kicked again. When they were bored kicking him they tied ropes around his wrists and hung him from the steel joists that ran across the ceiling. He was hit like a punchbag in a boxing club.

By the second day, most of Will's body was black, red or blue. He couldn't raise his head or stand up straight. Gomez came in to see him. "You're still not dead," he smiled as he walked out the cell door. As it clanked shut Gomez opened the peephole. "My sister's looking after your boyfriend by the way."

Mentally, Will was in a difficult place. Desperately trying to keep himself in a position where he could still could make good decisions, he was physically at a point where he knew he could collapse at any point. "Fuck this up," he said to himself, "and this is game over for-fucking-ever." The bit that kept him going was that Robbo was still in this too.

On the second night, having been kicked, punched and beaten again, hour after hour, still handcuffed and still hooded, someone brought both Will and Robbo a drink of water. She made the mistake of bringing it in solid glasses. Robbo drank the water, smashed the glass on the floor and stuck what was left of it straight into his gaoler's neck. Being hooded, he missed the primary target and caused only superficial damage.

Robbo's punishment was a night-long beating. Will could hear it and could do nothing about it; it was the longest night of his life up to then. The next morning he heard the familiar female voice again, not the one who had brought them both water that night, but Gomez's sister.

Just as Will was thinking about Robbo again as he woke, he was kicked in the base of his spine by another of the guards. He tried to stand up but couldn't. The guard kicked him again in the same spot. Again, Will tried to stand up, but fell to the floor. The next kick came to the back of his neck and the beating that followed lasted hours. Will's slip into unconsciousness was the best thing that happened to him that day.

He came round to discover Gomez sitting on a chair opposite him. "You have interrupted my schedule," he said, "so I decided to have a little fun personally". Another man handed him a carton of cocktail sticks and a small hammer before taking Will's hand and kneeling on it, anchoring it to the floor of the cell. "Your boyfriend's enjoying the hospitality of some of the other prisoners" said Gomez. Will hadn't heard any screaming from Robbo for a while before he passed out, so it was entirely possible.

Gomez knelt down and placed one cocktail stick under each of Will's fingernails. He grinned before slapping Will across the face and then slowly tapping on the end of each stick with his little hammer. He knocked them all in until they reached beyond the nail bed. This was a pain unlike any other Will had experienced and his eyes shut as he tried not to scream. Then Will's other hand was taken and the routine repeated. "There, now you look a bit like Wolverine," he whispered. Then Gomez broke the exposed parts of the cocktail sticks off so that Will had no chance of removing them. He passed out again.

CHAPTER EIGHT

Comrades…

Bill was sitting in the Captain's quarters of the USS Kearsarge, the amphibious assault ship just off the Panama Canal, discussing what the next move should be.

"Bill," said Captain Vince Young, "that's two scheduled radio calls they've missed. They're either dead or running for Guyana or Brazil right now. What do you want me to do?"

"Let's just go Vince. Let's just get in there and find them, and grab Gomez if we can."

"We don't even know if he's there Bill."

"Look, the Brit specialty about knowing how many paces before you turn right and then how many before you turn left and which door to kick in was a nice-to-have. It's not a requirement. These boys are raring to go." Bill was pointing at the door of the Captain's cabin, notionally indicating the twenty-four strong Delta Force team which was onboard. He paused, recognising that he had become excitable. "Besides, those are my friends out there. And they were doing us a favour."

"Favour or no favour Bill, you know it's not my call, or yours. And those Delta boys will volunteer for anything if it involves shooting at people, let's ask the question shall we?" Bill sipped his coffee and nodded silently as Captain Young picked up the secure phone in his bunk and made a call to the Pentagon.

In a room with no windows in Washington a junior officer took the call. Several of her contemporaries were watching television or reading books – it was the night shift. Lucy, however, was extremely committed and very happy to be doing the job she was, and her boyfriend had just given her tickets to the Russian State Ballet at the Kennedy Center for her birthday so she was upbeat. "Pentagon Situation Room, how can I help you Sir or Ma'am?" came the bouncy answer.

Captain Young hated the style of many of his contemporaries who simply barked the name of the person they wanted to talk to with no other comment. He considered himself old-fashioned and prided himself that manners still mattered.

"Could I speak to the Secretary of Defense please?" he asked.

"I'm afraid he's unavailable at present Sir," was the response. "Can I take your name and a message?"

"My name is Captain Vincent Young and I am the Captain of the USS Kearsarge," he responded quietly, "and what is your name Miss?"

The voice on the other end of the phone remained calm and measured. "You're speaking with Army Lieutenant Lucy Jackson Sir." Lucy knew exactly who she was speaking to and was aware that she was now talking to one of the most decorated officers in the US Navy.

"Thank you Lucy," said the Captain. "I'm sitting here with the Deputy Director of Operations for the CIA, we're in the Caribbean by the way, and he wants to do something we haven't quite agreed on so we need to talk to the Secretary, and we need to do it now. Would you be good enough to wake him up? I'll apologise to his wife when we get back."

Richard Holland's bedside phone rang, as it often did, halfway through the night. He was now accustomed to this and sat up fairly quickly, taking the encrypted cellphone with him as he left the bedroom to try to avoid disrupting his wife's sleep.

"Too late," called Maggie Holland, as she turned the light on.

"Sorry honey," he said. "Work." He pressed the answer key. "Holland."

Lucy had done this several times now. "Good morning Mr Secretary," she said, "I'm sorry to disturb you at this hour but I have the Captain of the Kearsarge on the line, and he'd like to talk to you urgently Sir."

"Vince? Put him through."

Vince and Bill had made eye-contact during the wait. "If this goes wrong...?" Vince suggested.

"It won't," said Bill, eyes twinkling. "I'll be going with them."

"Don't make me take the Lord's good name in vain, Victoria hates it when I do that," said the Captain. There was a picture of him and his wife on their wedding day outside their Baptist church in Michigan by his bunk. He pointed to it.

He was interrupted by the voice of Lieutenant Lucy Jackson. "The Secretary is on the line for you now Sir," she said, "please go ahead. This call is encrypted to Secret US Ears only."

"Vince! What the hell is it this time? You've woken up Maggie again you know." The scolding was good natured.

"I apologise Mr Secretary. You know I wouldn't do this if it weren't urgent. I promise to bring her chocolates next time I'm in town."

"You'd better. And proper ones I mean. Belgian or Swiss or something. None of that Scandinavian crap you came back with last time. Tasted like sheepshit."

Vince laughed. "I won't ask Mr Secretary."

"Well what do you want to ask me Vince? It's four o' clock in the goddam morning here."

Vince's voice became serious. "I'm here with the Deputy Director of Operations of the Agency. He's asking for a green light on Operation Bleak House."

"Bleak House? Are you serious? Have you found him?"

"No Sir. We haven't found him, we've lost the scouts." Vince looked up at Bill, the two men knowing the seriousness of the question that was being asked and the implications of the answer. It was not a time for levity.

"I get a lot of calls Vince. Am I correct in remembering that the scouts on this one aren't natives."

"Correct Sir. It's the cousins."

Bill looked down at the floor of the cabin, shaking his head; he had a good idea where this was going. There was a long pause before the Captain heard the Secretary's voice again.

"And how many are you thinking of sending in?" Holland asked.

"Plan is for twenty four Delta, three crew in each of the two Sea Knight helicopters, two times Apache cover," he paused again and then spoke slowly, "and Bill wants to go too."

"I don't like Bill," said the Defense Secretary.

"I don't like him either, not many people do" Vince responded, "but he can be quite persuasive."

"What bullshit did he come out with this time?" was the question.

"No man left behind Sir."

"And that applies to the cousins as well now?"

Vince simply repeated the mantra. "No man left behind Sir."

"That's a shitload of talent we could lose if this goes wrong you know. And the political fallout is huge. And for what? To bring back a couple of corpses?"

Bill could hear the Defense Secretary's comments on the call. Vince had been gracious enough to turn the volume up as high as possible and had left the handset on his small desk. There was no speakerphone option. Bill grabbed his notebook out and wrote a message very quickly.

Vince read it and nodded to his friend. "They'd do the same for us Mr Secretary."

Being the US Defense Secretary had its perks. This wasn't one of them and Holland knew he had to ask the question. "How much time do I have to call it?" he asked.

Vince didn't hesitate. "Now is the time, Sir," he answered.

"You people are gonna give me an ulcer," he said. He looked up at his favourite photograph that wasn't of his family on the wall in front of him on the landing. Three men sat beside each other, each a leader with enormous responsibility. President Roosevelt sat in the middle, Prime Minister Churchill to his left, and Stalin to his right had been felt-penned out by the Defence Secretary's four year old nephew, at the Defence Secretary's request. The decision was made, "Get 'em back," he said, and killed the call.

"Everything okay honey?" asked Maggie.

"Everything's fine dear. Vince owes you more chocolates and the Brits owe me a favour. Go back to sleep."

CHAPTER NINE

Rescue…

The Officer Commanding the Delta Force team looked around the briefing room. "Everyone clear?" he asked, "any questions?" Major Steve Moyles had spent the last half an hour going through the hurriedly re-written plan to assault the prison. The original plan had been a silent approach, once the exact location of Gomez had been identified and Will and Robbo could provide sketch-maps of the interior of the complex. Steve had worked quickly with Master Sergeant Will Williamson, known to everyone as 'Willow', to re-jig the approach. There were no questions and no visible dissent about the new way to do things. "Okay, one last thing. Bill Reeves is coming with us, make sure he is behind you at all times, I do not want this man in the line of fire," he said, pointing at Bill, who was sitting by the entrance of the briefing room. Major Moyles turned to his Master Sergeant. "Anything I've forgotten Willow?" he asked.

"One thing if I may Sir?" Willow turned to the screen behind him where three photographs were projected, one of Will, one of Robbo and one of Gomez. "The priority is the two Brits," he said, "on this one, Gomez is a bonus. Let's not take our eye off the prize but we've only got one chance to get them out, we've got the rest of his shitty life to hunt Gomez." Willow eyed every man in the room. "And something you need to think about gentlemen. If these two crazy Limeys are still in that prison," he pointed at the meticulously prepared model on the briefing room floor, "and if they're still alive, they will not be looking like their passport photos."

A hand was raised at the back of the room and Willow acknowledged it. "Yes,"

Mike Winter was one of the newest members of this particular team but was confident enough to know that any question he asked would be responded to without ridicule.

"Sirs," he asked, addressing both the Officer and the Master Sergeant, "what about the prisoners?"

Willow looked to his team leader, admitting, "Good point. We didn't cover that Sir, and this is politics not tactics. Your arena."

"They are prisoners of a sovereign state and we have no idea what they are in there for. They could be rapists, murderers, paedophiles or thieves. They could also be political activists, kidnapped tourists or the personal enemies of a drug baron. I don't know, you don't know, and we sure as shit won't have the time to ask them all. This is not about nation-building or the promotion of democracy, this is about getting a couple of scouts out who were doing us a favour. As Bill has said, they would do the same for us if the tables were turned." The atmosphere in the room was subdued. "I do not have to remind you though gentlemen, that you have the full authority of the United States government to open fire on anyone whom you consider to be a threat to you or your fellow soldiers."

A shout came from the back of the room, "Hooah!" The cry was repeated by every man present except for two, one was the Captain of the USS Kearsarge, standing at the back of the room with his arms folded and shaking his head while looking at Bill Reeves, who was the only other man who didn't feel the requirement to psyche himself up.

"It'll be fine," said Bill to Vince as they left the briefing room. "What could possibly go wrong?" he added with a grin.

* * *

It was dark when the troops boarded the helicopters on the flight deck, but dawn was breaking by the time they approached the prison. The two Apache attack helicopters had flanked the Sea Knight Chinooks on the approach but now took the lead in the last few minutes to target, flying low and fast. The light level had reached the point where both pilots had snapped their night vision systems up onto their helmets and flew without assistance.

"Two towers, either side of the main gate," radioed the pilot of the lead Apache helicopter.

"Roger that, Zulu One," came the response. "Will you engage?"

"Engaging now, Zulu Two. Mop up if I miss anything."
The voices sounded disconnected, not quite human, as they were
processed through the encrypted radio transmission.

Zulu One opened fire and the wooden eastern watchtower
disintegrated. Switching his aim to the western tower the pilot
destroyed most of it bar a few planks in the ground.

Zulu One provided cover while the first Sea Knight,
designated X-Ray One, landed on the approach road just outside
the gates. The pilot turned the helicopter as she landed so the
assault force could run directly out of the tailgate at the target.
Gold Team blew the perimeter gates off shortly after
disembarking and secured the central compound, having shot
dead four guards in the process.

"All clear," the Gold Team leader radioed, and with that
X-Ray Two landed in the courtyard and the remaining twelve
members of the assault team ran out. There was surprisingly
little response to the incursion, although the sporadic shots from
some windows resulted in overwhelming firepower being
directed at them by the troops on the ground and from the
Apaches. X-Ray One and Two remained on the ground, engines
running, as the troops entered the main detention facility. Four
men were left behind to provide a security cordon for the
helicopters. The plan included a built in redundancy for one of
the aircraft, whether mechanical failure or physical attack; one of
the Sea Knights could take everyone back to the Kearsarge, but it
was naturally preferable to keep both helicopters flying if
possible. The Apaches remained hovering, but they couldn't do
so for long, having much smaller fuel tanks than the Sea Knights.
The Kearsarge was making best possible speed towards them but
they still only had less than ten minutes on target before they
would have to return as their fuel ran out. Major Moyles and
Willow had done the sums with the pilots when they put the plan
together. While the attack helicopters might not be necessary
once the ground force had been deployed, the extraction through
hostile Venezuelan airspace might still require an escort with the
ability to deploy some heavy weaponry, something which the Sea
Knights did not have.

Moyles and his team moved fast. Blasting open the main
door with somewhat less finesse than Will had opened it they

flooded through the corridors shouting, "Red Bus", the code word for the extraction plan.

Will, pulled back into consciousness once again by the noise of the airborne assault, managed to gather his senses. "Black Cab," he repeatedly shouted back the response code they'd agreed. The Delta team found him quickly, and a single shotgun blast to the lock opened the door. The prisoners in the rest of the facility had also been woken and were screaming to be released, banging on their cell doors with anything they could find. With the combination of the gunfire and the shouting it was difficult for Will to hear the instructions he was being given by Mike Winter, the most recent recruit who had so thoughtfully questioned what to do with the other prisoners. Mike ripped the hood off Will's head and pulled him to a standing position.

"Time to get you out of here," he shouted, pulling his knife from his belt and cutting Will's plasticuffs in one swift motion.

"Robbo," gasped Will, "have you got Robbo?"

"Let me check."

The Silver Assault Team had found Robbo, as well as Gomez and his sister, identified by Bill. Will needed assistance to walk and had wrapped himself in the thin grey blanket from his cell while he was taken to them.

Bill looked up at him as he entered the cell. "I'm really sorry," he said, his eyes misty. Will had never seen his old friend like this before. Bill pulled back the blanket to reveal Robbo's naked corpse, black and blue from the beatings and covered in crusted blood.

Will stared at the body of his brutally tortured former comrade in arms, a new strength building in him, as it did every time his world changed. Bill looked up at him from the low prison stool he was sitting on, "We haven't much time," he said.

Will's senses were sharp again. "No. Understood. We're bringing him back though?" he asked.

"No man left behind," came the instant response from Bill.

"What about these two?" he asked, indicating Gomez and his sister.

"We want him alive," said Bill, "he's got important information. She's nothing." The fear in Mathilde Gomez's eyes was evident as her pupils widened. Will looked at her straight in the face as Bill, unasked, handed Will his pistol. "Let's go," he said to the soldiers in the cell with him. Turning, he said to Will, "We've really got to move mate."

"Can you bring me two stretcher teams?" Will asked.

"Done."

"Was it you who cut his eyes out?" Will asked Mathilde Gomez. She looked at the floor and started to sob. The blackened and clearly burnt remnants of Robbo's eye sockets were the most startling elements of his massively abused body.

"What are you going to do to me that means I'll need a stretcher?" she asked.

"Absolutely nothing," Will replied, "it's not for you."

"But you asked for two teams," she cried.

Will stood up and the thin grey blanket fell from his shoulders. As he stood there naked he raised Bill's pistol, pointed it at Mathilde's head long enough for her to know she was about to die. As he applied pressure on the trigger the pain from the cocktail stick still under his fingernail was excruciating, so he pushed his finger further through the trigger guard and then fired a single shot. She slumped to the floor, leaving a red stain on the wall behind her where she had been sitting.

Gomez attempted a smile. "I will tell you everything you want to know," he said. "There is no need for a stretcher team. I get it. I get it. One stretcher for me and one stretcher for your companion. But, as I said, I will tell you everything you want to know. No need for stretcher."

"Yes you will and yes there is," said Will, "you should never underestimate the things I will do." With that he fired a shot into each of Gomez's kneecaps, a man who would never walk again and whose removal from Venezuela was never acknowledged by the American, British or Venezuelan governments.

* * *

The flight back to the Kearsarge was uninterrupted and Will took the opportunity to sleep as much as he could, although he and Bill went through a quick debrief. The Delta troops had thoughtfully put Robbo's body on the other Sea Knight – Will would have felt disrespectful falling asleep in the same helicopter. After medical treatment on the ship he found himself clothed in a boilersuit and sitting in the Captain's cabin, along with Bill. The doctors had been able to remove all the narrow wooden sticks from his nails, not without considerable pain, but his hands remained bandaged to prevent infection.

Captain Young walked in and as Will attempted to stand he waved him down. "Sorry about your man," he said, "must've been a brave guy."

"Yes sir," said Will.

Captain Vincent Young looked at the physically broken human being in front of him and then turned to Bill. "Bill, I do believe this is all your fault," he said.

"I do believe it is Captain," Bill answered.

"This man had the courtesy to attempt to stand when I came in, simply because I am the Captain of this ship. This is a man who has endured two nights and three days of pain I couldn't imagine. This is a man whose colleague lies in our morgue and is a significant contributor to the reason why we have Alberto Gomez in our Brig." Captain Young's gaze turned to Will again.

Will smiled. "If you're about to give me one of those bloody 'Commander's Coins of Excellence' that you Yanks are so damn fond of, can I pass on that?" he said. Now it was the Captain's turn to smile.

"I suspect Bill never told you I did an exchange posting with the Royal Navy?" Vince asked.

"No, he missed that one off on his briefing points on the way back. Fair one though, I was trying to get my head down."

"I learned a lot of things from the Royal Navy, especially about morale. You know the US Navy is alcohol-free while at sea?"

"Depressingly, yes," Will answered.

"Well, that's every ship apart from the USS Kearsarge," Vince said, "and as Bill is not technically a member of the Navy, and you are definitely not, I think..." he paused, reaching into the storage area under his bunk and pulling out a cardboard tube, "this is in order." Vince opened the tube wrapped in brown paper and pulled out a bottle of Lagavulin whisky. "Got introduced to this when they had me up at Faslane. Tell anyone on this ship or anyone ever that this happened and I will come looking for you." He poured generous measures into the three plastic cups he retrieved from his sink. "Sorry about the cups," he said, "and here's to Robbo." The Captain lifted his white plastic toothbrush cup and the other two men raised theirs, Will cupping it like a hot drink on a cold day. Will smiled sadly and the three of them toasted the fallen man. Although Will knew that he wouldn't have the horrendous experience of having to press the doorbell of the married quarters of Robbo's widow that night, (that task fell to the Quartermaster), he knew he would be having to talk through what had happened with her in the coming days when he got back. His mind raced as he thought about which parts of the story he would include and which bits he would leave out.

"Robbo", said Will. There was a brief silence.

"Anything we can do for you?" asked Captain Vince.

"Cheeseburger would be good," said Will. "Robbo reckoned you guys were the best in the world at cheeseburgers."

* * *

In his office in Chicago a man called Paul Gilmour got the call about the attack on the prison in Venezuela for which he had the contract to provide security guards and prison officers. His private security company was already on the verge of bankruptcy, having received very bad press after several of his employees had posted personal videos of obvious human rights abuses in Iraq and Afghanistan on the internet. The stock market value of 'Gilmour Land Security' had plummeted. He spoke with his chief legal advisor quickly after he heard the news about what had happened at the prison. There would be a significant amount of compensation to be paid to the families of the dead, and it was likely that the other three contracts he had would not be renewed and his bid to build two new prisons would be rejected. The Venezuelan government was embarrassed and the drug barons whose influence reached the highest levels had made clear both their fear and anger. Gilmour needed a new business model, and soon he would receive an offer he couldn't refuse.

* * *

Just before Will boarded his flight back to the UK, Susan, the lady who had driven him to the port several days earlier and whose daughter he had been engaged to, drove into the hangar where the CIA Learjet was waiting for him. "I thought you might be interested in this," she said, handing him a file. "We don't like him very much. If you ever get the opportunity…" she said, deliberately not finishing the sentence.

Will raised his eyebrows, confused.

"He's an American citizen, we can't, well you know, we just can't, not when he's in America anyway. But feel free to if the possibility ever comes up."

"Who is he?"

"He's the man who made money out of letting Gomez live in that prison."

Will smiled, "Well in that case, I hope I get the opportunity to meet him one day." Susan hugged him. "Ooh! Not too tight," he said, wincing with the pain.

"She'd have been very proud of you," Susan added, kissing him on the cheek. And with that she turned, not wanting him to see the tears rolling down her face as she walked back to the car.

CHAPTER TEN

Another Job Interview...

The Commanding Officer of the Special Reconnaissance Regiment visited Will in the recovery ward the morning after he got back to the UK. "Can you walk?" he asked brusquely.

"Yes Sir."

"Then get dressed. We have a train to catch." The two nurses who had been assigned to him helped him pack, not that there was much to put in the small holdall he arrived with. Rachel and Charlotte walked with him to the hospital lobby.

"I don't know, and I don't want to know how you ended up like this, but we'll miss you Will," said Charlotte, squeezing his forearm gently, deliberately avoiding his hands. Lucy kissed him on the cheek.

"Don't worry girls. You see the scary looking guy by the door?" he said, looking towards his Commanding Officer. They both nodded their assent. "Well the reason he's dragging me out of here probably means he wants me to do something which will result in me coming back here pretty soon."

The medical staff at the hospital were used to not asking too many questions, or if they did, being told not to. Will smiled at them and headed for the exit.

Will and his CO spoke very quietly on the train to London. Will learned that he was heading for a meeting with the Prime Minister and the Chairman of the Intelligence and Security Committee. That was about as much as his boss was willing, or able, to tell him.

"I'm not really dressed for it," he ventured, looking down at the casual shirt and chinos he was wearing.

Johnson and the Prime Minister were waiting for him in the Prime Minister's private office. Both stood up and everyone shook hands except Will, who apologised while indicating his bandages. Ffi walked in from the adjacent office and took a seat in the corner window, pen and paper in hand.

Will sat in anticipation, calm, but curious and confused. He had no idea what was about to come next. Sometimes he relished situations like this, today he did not.

"Major Richards," said the Prime Minister, "I understand you've been in hospital as a result of recent operational activity."

Will couldn't resist the temptation, "Yes Sir, and I suspect my premature departure from that institution may be the reason why we're all sitting here together today," he beamed.

The Prime Minister could not stop himself from looking a little irritated. He turned to Johnson, asking, "And this is the man you're recommending for this position?"

Johnson responded quickly, "This is the man who has been recommended to us by people who know a lot more about it than you and I do Prime Minister."

There was a knock at the door and without waiting for a response General Jim Green walked into the room. Will stood up, as did his CO. "Prime Minister", he said, and then acknowledging his fellow officers waved them back into their seats.

"General," asked the Prime Minister, "are you sure this is the right man for the job?"

Will was losing his patience, but remained measured. "Sirs, I don't want to be rude, but could someone tell me why I'm here?"

The Prime Minister looked at his briefing notes. "You appear to be quite a capable chap Major Richards."

"Thank you Sir," Will replied. "So do you, not a bad job title."

The Prime Minister could not help himself from smiling. "Your superiors speak very highly of you, the Americans have been gushing in their praise, but then that doesn't count for much, and for some reason Ffi..." He broke off and looked at Ffi, who looked up from her note-taking, "and Ffi always smiles when anyone mentions your name."

Ffi looked embarrassed, "Do I?" she asked, blushing slightly.

"Yes, you're doing it again now." The Prime Minister stared intently at Will. "One question," he said. "Why have I been listening to influential civil servants and a Two Star General referring to you as the Milk Tray Man for the last 24 hours?"

It was Will's turn to look embarrassed, and Ffi blushed even more visibly. Will looked first to his CO, then to General Green, and then finally back to the Prime Minister. "That all started a few years ago Sir. We were doing a job in Cyprus, and Ffi was our Home Office liaison officer. That's how I first met her, well sort of. I was in daily contact with her but she was in London and we were in the Mediterranean. She told me that her boyfriend had just dumped her – clearly not a bright individual. Anyway it turned out that we flew back on Valentine's Day, so I bought a box of chocolates at Heathrow and on the way back to Hereford we diverted to the heliport at Battersea. Ffi had been sent a message to meet us there and so when we arrived I just jumped out of the helicopter, gave her the chocolates and jumped back in." The Prime Minister looked puzzled. "Seemed like a nice thing to do," said Will, by way of explanation. The PM raised an eyebrow. "And the pilot needed to get his flying hours in anyway so it didn't cost the taxpayer anything," he added hurriedly.

General Green broke the silence. "You wanted someone with imagination," he said to Johnson.

The Prime Minister stood up, followed quickly by the three officers. He extended his hand to Will, who took it between both his bandaged palms. "Congratulations, you have the job," he said.

"That's great," said Will, "what is it?"

"I'll let the Chairman go through that with you." The Prime Minister pushed a button on his desk and a secretary appeared and escorted the men to a private conference room. David Marshall turned to Ffi. "Did you have a thing with him?" he asked.

"No, no, not at all, he's just a nice guy," she laughed.

"Nice enough to divert Special Forces helicopters to bring you a box of chocolates?" asked the Prime Minister, eyebrows raised.

"You don't understand Prime Minister. At the time, Will was engaged."

"That's not making it sound any better," he responded. "And where is the engagee now?"

"She's a star on the wall at Langley. American, obviously. Worked for the Political Action Group in the Special Activities Division of the CIA. Killed in Kazakhstan, body never found."

"Jesus Christ," said Marshall slowly, dropping his pen on his desk.

"Yep," said Ffi, taking a sip from her glass of water, "and much as I love him, and he is kind of cute too, I've never even entertained the idea of being his girlfriend."

"How come?" the Prime Minister asked.

"Simple," she replied, "he's still in love with Sarah, always will be." She stood up and walked to the window. "The thing you have to understand about Will, and this is very important, is that while he is a very nice, affable and amusing guy, and blessed with the gift of exceptional clarity of thought and imagination, he really doesn't care about himself. You can insult him, betray him, stab him, shoot him, whatever. He really doesn't give a shit if he lives or dies. Genuinely. I've had bad days where I've called him and he's listened to me sobbing over the phone for hours. He listens better than my girlfriends do. And the next day he's gone out and planned something where people get killed. And you know what, I've never had a phone call from him where he's moaned or whinged about anything, and he's got more invested in the bank of "Christ, that sucks", than anyone I know."

The Prime Minister smiled. "You're a little bit in love with him, aren't you?" he asked.

"A little bit," she said, "but never more than that."

"And why's that?"

"Self-preservation. He'll never love anyone like he loved Sarah, and besides, the man is walking target practice for every lunatic he goes up against, which happens quite a lot. He put on a good show for you today."

"You've lost me there Ffi."

"Prime Minister, Will can barely walk at the moment. He discharged himself from hospital this morning because you asked to see him."

David Marshall looked humbled. He took his glasses off and rubbed his eyes. Nodding, he said, "I think we got the right guy then."

Back in the conference room Will limped to an armchair and slumped into it. He turned to Johnson, "What's the gig?" he asked.

"We'd like you to set something up," he started, and over the course of the next hour he explained how he wanted someone to plan for and co-ordinate the interventions and responses to the unexpected. "Terrorists, train crashes, chemical spills, natural disasters, the remit is unlimited. Just think about what can go wrong, catastrophically wrong, by accident or design, and think of a way to stop it before it happens or fix it when it does. That's your job," he finished.

"That's a big job," said Will.

"Can you do it?" Johnson asked.

"Yep. But it'll take a bit of time."

"How much do you need?"

Will thought for a moment. "Off the top of my head I'd say we could probably put something together in six months, given we had the right budget."

"And what would that be?" came the question.

"I'm not an accountant Mr Johnson. I'd have to give you the bill at the end of the six months."

Johnson laughed. "You sound like me when I used to run a union. Don't worry about cash, I've found out how to get that out of the government. You up for the job then?"

"Yeah, I'm in," said Will. When the two men stood up, Johnson clapped him on the back. Will winced so briefly that Johnson didn't even notice, although he did notice the blood seeping into Will's shirt as the three officers left the room. Will turned just as he was about to leave the room. "What do you want to call it?" he asked.

"I've been working on that one," said Johnson, grinning proudly. "What do you think of 'Task Force Nightshade'?"

Will laughed in Johnson's face. "You're not serious!"

"Of course I'm serious. I think it sounds quite sort of special operations-like. You know, SEAL Team Six and all that."

"Yes Sir, but we leave things like that to our American friends. You've been watching too many Hollywood films. The press will be all over that in days once the civil servants start gobbing off in the Westminster bars. I'd much prefer something which barely raises an eyebrow, the most innocuous sounding title we can think of would be best."

"Alright then," said Johnson, "Call it what you want. I just want you to put a group together that can plan for the contingencies we've just discussed."

"That'll do then," said Will, as he turned again and limped down the corridor. "Contingency Planning Group," he shouted, "perfect."

Johnson stared at his shoes. He was rather proud of coming up with the name Task Force Nightshade. "Hmmm," he muttered to himself, somewhat deflated. He decided that while for those who even needed to know the existence of the capability, the 'Contingency Planning Group' would suffice, but all the files in his private office would refer to Task Force Nightshade.

As they walked down the corridor Will's CO turned to him. "Well done Will," he said.

"Thank you Sir."

"As for you," he said, turning to his own boss, the Director of Special Forces, "got any recommendations for my next Ops Officer or are there any others of my diamonds you'd like to poach?"

General Green stared straight ahead as he walked. "Be quiet Philip, or you'll be buying the first round, not me, and the first round is going to be champagne."

"Where are we headed?" asked Will.

"Jesus Will, sometimes you are such a Philistine."

"Thank you Sir, years of training."

"We are going," said the General imperiously, "to the champagne table at the Landmark hotel, where we have a reservation, and where an old friend wants to say hello."

The General's chauffeur driven Jaguar swept out of the gates of Downing Street and the three men arrived shortly afterwards at the hotel. Paula greeted them as they entered the bar. "Mr Reeves is at his usual table," she said, smiling as sweetly as always. As they turned to walk to the corner table, Paula caught Will's hand and she saw his face contort. "Sir, you are bleeding," she said, having noted the reddish-brown stain on the back of Will's white shirt.

Will sighed. "Shit, not again. Sorry, this keeps happening.

"Come with me," said Paula. She took him to the staff bathroom and ordered him to take off his shirt. "I do not allow bleeding men in my bar," she told him directly. She took a fresh flannel to the wound on his back and washed away the blood. There," she said, "it has stopped bleeding. Put this on." She had grabbed a freshly starched waiter's shirt from a hanger in the cupboard and gave it to him, simultaneously throwing his own shirt into the bin.

Bill Reeves stood up as Will approached the table. His champagne was already poured. "Sorry about Venezuela," he said. "And Robbo," he added.

Will lowered his head in acknowledgement. "It happens."

"We've paid off the mortgage on his house and we've given his wife a trust fund for the two girls which'll get them through college, if they want to go."

"Widow," Will corrected him.

"Sorry, didn't mean to offend," said Bill.

"None taken. Jesus, are we just going to sit here talking or drink this stuff?"

CHAPTER ELEVEN

Six months of work…

When Will actually had to do thinking rather than doing he always did the same thing, and so once again he rented the beautiful cottage on Gold Hill in Shaftesbury which he and Sarah had stayed in years earlier. He put the picture of her which he always carried in the window, and lit the fire. Then he opened a bottle of red wine and played the baby grand piano at the top of the steep stairs which led down to the kitchen. The cottage was built into the side of a steep valley, quite how it hadn't fallen down the slope was a mystery to Will, and he remembered Sarah mentioning it the first time they had stayed there.

Too many glasses of red wine later Will sat on the floor in front of the fire with his notebook and a fountain pen. The page remained untouched for some time. "I'm Winnie the bloody Pooh", he said to himself, "thinking makes my brain hurt".

Then a realisation came to him, and while confronting the problem was welcome, the answer to the question was somewhat overwhelming. "Shit," he said out loud, "I have to write the Business Continuity and Crisis Management Plan for the bloody country." He stared into the flames for a few minutes, dwelling on the size of the task he had been asked to carry out. He turned to the photograph. "Sarah, I'm going to the pub. I may be some time."

* * *

The next morning Will woke with a sore head, but a notebook full of ideas. He spent the next four days in the cosy little cottage thinking of everything that could affect the stability of the country. He sat in the garden drinking Scotch and looking out over the valley as the sun dipped behind the hills and the house lights were switched on in the distance. He stared through the morning mist and leafed through history books trying to understand how empires and establishments fell. He paced up and down in the kitchen reading books on economics and lay in bed turning the pages of encyclopaedias. He was a fast learner and by the end of the week he didn't know how to solve the myriad problems he had identified, but he had listed them and had a list of people he wanted to speak to who he had concluded could help him. Will Richards had written a shopping list of people.

His first stop was at the Co-Operative supermarket at the top of the hill. There was a machine in the lobby which printed business cards. They were cheap and unprofessional but Will decided he had to start somewhere. He laughed at himself as he typed in the details to be printed. "Keep it simple," he thought, and less than two minutes later fifty cards fell out of the machine. "Contingency Planning Group," they announced, with Will's name underneath. The only contact details were the central switchboard for the Ministry of Defence and 999. Will smiled. "Got to start somewhere," he thought, stuffing the cards into his wallet and walking to his car. He drove to Hereford.

"I've been expecting you," said the Commanding Officer of 22 SAS as Will walked into his office. The two men shook hands. "Sit down," was the instruction. Will did as he was told and over the course of the next hour explained his vision for a nationwide co-ordinating capability that would be able to respond to any national security threat to the United Kingdom, and hopefully, spot them before they happened.

The Commander of the Special Air Service looked unimpressed. "And what do you think we do and prepare for here on a daily basis?" he asked, somewhat testily.

Will smiled, "Lots of very good things," he answered, "but what's your plan if there's an earthquake and the Severn Bridge falls into the river?"

There was a moment's silence and then the CO stood up and extended his hand again. "What are you going to call this bastard child that you're setting up Major Richards?" Will handed him one of his newly made business cards as he returned the handshake. "Where the hell did you get this, your local corner store?"

"No Sir, that comes from a proper supermarket."

Will left Hereford and spent the next few weeks on the road. One by one he ticked off his shopping list, visiting the military units of the Special Boat Service, his home unit of the Special Reconnaissance Regiment and the Special Forces Support Group. He had lunch at the Savoy Hotel with the Association of Chief Police Officers. He had afternoon tea with the Director of the Meteorological Office at the Landmark, where Paula once again ensured they were able to talk in confidence. "At least you've stopped bleeding," was her parting remark as they left.

He addressed the Chiefs of the General Staff, the Prime Minister and Her Majesty the Queen. Once they had all concluded that he wasn't a complete idiot he got down to the really difficult business, and started buying real estate and logistical capability which would not appear on government books. That process resulted in him recruiting some surprising people, one of whom was a teenage mugger who really picked on the wrong man when Will was walking back to his hotel after dinner with friends.

After six months, and many more meetings, Will was reasonably confident he'd got things covered. He handed David Johnson the documents covering the expenses to-date and the projected annual expenditure. He was expecting to be shouted at.

"Nice work, well done," was the response.

CHAPTER TWELVE

Present Day…

After his meeting with Hannah at the newspaper offices, Will decided to walk the couple of miles to his sister's flat in the Limehouse Marina, stopping on his way at an off-licence to buy her a bottle of wine. She only drank white and Will only ever bought her the best – he was grateful to her for letting him use her flat as a bolthole, it was modern with large windows and had a spacious balcony, in stark contrast to the dingy and noisy basement flat in Kilburn he'd been given by the army.

He had his own key and let himself in. Lucy had left him a note on the low table in the living room. "At soundcheck. Beer in fridge. See you later. X." Will walked into the kitchen, swapped a beer bottle for the wine he'd bought and went out to the balcony. After loosening his tie and taking his shoes off he leaned back in one of Lucy's extremely comfortable beanbag chairs. He had a habit of talking out loud when he was alone. "Well, perhaps," he mused," we've finally got something to do. And are you, Rebecca Taylor, whoever you are and whatever your real name is, going to get the clue? I bloody hope so, because this is both interesting and serious at the same time. Six months it's taken me to set this thing up and now we are pressing the 'go' button." He raised his beer as if in a toast. "Here's to you Rebecca, let's hope you're for real."

* * *

Jan at reception was still there as Hannah left the newspaper offices. "Everything alright?" she asked.

"Just peachy," said Hannah, raising her eyebrows.

"Interesting place to work innit?" said Jan in her Estuary English.

"I think that's what you English people call 'understatement'," said Hannah smiling.

"Have a good evening darlin'," she called as Hannah approached the revolving doors.

"You too," shouted Hannah, waving without looking back. She took the Docklands Light Railway back but instead of going home, she phoned her neighbour Susie and asked if they could just go straight to the pub. Susie had had another crappy day at the department store in Oxford Street - were there any other kinds - and was delighted to oblige.

Hannah waited for her at the bottom of the station steps. Susie may have had yet another miserable experience at work but she always smiled, genuinely. "Hey hon, how you been?" she asked, linking arms with Hannah as they walked to the pub.

"You know, same old, same old," she said, but Susie knew there was something different.

She tugged on Hannah's arm. "Bluffer. Come on, what is it? You meet a guy? You meet a girl?" she teased.

"I met a guy," answered Hannah.

"Ooh!"

"But it's not what you think," she added quickly. "Just weird. All weird."

"And?" Susie pleaded. "Tell, tell, tell."

"You promise not to talk to anyone else about this?"

"Scout's honour," said Susie, raising her hand.

"Okay, well to summarise, this guy comes in, gives me his phone, I call the owner of the paper and we put a made-up death announcement in tomorrow's edition."

"Sounds exciting!" Susie sang as they descended the steps to the pub. "I always knew you'd get a great story," she said, patting Hannah's hand. The great thing about Susie was that she knew when to stop asking questions. A fair few people at work just thought she was a ditzy blonde who didn't understand complexity, and sometimes Susie played up to that. The reality was quite the opposite.

* * *

Will walked down to the pub his sister was going to be playing at that night. He hadn't seen her perform for a couple of months and was looking forward to it. He loved the way dusk fell over the marina and he lingered on a footbridge just outside the pub, listening to the muffled sound of the good-natured voices inside. Looking across the river Will wondered if something seismic was about to happen. The codename 'Rebecca Taylor' was known to only eight people. It had been chosen to be as innocuous as the name of the Contingency Planning Group – it wouldn't have come up by accident at the Chinese Embassy. Whoever she was, she knew something and wanted to say hello. Will was still hoping that she knew more than just the name, and would look a bit harder than the obvious, which is why he had chosen the newspaper announcement so carefully.

He heard his sister's voice introducing the band to the packed bar and walked down the old stone steps to the quayside.

"Good evening everyone. I'm Lucy Milton and these are, as they hate to be called, the Miltonette's." Lucy raised her arm in the direction of the band.

There was a generous round of applause. It was approaching Christmas and despite the dark evenings and cold, wet weather, people were generally predisposed to celebrating rather than indifference.

"We've never played here before, despite the fact that I live just around the corner," she smiled coquettishly. "The new album's just out, available from all good record stores and from behind the bar," she announced. "Thank you Michael," she said, acknowledging the landlord. "But tonight we're playing the tunes as requested by you guys during the week."

Michael walked over with a glass jar full of business cards and put it on Lucy's piano. "Okay, the rules were, one card per customer, rhythm and blues or soul music only. Your card gets picked, you get a free drink." A cheer went up from the drinkers. Lucy pulled a card from the jar and was about to read it out when she spotted Will approaching the bar. Tony Fletcher, an accountant with an international shipping firm would not get his free drink that evening, nor would he get to hear Son of a Preacher Man.

"Okay then," said Lucy, cupping Tony's business card. "This is for Will Richards of The Contingency Planning Group, and this is Gimme Some Lovin".

Will looked across at Lucy as the band kicked in, slowly shaking his head as she smiled at him. "You," he mouthed.

At almost the same moment Hannah realised what she'd just heard and looked around the bar frantically. "You alright?" asked Susie.

"No," came the definite response. Hannah put her wine glass down and scoured the bar, eventually spotting Will. She walked over to him with a face like thunder. "Are you following me?" she asked.

Although surprised by the turn of events, Will was relaxed. "No," he answered.

"Well, it sure seems like you are."

"If I were following you do you really think I'd ask that singer to call out my name, something I know she couldn't have done genuinely because I know I haven't put a business card in that jar," he said. "Hey, I know it's all a bit weird. Let me get you a drink," he offered.

Hannah looked at the floor briefly. "How the hell does she know who you are then?" she asked.

"Umm, that would be because I'm her brother."

"I'm with a friend actually, I should get back to her." Susie had been watching Hannah during the exchange.

"No dramas," said Will, "although, I just got a free drink. What would your friend like?"

"She'd probably like to be left alone, just like me," Hannah answered.

As she turned to leave Will reached for her hand. "Hannah, we're the good guys," he said, trying to reassure her.

"You better be," she replied, as she turned away.

* * *

Several hours later on Lucy's balcony she was sipping a glass of the wine that Will had bought her and he was enjoying another beer. She went to light another cigarette.

"You know, apart from killing yourself, you are killing the tastebuds that would help you to enjoy that seriously expensive wine properly," he mused.

"If you're gonna sing the blues properly, you really need to smoke," she shot back.

The two of them gazed at the now cloudless winter sky. "Something's going on isn't it?" Lucy asked, glancing across at him.

"I do believe it is. Yes."

"Can't talk about it?" she asked casually. There was no response. After a pause she said, "That girl at the bar, she's something do with it isn't she?" There was still no response. "Do you like her?"

"Not going there Lucy," was the response.

"Will, it's been seven years. You have got to let go of Sarah at some point."

"Agreed," he said, "But I haven't reached that point yet."

CHAPTER THIRTEEN

Thursday…

Margret had spent the early part of the morning signing in all the correspondence for the Chief of the Naval Staff, as she had done for nearly two decades. Her office in the Admiralty building was small and cluttered and although the one window in it was small, it looked out over the Police memorial in St James's Park. Margret's father had been a policeman, killed in the war by a German bombing raid, and it gave her comfort to think that he was not forgotten. She had stamped, dated and initialled all the morning's documents, and placed them in the pink folder marked "Top Secret – UK Eyes Only", as she had done since she could remember. Margret was nearing retirement, and had hoped that her last few months would be quiet ones. Having seen the morning's post however, she knew that today, at least, was going to be what she always referred to when speaking to her husband as "one of those, you know, slightly 'shouty' days".

Margret was generally and genuinely what all her colleagues referred to as sweetly dispositioned. It was unusual therefore for her to leave the tiny Registry, pink binder in hand, with a look of resignation and misery. A colleague passed her in the corridor and did a double take as his smile was not returned. He was on his way to yet another anonymous budgetary sub-committee of no import and the perceived snub set him up for an entirely miserable day.

Margret continued down the corridor to the outer office of the Chief of the Naval Staff, Admiral Sir James Dudgeon. The door, as always, was open.

"Hello Margret," came a cheery greeting from the Lieutenant Commander who had the completely unrewarding job of the lowest ranking of the aides-de-camp to the Admiral. "How are you this morning?" he asked. Margret just looked at him and handed over the folder. "Oh dear. Oh dear, oh dear, oh dear," he said. "Shouty day?"

"I think so yes, Lieutenant Commander."

"Margret, I've been here a month now, how many times do I have to ask you to call me Richard?"

"Well, I've only got two and half months left, so maybe you can keep trying until then," she answered.

"Then I shall. Anyway, what's the damage this morning? What," he piped cheerily, "is the reason for this morning's requirement for ear defenders?"

"It's the naval spending review. I know he knows what's in it but today he has to sign it off."

"Oh shit." Even the energetic Lieutenant Commander seemed to have the wind taken out of his sails. "Forgive me Margret but he is going to go absolutely..."

"Fucking ballistic," she finished his sentence for him. "I know." The Lieutenant Commander raised his head from his hands in astonishment. She smiled. "Lieutenant Commander, I've worked in the Admiralty long enough to have picked up the language of sailors. Now that one," she nodded to the Admiral's office door, "has got to be the pick of the bunch. Tread carefully." Margret left the outer office and quickly headed for the sanctuary of the Registry.

Lieutenant Commander Richard Reeves briefly skimmed the contents of the morning briefings and papers that Margret had brought him. There were a lot of the usual routine annoyances, requests for fuel for training exercises and concerns about Chinese naval manoeuvres in the East China Sea. But there was one document which Richard knew was going to take the roof off that morning. Unlike the encyclopaedic-sized document which was its predecessor, this one ran to only two pages, summarizing the findings of the Defence Select Committee and six month's worth of what seemed like endless discussions. These were no longer recommendations, these were findings, and today was the day they had to be signed off. Neatly punch-holed and bound with a treasury tag by Margret, the first page was a letter from the Prime Minister.

"Dear Admiral Dudgeon,

I know this is a task which you will not take any pleasure in, and I am sorry that I have to ask you to do it, but the findings have been passed by Cabinet and Parliament and are now required to be signed-off by you. Let me assure you that your strong and well argued objections were taken into account at all stages and as a result we have tried to make the impact on the Royal Navy as minimal as possible.

I am confident that the Royal Navy will still be able to project power around the globe and act as a force for good in the international arena, in concert with our allies.

Sincerely,

David Marshall"

Richard steeled himself for the task. There was no point trying to hide this stuff at the back of the folder so he put it straight to the top and carried it to the Admiral's inner office door. He knocked and then waited before entering. He had made the mistake of knocking and entering on his first day in the role. He had no desire to repeat the experience. Admiral Dudgeon had a fierce reputation, and for a good reason.

"Come," came the shout from inside.

Richard walked in. "Good morning Sir." The Admiral did not look up from the papers he was marking with a fountain pen filled with green ink. He held his hand out for today's first sight file. Richard was becoming accustomed to the Admiral's nature.

"Anything interesting?" Admiral Dudgeon asked.

"I wouldn't call it interesting Sir, I'd call it the spending review." Richard knew he was not going to enjoy the next few hours but he wasn't about to shirk from the reality of the situation.

Dudgeon looked up slowly. "So it's here is it? This is the day I have to kill the Royal Navy? Thirty years of service and now I have to destroy the very thing that put me in this chair?"

"I'm not sure it's for me to comment," Richard answered.

"Sit down Richard." This was a surprising turn of events. The Admiral had only ever referred to him as Lieutenant Commander Reeves and Richard had expected him to at least shout some sort of obscenity at the messenger. He pulled out one of the buttoned-leather chairs from the Admiral's conference table and sat down, more apprehensive now than he had been when he knocked on the door. Admiral Dudgeon raised himself slowly from his desk, and turned to the cabinet behind him. Taking a small key from his pocket he opened one of the mahogany doors and withdrew two crystal tumblers and a bottle of single malt whisky. "I know that traditionalists will say this should be rum, but I'm not a traditionalist Richard, I'm a pragmatist, and I've never been able to stomach the stuff truth be told. Bloody awful. Bit like that spending review."

Richard was unsure how to respond. "It might be a bit early for me Sir." It was just gone ten o' clock.

"Nonsense. Absolute nonsense. It's not too early Mr Reeves. It's too blasted late is what it is." He nodded at the bottle as he opened it. "See this, I was saving this for an appropriate moment. Was a christening gift from my Grandfather. Probably worth a bloody fortune by now. Probably was then actually. Anyway, doesn't matter. This is an appropriate moment. Shall we toast the death of the Royal Navy, the finest military force the world has ever seen?"

"Sir, with the greatest respect," Richard began.

Admiral Dudgeon's voice rose just a little, but the venom that was barely concealed in it was enough to make Richard stare at the luxurious dark blue carpet with the insignia of the Royal Navy threaded into it in the middle of the room. "Stop there Mr Reeves." Dudgeon was pouring the whisky now. "Speak your mind. And don't tart it up with that 'greatest respect' crap. I never used it and I've been around long enough to know it's the language of cowards and sycophants."

Richard pursed his lips. How to respond? "I was simply going to say Sir that I'm not sure I could actually toast the death of the Royal Navy. Simple as that."

Admiral Dudgeon handed Richard his glass. "Well said young man. But don't tell me I'm not wrong. I didn't get here by being an idiot and you didn't get there by being an idiot. You're a very bright and capable officer Reeves. You think I don't personally appoint my naval assistants?"

"No Sir. I mean, yes Sir, I'm sure you do."

Dudgeon threw his neck back and consumed the contents of his tumbler.

"Damn right!" He poured himself another measure. "So you should be smart enough to know that this is game over. Right here! Right now! There is no going back from this." He paused briefly. "I cannot, and will not, allow myself to be the person who history records as the man who lost the Royal Navy. Not going to happen." The second measure was downed.

"Sir, with..." Richard stopped himself as he received a severe glare from the Admiral. "Sir, no-one's happy about what's coming. It's very difficult. But the Navy still exists, it's just smaller."

"Just!" spat Dudgeon, "Just! Perhaps you're not as bright as I thought."

Margret was right, thought Richard, it was going to be a 'shouty' day after all. The Admiral walked to the window where the view looked over Horseguards Parade. It was the Grenadier Guards' turn to troop their Colour that summer and they were rehearsing the complex and intricate drill moves to the beat of a single bass drum before the official birthday parade for the Queen. The Regimental Sergeant Major was berating at high volume a young officer who had failed to issue a drill order to his guardsmen. Dudgeon couldn't make out the exact words but the way the Sergeant Major had bellowed at the bass drummer to stop beating and was pointing his v-shaped pace stick at the Guard Commander left no-one in any doubt as to his displeasure. "You see this Richard," the Admiral asked. "Come here, have a look out this window."

Richard put his glass down and walked over. He was completely unsure what was coming next – he had been addressed formally and informally, casually and directly. This was already the most unusual day he had experienced since starting his posting at the Admiralty.

"What do you see?" asked the Chief of the Naval Staff.

"Soldiers Sir. Trooping the Colour rehearsal," Richard responded.

"You're missing the point Richard." The Admiral's voice had returned to normal pitch and volume. "What you're seeing is tradition. Military capability. See that chap with the bass drum? All on his own. Where's the rest of the band?"

"I don't know Sir," came the honest response.

"Well they're not in their bunks sleeping off the night before are they? They're rehearsing too. And this one lone chap comes out here and beats out the time for these men to make sure they don't embarrass themselves in front of each other or Her Majesty."

"Yes Sir. Sorry, I'm not sure where you're going with this."

"Sit down and finish that whisky Richard. I am about to make it crystal clear." The Admiral poured his third glass. "What is this I am about to sign?" he asked, tapping the pink folder with his fingertips. Just as Richard was desperately trying to form a non-explosive response Dudgeon got in first. "I am about to sign the death-knell not just of the Royal Navy but of the United Kingdom. You know what I'm about to put my name to. No carrier capability. The abolition of the Fleet Air Arm. The sale for scrap of the minesweepers. And, most appallingly, the running down of the submarine fleet with no plan for renewal of the boats or what they carry. No independent nuclear deterrent equals no guaranteed permanent seat on the UN Security Council. We can scarcely police our own fishing waters. We're down to half a dozen frigates and destroyers. The Americans aren't just laughing at us any more, they're turning their sterns and sailing away. There are drug smugglers in the Caribbean and pirates off the east and west coasts of Africa who will be listening to the BBC World Service tonight and pissing themselves laughing. We're out of the game Ricky. We just turned into Belgium. Those bandsmen you can't see rehearsing in their band hall you're unaware of are still rehearsing. And they'll probably be damned good. Take away their trumpets and trombones and drums and flutes and see how good they'd be after ten years. A ship can't be in two places at once, I don't care how advanced it is, and a navy can't exercise and prepare for the worst when there're no damned ships and even if there were no-one would know how to drive them."

"It's difficult Sir, I know," Richard responded.

"It's bloody treason is what it is," whispered the Admiral, before smashing his glass down on the table. He had started pacing the office, staring fiercely at the paintings of some of the most famous ships in the Navy's history. "See that?" He pointed at one of the older oil paintings of a wooden ship engaging a Spanish galleon. "What is it?"

"That's the Ark Royal Sir."

"Correct. Commissioned?"

"Fifteen eighty-seven," Richard answered.

"Correct again. Dartmouth Naval College gets a point for still getting some things right. Have another drink." It was more of an instruction than a request and Richard noticed that he had actually finished his whisky. He picked up the bottle and poured himself a slightly larger measure than he thought sensible, but he thought he might as well settle himself in with a bit of anaesthetic to endure what he felt was imminent.

"Now then Richard, like I said, I'm not a traditionalist, I'm a pragmatist. There is a reason we now build our ships out of metal and not wood. This is entirely sensible. There is a reason we use rocket powered missiles and not thumping great cannon balls to deter and defeat the enemies of the realm. But now we have to ask ourselves, really ask ourselves, who are the enemies of the realm? Are they the jihadists in the caves learning how to build bombs or the people who have stripped us of our capability to blow them to bloody pieces?" The Admiral looked Richard straight in the eyes. "It's both Richard, both."

Dudgeon poured himself yet another drink and gulped it back quickly. "Right, I've got some people to see. I won't be back in the office today Richard, see you Monday."

"Yes Sir, do you want me to leave these here or take them back to the Registry?" Richard asked, pointing at the papers.

"Yes, if you would take them back. I can't stomach the sight of them. It'll take me at least a long weekend to get over what I'm doing here." Richard swigged the rest of his whisky and stood up to collect the files. "You got a girlfriend Richard?" the Admiral asked. It was the first time Dudgeon had ever expressed any interest in Richard's personal life.

"Fiance actually Sir."

"Good show. What does she do?"

"Nothing at the moment. Just got back from Borneo. She's a nurse. Team medic for a Raleigh International expedition. She's got a new job starting in a couple of weeks at St Thomas's".

"Good for her. Well, take her out for lunch and have the afternoon off." Richard did a double take. "Don't look so bloody surprised man, and take the opportunity before I change my mind."

Richard smiled. "Thank you Sir. Wasn't expecting that," he said.

"And I wasn't bloody expecting that," said the Admiral, pointing at the pink folder, "well I was expecting it, obviously, but I never thought the day would come. A day for surprises eh Richard?" He clapped Richard on the shoulder and went for his overcoat hanging on the back of the office door. Richard walked around the desk to retrieve the file. As he did so, he saw the Admiral's notebook lying open on the centre of the desk. It was not in Richard's nature to be nosey but one piece of writing stood apart from all the rest. In amongst the sea of green fountain pen scribbling was a red circle drawn with a marker pen. Inside the circle was written 'C.P.G. Specialist UK response to imminent threat'. Underneath that was written 'Cabinet unaware. Could it derail?' It was underlined three times.

Admiral Dudgeon turned around as he slipped his right arm into his coat sleeve. "Oh, and bring me that would you Richard," indicating the notebook. The Admiral seemed a little agitated.

"Of course Sir." Richard closed the leather-bound notebook in one hand, picked the briefing papers up in his other and walked to the door.

"Thank you," said the Admiral as Richard handed him the notebook. "So what's the name of your fiancé then?"

"Esther Sir"

"Esther. Very pretty name. And where are you going to take her for lunch then?" Dudgeon asked.

"Probably the British Museum Sir. She likes it there."

"Interesting choice considering what we've just been talking about," said the Admiral with a raised eyebrow.

"It's been a while now Sir. I'm sure we'll be fine. Thanks for the drink, and the afternoon off, much appreciated. See you on Monday." Richard walked back to the Registry. Margret had long learned to recognise people's footsteps down the hall and looked up inquisitively as Richard entered.

"Well?" she asked.

"Well what?" Richard replied.

"Is that whisky I can smell?"

"Yep."

"I thought he was going to go apoplectic."

"Well he kind of did. But in an unusually quiet way. I mean, he got a bit animated once or twice, but it really wasn't the reaction I expected. He's actually given me the rest of the day off and told me to take Esther out to lunch," Richard explained, looking very puzzled.

"Good Lord," Margret said. "He's never done anything like that before."

"He said it was a day for surprises Margret," Richard said as he put the file back in the secure cabinet.

"So, he's not signed it then," she asked.

"Nope. Says he needs the weekend to compose himself. Don't blame him really. It's hit him hard. He must have had about four doubles in there, but still completely coherent. I'm feeling a bit woozy myself to be honest but he was as clear-eyed and articulate as they come."

Margret closed the cabinet and spun the lock. "Well, if he's out for the day and you're off, then..." she smiled at Richard.

"Yes, of course Margret. Off you go. Any particular plans?" he asked.

Margret looked thoughtful. "Well, I suspect I shall probably take myself for afternoon tea at Fortnum's. It's a very pleasant way to lose an afternoon."

"I've never been," Richard replied. Then, hesitantly, he asked, "Don't you have to book that? It must get really busy."

"It does indeed. But I have a secret weapon."

Richard looked puzzled. "A secret weapon?"

"My husband. He's the manager." Margret was putting her coat on as she turned to Richard and said, "He must quite like you, you know. Both your predecessors were sacked within a week. You've lasted quite a long time considering."

"Great," said Richard, "that's comforting. Well have a lovely time. " Margret smiled and walked down the corridor to the lift. Richard returned to his office and phoned Esther. Esther was putting photos of her time in Borneo into a scrapbook when the phone rang.

"Hello sweetheart, how are you? Richard asked.

"Bored, bored, bored," she answered. "I'm sick of this bloody scrapbook and I'm sick of being stuck in this pokey little flat." Richard had been given a flat in Limehouse in East London for the duration of his posting – he was completely unaware that he lived in the flat above Will Richard's sister's. It overlooked the marina, and he thought it was terrific, the first time he'd actually lived in something that wasn't just a room with a sink in it or a bunk on a ship. Esther, having just returned from the jungle, longed for something less boxy than a one-bedroom flat in a yuppy development. "I can't wait to get back on the wards again," she said.

"Yes, with all the joy of London commuting. You haven't experienced that yet. Speaking of which, I'm going to be late tonight."

"Oh no, not again Richard. What is it this time?" Esther moaned. She was still coming to terms with Richard's new role.

"Top Secret, I'm afraid."

"I'm bored of that as well."

"Alright then. Just kidding, you fancy lunch?" He was smiling as he cleared up the papers on his desk.

"Seriously?" she asked.

"Well I'd rather not have a serious lunch, I'd prefer a casual one, but if you insist..." Richard knew that she would be rolling her eyes at that one.

"You're not funny."

"Yes I am."

"Are not."

"Am so." Richard and Esther always bantered like children in a playground.

"So where are you taking me?" she asked.

"British Museum. Fancy it?" Esther was beaming. She loved the British Museum. "See you there in about forty minutes."

Richard walked and Esther took the bus. Esther found him sitting in the glass covered Great Court atrium staring at the seemingly impossible ceiling. During his walk he had had time to think about some of the things the Admiral had said. And he was looking pensive.

"You alright?" she asked. He stood up and as she leant forward to kiss him she suddenly started back. "Have you been drinking?" She'd met enough sailors to know that wasn't necessarily unusual, and the medical profession wasn't exactly renowned for its alcohol discipline, so Esther was sure she could smell whisky, and Richard hardly ever drank spirits.

"Yeah, but I'm fine. Come on." They walked up the staircase to the restaurant above the reading room. After they sat down Esther gave him one of her direct stares, the one she used when she asked patients if their family had smuggled alcohol onto the ward.

"What's going on?" she asked.

"What do you mean?" he asked back.

"Since you got this posting you've been working all hours. Now suddenly you've got the afternoon off and you're doing that thing you do."

"What thing?" Richard was, as usual, doing his worst impression of pretending not to know what Esther was talking about.

"You know that thing. The, 'I'm pretending there isn't a thing going on when there clearly is' thing. Something's unusual here Richard, what is it?" He was fiddling with his cutlery. "And you're fiddling with your cutlery. You only do that when you're thinking about a 'thing'." She used her fingers to indicate the quotation marks.

Richard scrunched his face and looked to the ceiling. "Well," he hesitated, "it's the boss, he was just really odd this morning, not himself." Esther leaned forwards, placing her chin in her hands.

"You mean he was actually nice?" she asked.

"Not exactly nice. But he said some things which I didn't really concentrate on at the time, but which are sort of, well, resonating now." Richard was still trying to organise his own thoughts.

"What like?" Esther asked.

Just as Richard was about to start explaining his thought processes the waiter came over and took their order. Esther knew he was about to say something and had stopped. After the waiter had left she said, "You can't talk about it can you?"

Richard was still hesitant. "Well, I can," he said, "with you, but I don't want the world to know."

Esther was halfway to putting her napkin in her lap and simply stopped, placing it gently back on the table. "Richard, what on earth is bothering you?"

"I'm not sure. You know about the whole Defence Review thing?" Esther nodded and sipped her glass of water. "Well, Dudgeon said some odd things this morning. He talked about not being the man to destroy the Royal Navy and about being a pragmatist and, just, well, it was just odd."

Esther smiled at him. "Sometimes people are just odd. You're being odd. Look at that guy over there," she said, "the one with the glasses." There was indeed a man two tables across from them with a buttoned-up coat and yellow scarf who looked like a cross between the bears Paddington and Rupert. He was reading a very thick book and talking to himself as he did so. "He's pretty odd," Esther said.

"Yes, but he's not the Chief of the Naval Staff is he? This is the British Museum, it's full of weirdos. Dudgeon's up to something or on to something. The more I think about it the more convinced I am." Richard stopped talking and smiled as their waiter brought them their lunch.

"Is there something in particular...?" Esther ventured.

Richard thought. "No. Well, yes and no. I don't know. I'm probably just making stuff up in my head. I saw something on Dudgeon's desk today, something I probably shouldn't have, and I want to know what the hell it means." Richard leaned back in his chair. This was a tough one. His hands went to the back of his head and his eyes flicked from left to right as he deliberated what to do next. The more he thought about what he had heard that morning the more worried he was getting about the Admiral's intentions. He leaned forward and took Esther's hand. "Sweetheart, I need to talk to your Dad."

"Jesus. Is it that serious?" Her eyes widened.

"Almost certainly not. I'm probably jumping at shadows but there's something here that's not right. My head's a bit fuzzy from the whisky that Dudgeon gave me so I'm probably not thinking straight," he said.

"Okay then, to borrow one of your most memorable phrases, what's the worst case scenario?"

"I think," he said, "I think, the worst case scenario is possibly that Dudgeon is trying to put some sort of off-the-record military capability together to counteract the effects of the defence cuts."

Esther laughed. "That's ridiculous. How could he do that?" she asked.

Richard held his hands up as if in surrender. "I don't know honey. I don't know. This is Britain, not Somalia. But the idea of senior military officers operating outside parliamentary instructions scares the hell out of me."

Esther laughed. "And a good thing too."

Richard did not return her warm look. "You remember the Undergound attack?" he asked.

"Of course I do stupid. How couldn't I?" Esther was despatched with the ambulance fleet to King's Cross that day and had seen things she never wanted to see again.

"When you triage the wounded what do you do?"

"Well there's loads of things. You start with..."

Richard cut her off. "What about the ones that are shouting?" he asked.

Esther put her knife and fork down. "Okay. Alright. I see where you're going with this. Leave the screaming ones, deal with the quiet ones. It's not quite as simple as that but there's a lot of sense in it, providing the patients are still breathing and have a pulse."

Richard looked around to make sure no-one was listening in to their conversation. "You know what Margret calls Dudgeon?" he asked.

Esther smiled again. She had a beautiful smile and this time Richard couldn't help but mirror it. "Mmmhmm. She calls him 'Mr Shouty'."

"Yep. But today, with one exception, he was just 'Mr Talky'. This is a guy who goes mental when I put too much milk in his coffee." Richard was whispering now. "Honey, he just got asked to sign off the biggest strategic defence cut in our history, and instead of turning into the Grade A lunatic that he often does, he pulled out a vintage bottle of Scotch and gave me the afternoon off. Absence of the normal..."

This time she finished his sentence for him. "Presence of the abnormal." It was his turn to laugh. She took his hand. "You have taught me well, Obi-Wan. But why Dad?"

"I just want to check if it's something he knows about or not. Like I say, it's probably nothing, and you know I said I'd never take advantage or take the piss or anything, and I meant it. Mean it. But can you give him a call? I just want to run it by him."

Esther squeezed his hand. "Let me call him now."

* * *

Esther's father, Edward Walsh, was in his office meeting an old friend from Canada when his mobile phone rang. Edward had many phones, landlines and mobile, but this was the one he reserved exclusively for his wife, daughter, and two sons. They knew not to ring it during office hours unless it was very, very important. Edward picked the phone off the desk and saw it was Esther. He looked across at Andrew, a contemporary from their time at Oxford, and simply said, "Esther. Sorry."

"I know the score Ed. I'm just the same. Let's pick this up later. Got a whole heap of paperwork to get through anyways."

"Thanks Andy. Drinks Thursday, yes?" Andrew Vincent gathered his papers together and put them in his briefcase, giving Edward a thumbs-up.

"Wouldn't miss it," he mouthed as he walked out of Ed's office. In the outer office he turned to the plain looking girl who never bluffed him when he asked to see Ed. "Take care Annie. Have a good week-end."

"Thank you Ambassador," she replied. "You too."

Back in his office, Edward jabbed the answer button. "Hello sweetheart, what's up?" Esther was a bright girl and he knew she wouldn't be calling on a flight of fancy.

Esther's voice was serious. "Daddy, can we see you tonight?" she asked. As they sat in the British Museum restaurant, Richard was staring at his fiancé like she was his estate agent putting in an offer on a house.

"We?"

"Yes, well, Richard would like to speak to you about something."

Edward liked Richard, and knew that he wouldn't have asked his daughter, and his daughter would not have called him, unless there was a damn good reason for it. "Alright then. Drinks tonight. The club, seven o' clock. That suit you?" he asked.

"Thanks Dad," Esther replied. She switched her phone off and looked across at Richard. "Done, now you get to spend the rest of the day taking me round the Asia exhibits."

"Thanks honey." Richard leaned over the table and kissed her.

Annie tapped on Edward's office door and came in to collect the outgoing correspondence. "Thanks Annie", Edward said as he scribbled his signature on the bottom of one last document before throwing it in the 'out' tray.

Annie went back to her desk. She had joined the civil service fast track scheme after graduating with a first class honours degree from Durham, and although she was doing what she described to her friends as 'just' clerical work, she couldn't believe her luck at her first placement.

She took the ink-stamp from the top right draw of her desk as she did every afternoon. She adjusted the date and wobbled it on her ink-pad. She then took each document from the out tray and stamped them one by one.

'Office of the Home Secretary.'

CHAPTER FOURTEEN

Thursday evening…

"He'll be in the bar," said Esther as she and Will walked into the lobby of the Oxford and Cambridge Club on Pall Mall. "And he'll have opened a bottle of Club Claret. There will be a glass for you and a glass for me. If you order anything else he will be offended."

"Thank you for the briefing."

The Home Secretary stood up as his daughter and her fiancé approached. Kissing his daughter first and then shaking hands with Richard he invited them to take a seat.

"Nice place," said Richard, taking in the surroundings. The ceiling was high and the portraits on the wall, luxurious carpet and leather chairs made for an indulgent atmosphere.

"Have you not been here before?" Edward asked. He looked confused, "I'm sure we've had dinner here before."

"No Sir," Richard responded.

The Home Secretary pointed a finger at him as he poured the wine. "I've told you before Richard, the name's Edward. When we're here with Esther I'm not the Home Secretary and you're not a Lieutenant Commander. Understood?"

Esther interjected, "Actually Daddy, it is a bit like that this evening."

Edward looked perplexed. "Esther, today I have had to deal with the Argentinean ambassador, woman is a complete fruitcake, and a very, very angry German Chancellor who has just discovered that the Bundesnachrichtendienst has passed details of…"

Esther interrupted again, "Sorry Dad, the what?"

"German spies," he continued without missing a beat, "actually what they've done is not something we should be discussing. Anyway, here's the point. Why is it that when I get to share a few stolen moments with my daughter and her charming fiancé I have to play grown-up politics?" He leaned back in his chair.

The bar was reasonably busy but Richard was confident no-one could overhear their conversation. He leaned forward. "Edward, I have never taken advantage of the relationship I have with your daughter and your position in government, nor would I ever seek to. I am not attempting to take advantage of it now, but I'm worried about something, probably pointlessly, and you're the only person I know who it seems worthwhile to talk to."

"I'm listening," said the Home Secretary, "but not here. Grab that bottle would you?" He led them up the grand marble staircase of the club and into the South Library, which was unoccupied. They sat by the fire.

Esther smiled at Richard. "Dad used to work in Army Intelligence," she said.

"Really?" Richard asked, surprised.

"Really," Edward replied, "but don't get too excited, it was mostly about sticking pins in maps and reading really boring books. But I do have a thing about people listening in to my conversations, and I suspect this is going to be one of the ones that I don't want to share just yet – you'd be surprised who's down there listening to things. Fire away Lieutenant Commander, the Home Secretary and Esther's Dad are both listening to you – I'm expecting this to be good."

Richard outlined the conversation he'd had with Admiral Dudgeon that morning, and how out of character it seemed. "I agree with you it seems a bit odd, but he's an Admiral about to have a very reduced Navy. I sympathise with him on that, I genuinely do, if the country had more money I'd be banging my fist on the table to give him more ships. But we don't. I can see his position."

Richard sighed. "It's probably nothing, maybe I'm over-reacting. Who knows?"

Edward stood up and said, "Right, well who's for dinner? My treat."

Richard was staring into the fireplace when something occurred to him. "Edward," he said quickly, "do you know what the CPG is?" The Home Secretary stopped in his tracks.

"Where did you hear about that?" he asked.

"I didn't. I read it. In Admiral Dudgeon's personal notebook. I wasn't snooping or anything, it was open on his desk when I handed it to him. It also said, 'Cabinet unaware. Could it derail?'"

The Home Secretary sat back down. "How many other people know about this?" he asked.

"No-one," said Richard, "we're it," he added, looking around. "There was something else about a specialist response to a threat to the UK, I can't remember exactly."

"Leave those, we're moving" said Edward, and he hurried his daughter and fiancé to the street. Edward's driver, who doubled as his close protection officer, pulled the Jaguar up in front of the steps.

"Daddy, what's going on?" asked Esther.

"You're going to Dorset. I will sort everything else out." He turned to the driver, "Billy, how many guns do you have?"

"Two Sir, one primary, one back-up."

There was a sense of urgency in the Home Secretary's voice. "Give the back-up to this man. He's a Royal Navy officer, he will have used these at Dartmouth."

Richard was looking at his future father-in-law with astonishment, as was Esther. "I have to make a call," was the only explanation.

* * *

Edward Walsh walked back into the club and hid himself in the only phone booth before calling Will. "Home Secretary," said Will, answering his mobile.

There were no pleasantries. "I'm sending you some people. One of them is my daughter, the other is her boyfriend. I will be five minutes behind them. Look after them."

"Omega site?" Will asked.

"Absolutely."

"Well, that's what we built it for."

And then the Home Secretary walked out of the Oxford and Cambridge Club and hailed a cab. He got out in front of a private road in west London which looked like it was manned by private security guards and protected by reinforced electronically operated gates.

He walked into the sitting room of the beautifully appointed townhouse where Will, Richard and Esther were waiting for him. Esther and Richard looked a little starstruck. "Tell him what you told me," said the Home Secretary, walking to the drinks cabinet.

Later, Will sat alone in the drawing room, staring at the flames of the fire as they were drawn up the chimney. "Shit," he said quietly, or at least he thought he'd said it quietly.

"Watch your language young man," said the housekeeper, as she bustled into the room quickly, poked the fire and started collecting the empty glasses.

"Jesus Christ Mrs 'H', you scared the shit out of me!" said Will, who had jumped in his chair when she came in.

"And don't blaspheme either," came the instructive Irish tone. There was a pause as she looked at him, somewhat maternally. "Are you about to do something stupid?" she asked.

"I think so, yes."

"Well for the love of God make sure you do it properly," she advised. As she was leaving the room she stopped, put her tray on a side table, bent down and kissed him on the forehead. "My father got killed in the war doing stupid things like you people. Despite what you might think, I actually quite like you, and at my age the only funeral I want to go to is my own, so whatever you're up to, don't get it wrong."

Will smiled at her. "You know, I've actually named the kettle after you, because it makes annoying noises too."

Mrs Hudson slapped him round the back of the head and picked up her tray. As she left she called, "and if there's anything else that needs tidying up you can do it yourself, you ungrateful little..." She didn't finish the sentence, out of respect for the Church.

CHAPTER FIFTEEN

Conspiracy...

Emma Harris was walking around her father's extensive formal gardens, glass of champagne in hand, thoroughly bored. There must have been almost two hundred guests at the Foreign Secretary's annual summer garden party, some were political colleagues, others civil servants who he worked with closely but the majority were the ambassadors of what her father described as "the first division" countries.

Emma hated these occasions, but her father insisted that she and her mother were present to ensure a picture of a happy family life came across to all present, which included some substantially influential media figures. It was far from happy, as well he knew. His wife, Alice, normally opened the gin at ten o' clock in the morning; it helped her to block out the feeling of betrayal after his near-constant string of affairs over the previous decade. She had concluded that she was clearly no longer sufficiently enticing for him – all his conquests had been pretty young things – but she also enjoyed the lifestyle and status of being the Foreign Secretary's wife too much to stand on principle and leave him. The dinners, the gala balls, the playing hostess to such famous and important people had beguiled her, and between that and the almost constant inebriation Emma was convinced that her mother was incapable of making a sound decision.

She was gazing out over the upper lake when a hand rested on her shoulder. "Emma darling," said her father, "I'd like you to meet Dimitry. Dimitry's the Defence Attache with the Russian Embassy."

Emma smiled and shook his hand. She knew exactly what her father was doing. She was blonde and young and pretty and no doubt there was a deal that her father needed to make with the Russian military in the imminent future. He walked away almost instantly. Emma rolled her eyes.

Dimitry was demure. "Miss Harris, it is a pleasure to meet you," he said, "but I can see that this pleasure is not mutual, so I will happily leave you alone if you prefer." He raised an eyebrow in anticipation. Though his knowledge of English was extensive, his accent was unmistakable.

"Your English is exceptional," she replied, "where did you learn?" She did not wish to be impolite after his kind gesture.

"Like everyone else," he smiled, "at school."

"Oh, you're funny," she mocked him. "Do all the spies get comedy lessons?"

"I'm not a spy," he said, "what makes you think that?"

Emma was sipping her champagne and nearly had to spit it out from laughing. "You're the Defence Attache from Russia! And you're pretending you're not a spy? I may only be twenty-two but I'm not galactically stupid."

"Miss Harris," he started.

Emma interrupted him. "Please, for God's sake call me Emma, I'm not a diplomat, I'm not in the government. My name is Emma."

"So what do you do Emma?" the tall Russian man asked.

"I'm a student," she replied, "final year of Philosophy, Politics and Economics."

"Which college?" Dimitry asked.

"Aren't you clever?" she asked back. "Magdalen." She looked up at him, "so which spy school did you go to?"

"I was in the GRU for a while, but now I am purely here in a liaison capacity," he replied, although he couldn't stop smirking as he answered her. He looked down at her glass and noticed it was empty. "I have a proposal for you," he said. "If you let me get you another glass of champagne will you take me up to the roof of the turret? I'd love to see the view from up there."

Emma decided she had nothing better to do and acquiesced. She got the keys to the tower door from the rack in the parlour. The family house was a substantial building and the number and variety of keys would have bewildered someone unfamiliar with them, but Emma had lived in the country seat her whole life. "Be careful," she said, turning round, "it gets really tight up here."

The spiral stone staircase was only just wide enough for one-way traffic. Emma led the way. Dimitry, who was a broad-shouldered man, was scuffing the shoulders of his brand new blazer on the dusty, spider-web covered walls of the staircase. "This thing cost me over three hundred pounds," he complained, attempting to dust himself off. "I make an attempt to fit in with English garden parties and look what happens to me."

Emma stopped and shot him a look. "You were the one who wanted to come up here," she said.

"That's true, I can't complain," he replied. When she opened the door onto the leaded roof of the tower Dimitry gasped. "Wow, what a view!"

"Yeah, it's pretty impressive isn't it," said Emma as she looked across the upper and lower lakes and the woods to the east. "I haven't been up here for years."

"How much of it is yours?" he asked.

"Well, technically it's not mine," she looked embarrassed, "yet. But the estate is as far as you can see."

"Every direction?"

"Yep. And the rest."

"I need to defect to Britain and marry a girl like you," he said, laughing.

"Well I can probably arrange half of that," she joked back.

Dimitry looked out over the rolling Surrey hills. "I think I'm too old for you Emma," he said, before looking back at her.

Emma had had sufficient champagne to play the game, and smiling, responded, "That wasn't the half I was offering Mr Russian Spy." She paused, thinking for a moment. "How would you actually do it though, if you wanted to defect. Just walk into MI5 or MI6 or something?"

Dimitry laughed again. "They would kick me straight out of the door," he said. "You can't just go walking into intelligence agencies or embassies and say you want to defect. It is the worst possible thing to do. Everyone will be suspicious of you and think you are a double agent or part of an entrapment operation. It's too basic, it's what the, how do you phrase it...?"

He thought for a moment. "I understand everyone here is Division One, yes? Well that's the kind of thing that Division Four does."

Emma smiled again. "So you're not a spy then?"

Dimitry finished his champagne. "I'm not a spy," he said. "I just work with them. You think your father is any different?"

Emma had no time at all for her father and hadn't for years. He had always been distant, had a capacity for nastiness and after his betrayal of her mother had openly demonstrated a cruelty for which he seemed to have no remorse. But she didn't like the way the conversation had turned and her face obviously showed this.

"I'm sorry," said Dimitry, "I did not want to upset or offend you."

Emma looked up, reconciled quickly. "So, did he get what he wanted today?" she asked.

"If by that you mean did his introduction to his beautiful, intriguing and intelligent daughter mean that we would widen intelligence sharing with the United Kingdom about Islamic extremism? Well, that one was already in the can, as our American friends say." Dimitry looked across from the tower at the view of the green fields and dotted copses, and the hedgerows full of wildlife. The sun was slowly dropping into the near horizon. "This is a beautiful country you have," he said. "But if you ever want to run away to mine, for God's sake don't come through the front door of the embassy. We'd kick you straight out and call MI5".

Emma laughed. "You're funny. And we're both out of champagne. And I need at least another couple of glasses before the dancing starts because I'm rubbish at dancing and I get all self conscious."

"My wife says the same about me," Dimitry replied. "She says I have something called 'rhythm bypass syndrome'."

"Your wife?" Emma asked.

"Yes, don't worry, you are perfectly safe with me. I think my children would hate me forever if I ever betrayed her."

* * *

Several days later and after dinner David Harris sat down with his old friend, Admiral Dudgeon, who would be staying overnight. The two had met as undergraduates at Cambridge just under thirty years earlier, and hit it off immediately. Both men were keen rowers and they shared a passion for politics, Harris quickly becoming Secretary of the University Young Conservative Association and the future Chief of the Naval Staff successfully running for President of the Cambridge Union, the prestigious debating society.

Dudgeon though, was always going to join the Royal Navy, as four generations of his family had done before him. Harris had a more specific ambition – he wanted the keys to 10 Downing Street. Both men progressed rapidly up their respective career ladders, Dudgeon becoming the youngest ever Captain of a nuclear submarine, Harris gaining a State Secretarial appointment in the Ministry of Defence at his first attempt. The men had stayed close ever since but there was a sense of thwarted ambition about both of them; Dudgeon had been removed from the shortlist for Chief of the Defence Staff by the Prime Minister himself, who thought Dudgeon was a warmonger, and Harris had been beaten to the leadership of his party by the same man, who was fifteen years his junior. Neither man cared much for the Prime Minister and both recognised that their careers had probably reached their zenith.

The grand drawing room was dimly lit, with ancestral portraits hanging on the oak panelled walls. "Drink?" Harris asked.

"Certainly," came the reply, "large one I think."

Harris walked across to his drinks cabinet, pointing up at the oar suspended on the wall above it. "Remember that?" he laughed. The oar was painted in the colours of Trinity College and the names of the successful crew of their final year's inter-collegiate competition were painted on the blade.

Dudgeon laughed. "How could I forget?" he asked.

Harris poured him a large scotch – he was fastidious in remembering the preferences of his friends and the people he did business with, he found it helpful in his line of business. "Sell any of our ships today then?" he asked, only half-joking.

"I swear to God David, we'll be commandeering those eights from the Cambridge boathouses at this rate."

Harris handed him his drink. "You know my thoughts on that Jim," he said.

Dudgeon sighed. "Is the P.M. only going to be happy when the entire fleet's been sold to bloody India and Australia?" he asked.

Harris sat down and gazed into the open fire. "It's not just the Navy Jim, he's closed just under a third of our embassies, and the prime ones that he can't close he's sold off and the staff are working out of bloody rented offices with flat pack furniture. It's no way to run a diplomatic corps."

Dudgeon nodded in agreement. "I don't think the man has any regard for Britain's status in the world. We're becoming a laughing stock."

There was a pause in the conversation and then Harris turned very serious. "I've been having some thoughts Jim."

Dudgeon looked up. "Thoughts?"

"Thoughts."

"What kind of thoughts David?"

"I can speak openly with you, can't I Jim?" asked the Foreign Secretary. "You know, Chatham House Rule, that kind of stuff."

Admiral Dudgeon shrugged. "How long have we known each other David? You know you don't have to ask me a question like that." He took another sip of his scotch, wondering what was coming next; whatever it was, it was likely to be explosive.

"You know I'm Deputy Prime Minister right?" Dudgeon didn't even bother to respond to that, and simply stared at his old friend. Harris spoke very slowly now, "If anything happens to Marshall I step up to the plate."

"Not sure where you're going with this David," said Dudgeon.

"This country is screwed Jim, and it's screwed because of David Marshall. We've lost sovereignty to the bloody European Union, we can't control our own borders, the armed forces are being decimated. On top of that we've got unemployed rioters burning down our high streets. Something has got to be done Jim. We," he paused for emphasis, "and people like us, have got to do something."

"I'm not sure I like where this is going David. What are you planning to do, call a vote of no confidence or something?"

The Foreign Secretary had finished his drink and stood up to refill it, gesturing towards his friend, who downed the remainder of his and handed over his glass. "The way I see it," he said, pouring the decanter, "this country's at a crossroads. This isn't something I've taken lightly; I've been watching and fighting our gradual decline for years, but I have concluded, and believe me Jim I have spent a great deal of time thinking about this, that we need to revolutionise the political debate in this country. David Marshall is not the man to initialise that revolution."

"And you are?" asked Dudgeon.

"Not on my own," came the response. "I will need assistance." There was a pregnant pause as the two men looked at each other, Dudgeon beginning to realise what might be being asked of him. The Foreign Secretary walked back across the expensively appointed yet understated room to his old friend and handed him his glass once more.

Dudgeon put his hand to his mouth and stared at the floor. Finally he looked up and said, "If you're asking what I think you're asking, that's treason David. You know there were rumours that Mountbatten made similar overtures to military chiefs in the seventies?" he asked.

"I've heard that, yes," he said.

"They told him to piss off."

"I heard that too."

There was another long silence. "What's your plan?"

"You remember Paul Gilmour?" he asked, pointing up at the oar again, where the name P A Gilmour was at the top of the list.

"Bow man, yeah, of course, only one of us to actually get a seat in the Boat Race. What's that got to do with anything?"

"You know what he did after Trinity?" came the next question.

"No, not a clue. Never saw him at any of the reunions or anything now I come to think about it."

"Let me tell you something about Gilmour. You'll remember he speaks with an American accent, but his mother was English, so he has dual nationality. Like rowing he always wanted to be the best, so he joined the British Army and went from Sandhurst to the Parachute Regiment to the Special Air Service."

"Good for him."

"Then he resigned his commission after two of his chaps got court martialled for beating up a terrorist in Somalia. You may recall the incident. The Prime Minister made a public statement that he could not and would not condone the actions of the British forces involved and that we must be seen to be acting under the law. The Somali shit in question had cut the head off an English woman's French husband in front of her the day before. They were both working for the Red Cross. That's why Gilmour's boys went in. And the P.M. decides that a couple of kicks to the bollocks for this unspeakable wanker are too much to bare."

"I do remember that actually," said Dudgeon, "Obviously I didn't realise Paul was connected with it."

"No, he kept his head down and stayed out of the papers. Want to know what he does now?"

"What?"

"Runs a private security company."

Dudgeon looked confused. "I'm not quite sure why you're telling me all this David. What's that got to do with getting rid of the PM?"

"He can help us. He's offered to help us."

Dudgeon noted that the Foreign Secretary had now started using the plural. "And in what way is that exactly?"

"I'm not going to beat about the bush Jim, he's got to go permanently, he can't be permitted to remain on the political scene, he's too dangerous."

Both men stared into the fire. After several minutes contemplation Admiral Sir James Dudgeon, Chief of the Naval Staff, looked up and asked, "Okay David, what's your plan?"

Neither man was aware that Emma had come down from her bedroom for a glass of water just as their discussion had started and, intrigued, had sat on one of the sixteenth century chairs in the hallway outside like a statue, almost too scared to breathe. She found it difficult to believe what she was hearing.

The Foreign Secretary stood up and started pacing slowly in front of the fire, whisky tumbler in hand. "We can't go for a leadership competition, he's far too popular for that." He stopped, looking to the ceiling, "I know more about that than any man." After a pause he turned, "And he's young, fit and healthy, no-one's going to believe he's too ill to continue in his post or that he's had a heart attack."

Dudgeon wasn't stupid. "So what are you thinking of? Car accident? Jesus David, you couldn't make something up more obvious."

"I was thinking of being slightly more creative than that. It's one thing killing the Prime Minister," he finally acknowledged explicitly, "it is yet another to make his death count for something. I don't just want Marshall out of the game and me in it at the highest level. I want his death to change attitudes in this country, back to the values and standards we once held dear."

Emma had one hand clasped over her mouth, the other was shaking and she was desperate not to spill any water or drop the glass.

"I've had hypothetical discussions with Gilmour."

"Hypothetical?"

"Yes, but he's not stupid of course. I told you what happened to him, he's highly sympathetic to the cause. Gilmour reckons he can make it look like an Islamic terrorist attack."

"Bloody hell David!"

"There's more. He's pretty confident he can make it look like a home-grown Islamic terrorist attack. The beauty of this is that it means we can set the agenda – greater counter-terrorist powers, stronger immigration laws." He paused for emphasis, "And significantly more resources for the armed forces."

Dudgeon smiled at this. "You don't need to bribe me David. But this is a serious, serious business. Who else have you talked to about this?"

"Apart from you and Paul Gilmour, no-one. Yet. But I will need to sound out several members of the Cabinet to see what they would do in the event of the PM's death." The Foreign Secretary waved away Dudgeon's questioning gaze. "No, no. Don't worry, I'm chairman of the Government Continuity Group, it's a perfectly reasonable question for me to bring up. I'll see how the others respond." Once more there was a pause. "And will you be able to sound out the other Chiefs?" he asked.

"And that would be because?" he let the question hang in the air.

"Because we might need to impose martial law Jim. We'll have to move quickly to pin the blame on British-born terrorists, and when I say quickly, I mean within twenty-four hours. We'll need to raid homes, produce martyrdom videos, pictures of the plotters, the whole lot. Whole boroughs of London, Birmingham, Manchester, Leeds, Bradford could be on fire." The Foreign Secretary waved his arms around as he listed the cities with large Islamic communities.

"This is potentially a very complicated plan you're putting together here David. It's not going to be easy to get all of that in place without leaving traces you know. I don't have the world's greatest opinion of our police service but when you put all those resources together with MI5's, we could find ourselves in a very uncomfortable place." Dudgeon looked sceptical.

The Foreign Secretary leant against the fireplace. "I know. That's why I need the backing of the military." He also, for the first time, looked unsure of himself.

"And...?"

"And the Home Secretary," came the earnest response. "I need Walsh on board to reign in the spooks. Otherwise, we're toast."

"Do you think he'll go for it?" Dudgeon asked.

"I have no idea, but I also know there's no love lost between him and the PM." He gazed into the flames again. "There's one other thing," he asked. "Have you ever heard of something called the Contingency Planning Group?"

"Can't say I have."

"I was in a COBRA meeting a few weeks ago," said Harris, referring to the Cabinet Office Briefing Room (A), from where the group got its name. "You get a lot of random chaps turning up to these things, depending on what country's gone tits up. As you know, the senior military attend in uniform, the intermediate ones tend to turn up in suits you can buy in the High Street." Admiral Dudgeon raised an eyebrow. "Sorry Jim, sorry.

Of course you know all this. Perhaps too many of these." The Foreign Secretary lifted his glass. "Anyway, this was a meeting about Mali, so no Navy staff present. Landlocked and all that."

"The Contingency Planning Group?" asked the Admiral.

"Ah yes. The Contingency Planning Group. There was a young chap, late thirties, early forties, waiting outside for the PM at the end of the meeting. Handed him a folder in the corridor, said he'd got everything in place, said that the brief he'd been given to ensure domestic security was complete and that in the event that things got out of hand, they could always rely on Rebecca Taylor." Harris left the name hanging.

"Never heard of her."

"Me neither. Or this bloody Planning Group. I want to know more about it Jim. Can you do some digging?"

"Of course. And what's the actual targeting plan?"

"I don't know yet. Gilmour's working on that." Both men finished their drinks. "Another?" asked the Foreign Secretary.

"I don't think so," said Dudgeon, "it's been a pretty heavy night. I think I should head for my bunk and sleep on this."

"But I can trust you, right, Jim?"

"You can trust me," came the reassuring response.

Hearing Admiral Dudgeon stand up and head for the entrance hall, Emma quietly stood up and headed back to the kitchen, knowing that every wooden stair on the grand oak staircase squeaked, even with her tiny frame. After Dudgeon had made his way to his room Emma didn't move for ten minutes. Ten minutes which felt like hours. But she also knew her father's habits and after she heard the decanter being poured once more she knew he would be in his favourite chair and asleep in moments. Sure enough, she heard the snoring shortly afterwards and tip-toed her way upstairs.

CHAPTER SIXTEEN

Thursday afternoon...

Admiral Dudgeon acknowledged all the military staff as he passed them on his way out of the Admiralty. Those in uniform saluted, those in suits braced up as they went by. Very few of the civilian staff actually recognised him, a factor which strengthened both his concern and resolve about the way things were going. Despite the tiresome and seemingly relentless push of the civil servants in the communications department, Dudgeon was convinced that the in-house, (in-house for crying out loud), inductions, magazines, pamphlets and workshops, (by Christ he hated the word workshop – what are we doing here, building fucking cars?), had done nothing to instil a culture of commitment and readiness to serve in a service which was in such distinct decline. It was a symptom. He passed painting after painting of naval victory, of heroic sacrifice and valour. He crossed the bridge over The Mall into Admiralty Arch and calmly strode down the magnificent staircase to street level.

Despite the season it was warm, and he concluded that, on second thoughts, there was no requirement for his overcoat. He left it at the reception desk with instructions that it be taken back up to his office. At least the reception staff recognised him. As he strode up to Pall Mall he pulled out his mobile phone and made the calls which he knew would define him one way or another. He deliberately used a number that would be recognised by the switchboard operators in order that he, or his message, would get through quickly.

Becky Wills was having a bad morning. She had split up with her boyfriend the night before. Her decision; she discovered he'd been cheating on her with her best friend from school. That said, she'd barely slept all night and was struggling with both emotional drain and physical exhaustion. As the Admiral's name flashed up on her screen she pushed the 'answer' button. "Good morning Sir, what can I do for you?" she asked.

"Ah, hello Becky, how are you?" Dudgeon asked. Becky nearly choked. He had never spoken to her by name and was normally very direct. She spoke without thinking.

"Just getting over a very messy boyfriend issue Sir. But then, I'm sure you've got much bigger problems than that to worry about."

"Indeed I have Becky, indeed I have. Is the Foreign Secretary available? Sorry for the short notice." Dudgeon had to raise his voice as he walked past what seemed to be the permanent roadworks and drilling at the junction of Haymarket and Pall Mall.

"He's in with the Transport Secretary at the moment Sir, but I can red light him and let him know you're after him," she said.

"No need, thank you. Could you just let him know that if he's available for lunch it's my shout and I'd like to recommend the veal."

"Certainly Sir. Whereabouts?" Becky asked.

"Oh, he'll know," Dudgeon answered and killed the call. Back to usual form then, Becky thought, as the Admiral had failed to even say goodbye. She sent a priority message through to the Foreign Secretary's phone and then pulled off her headphones and mic, throwing them on her desk and leaning back in her chair. Her purse was on her desk and she opened it to see the picture she had of her stupid boyfriend grinning while standing on the back of a speedboat off a southern Spanish beach. She pulled it out, looked at it briefly, and threw it in the bin. Seconds later she retrieved it, took a stapler from her top drawer and stapled his face repeatedly. Then she put the photograph back in her purse. "Bastard," she said. Becky never had the greatest self-esteem, and counted herself lucky to have the job she did. She didn't think she was particularly clever, or would ever amount to much. She probably thought she would never get another boyfriend, which is why she put the photo back in her purse. One thing Becky Wills could do though, was run. She could run very, very quickly indeed. If the physical education teacher at her appalling school had actually shown any interest or demonstrated any professional merit whatsoever, Becky would have been training with the British Athletics Team, not answering phones on a switchboard. Becky Wills could fly like the wind.

While she was stapling her ex-boyfriend's face, Dudgeon was putting in another call. "Mr Gilmour, how are you?" he asked.

"I'm tired of waiting Jim," came the steady response from a man with an American accent.

"In which case, let me take you out to lunch. My treat."

"What's on the menu today?" Again, the response was terse.

"I'm reliably informed that the veal is excellent," said Admiral Dudgeon.

"I've always been partial to veal," the American replied, "I'll see you there."

David Harris, Foreign Secretary and Deputy Prime Minister of the United Kingdom completed his meeting with the Transport Secretary, thoroughly bored with the idea of trying to sell British rail engineering expertise to struggling African countries – it all seemed like a complete waste of time. He walked into his outer office and sighed.

"Everything alright?" asked Becky.

Harris spoke softly. "No. I'm bored. I've been waiting for something to happen for ages and it never seems to be the right time. Meanwhile I have to listen to the Transport Secretary drone on about the advantages of small gauge railways for Sudan. I think I need a strong coffee to stop me from falling asleep". He crossed the office to a table where a kettle and some sachets of instant coffee and long life milk sat on a tray. As he switched the kettle on he turned to Becky. "This is ridiculous, isn't it?" he asked.

Becky didn't know what the question meant, let alone the answer, and could do nothing but look back at him, squeezing her lips together and looking blank. The Foreign Secretary knew that look well. He gestured at the cheap plastic kettle. "This! This!" he repeated. "I am the Foreign Secretary and Deputy Prime Minister of the United Kingdom. Do you think they have shit like this in the White House? Or the Kremlin? No, they'd have a proper bloody machine that made noises and things, and it would be someone's job to work it. This is the United bloody Kingdom for Christ's sake, not the Republic of Shittystan." Becky continued to look blankly at him and Harris composed himself. "Apologies," he said, "I just fear we're turning into a third rate nation."

"Some good news though," said Becky, smiling as hard as she could. "The Chief of the Naval Staff called while you were in your meeting. He would like you to join him for lunch and he said the veal was particularly recommended."

"Is that right?" asked Harris, flicking the kettle off and smiling broadly. Becky instinctively thought that this was what her boss had been waiting to happen. "Then it would be rude to stand him up, wouldn't it?"

"He said you'd know where," Becky called as Harris walked straight out of the office and down the corridor.

"Yes. Yes. Indeed," Harris called back as he strode towards the wide staircase which led to the entrance of the intimidating façade of the Foreign and Commonwealth Office. He walked quickly to the pre-designated location.

As he walked into the bar of the Oxford and Cambridge Club on Pall Mall he saw Dudgeon and Gilmour at a corner table. His pulse had increased a little but he tried to appear calm as he walked through the sumptuous room, with its deep leather chairs, beautiful mahogany tables and magnificent chandelier. An open fire was as yet unlit, but as he passed it he expected they might be there for the remainder of the afternoon, and he always liked it when the evening set in early, and the hypnotic effect of the flames prompted him to think on his plan.

Dudgeon and Gilmour stood up as he approached, Dudgeon holding a glass of Club Claret out for him. "Thank you," he said, "and how are we gentlemen?"

As they sat down the three men looked at each other, the smiles gone and faces that spoke of serious men about to do something serious. Paul Gilmour, a man who looked like he was still in his twenties despite having just turned forty, nodded to his companions. "Okay then. This is it. Here we are. I'm guessing you wouldn't have called if your boat hadn't turned up James?" he asked the Admiral.

Dudgeon smiled thinly. "If by 'boat' you are referring to the most advanced Naval Destroyer in the world, with the most capable air-defence and electronic warfare systems ever built by man, then yes. It has turned up, as you so poetically put it. And your people?" he left the question hanging.

Gilmour took a sip of his wine. "That's good," he said, placing his glass back on the table. He took his time. "My people are on their way," he said finally. "It's impossible that anyone will know."

Harris leaned forward, "And how many are there?" he asked.

"Enough," was the response. He turned to Harris, "And have you got that driver thing sorted out that we talked about?"

"You'll have to sacrifice one man, but I can get both of them to the garage no problem. It's probably best that the one who's going to die doesn't know it."

Gilmour lifted his wine glass and sipped again, then leant back in his seat. "That was always the plan." He looked out the window contemplatively and then back at the Foreign Secretary. "And you promise me that I will get every British Government security contract while you're in power?"

Harris smiled back at him. "That was the deal Paul. We'll make you even richer than you already are." He then turned his gaze to Admiral Dudgeon, "And you James, well you won't be just Chief of the Naval Staff, you'll be Chief of the Defence Staff, and I promise you I'll give you back your Royal Navy, one to be proud of." The three men chinked glasses in a toast. "Pleasure doing business with you gentlemen."

Gilmour chuckled to himself. "And also with you Mr. Prime Minister."

* * *

A visit to the Chinese Embassy

After the conversation she'd heard, Emma didn't sleep at all that night. The curtains in her bedroom were thick and heavy and the house was set in grounds so large that the loudest sounds she had ever heard during the night were the young deer which sometimes strayed onto the gravel drive. But she couldn't stop thinking about what her father had said. She tried and tried to think through the possibilities and to convince herself that she'd misunderstood the conversation, but every time she thought she'd found an alternative she ended up coming to the same, obvious, indisputable conclusion. The discussion could not be interpreted differently from the way she had heard it. Her father was plotting the assassination of the Prime Minister and a resultant coup d'etat, she was sure.

Emma showered and got dressed and headed for the kitchen to get some breakfast. Neither of her parents was awake and she was confident that they wouldn't be for several hours. The family had a permanent escort from the Diplomatic Protection Group, bodyguards from New Scotland Yard, and Patrick, on night duty that week, had, as usual, put the morning's newspapers on the kitchen table.

Emma flicked through them as she ate her cereal, not actually reading any of the articles she was looking at. Then she made the decision that would define her life. Without second guessing herself, she walked up to her father's study, a much smaller room than most people would have expected, and opened the red ministerial despatch box on his desk. He never locked it and frequently left secret documents strewn on the floor overnight. Emma took a handful of documents and photocopied them as quickly as she could, then put the originals back in the box. She didn't even pause to see what it was she was copying.

Twenty minutes later she was putting a small suitcase in the back of her car when David walked past.

"You off then Miss?" he asked.

"Yep," she replied, closing the boot. "London. Parties. Girl stuff," she said.

"Bedtime for me," Patrick replied, "I'm getting too old for nights."

And with that he walked off and Emma would never see him again. She climbed into the front seat of her car and held the steering wheel for a good minute before putting the key in the ignition. She was fairly confident things were about to change forever. She didn't quite know what she was doing, or what she was going to do, but she did know she had to get away, and get away quickly.

Despite being a student at Oxford she had a mews flat in Chelsea, courtesy of her mother, who couldn't conceive of the idea of her only daughter not having a place to stay in town. She drove calmly, not wishing to attract any attention. The garage door opened with the press of a remote control and closed behind her once she had driven in. Emma grabbed her bag and went upstairs to see what it was she'd actually copied. The whole thing felt like it had happened to someone else.

When she saw she had the Foreign Office's five year business strategy with Taiwan she still wasn't sure what to do. Emma had initially copied the documents to use as some sort of bargaining chip, she didn't know what for and what she might be able to secure with them; she was making much of this up as she went along. That was why she wanted to get away from the family home, it was all too close and immediate. If nothing else she knew she needed time and space to think, but that she also needed to act swiftly.

Emma made the executive decision to go to her favourite bar on the King's Road, The Rascal. Dylan the barman had her large glass of Shiraz ready by the time she'd walked from the entrance to the long brushed-aluminium bar.

"Hello Emma," he said, smiling. "And how are we today?" Dylan had a crush on Emma, and Emma knew, and Dylan knew that Emma knew so he made no attempt to hide it. But then, Dylan had a crush on just about every girl his age in West London.

Emma tried to smile back at him, but failed. "Hey," was all she could muster.

Dylan looked serious, "What's up sister?" he asked.

Emma took a sip of wine and looked up at him through her thick eyelashes. "Just girl stuff," she said, trying to avoid what she couldn't stop thinking about.

Dylan thought he might have a rare opportunity. "You know, if you ever want to talk about anything, I'm a very good listener," he said.

She smiled. "Thanks Dylan, I'll be fine."

Dylan kept trying. "In fact, you should hear me listen to my old vinyl collection. You have never heard anyone listen to vinyl records the way I do. I am an exceptionally gifted listener."

Emma laughed. "You see. That's better," he said. "That's what the Dylan-man can do. Make you smile. So when are you going to give me your number?" he asked. "When are you going to let Dylan show you a good time in old London town?"

Emma laughed again. "Dylan, I'm in a permanent relationship with the Bodleian Library, as well you know." She turned and headed for a table.

Despite his background, Dylan had lost his Caribbean accent when his parents moved to London when he was four, but could still muster a very serviceable version and knew how to exaggerate his body language. "Is it because I is black?" he shouted. "Posh white girl at Oxford. Is I not good enough for you?" The banter was good natured.

Emma turned, thankful that the bar was empty, "Yeah, that's right Dylan, it's because you is black," she mimicked him. "Now get back to your work, slaveboy."

Dylan swapped to an American mid-West accent and tugged his hair. "Yes sir Missy. You need any cotton picking?" Emma nearly spilled her glass from laughing. "You see," he said in his normal voice, "I can make you smile. You need to let me show you a good time."

Emma sat down and pulled out the papers she had copied from her bag. She recognised that she hadn't thought anything through properly and that now was the first time she had really had to contemplate what she was going to do since sitting, frozen, listening to her father and the Chief of the Naval Staff discuss the assassination of the Prime Minister.

She stared out of the window onto the small beer garden at the back of the bar. What to do, she thought. What. To. Do? She looked at the papers again, the header and footer on each page read, "Secret UK Eyes Only." Jesus Christ. I have no idea what I'm getting myself into here. Emma took another sip of wine and the solution hit her like a lightning bolt. She could go to the police and prove nothing. She could go to the press and prove nothing. She could, in fact, prove nothing to anyone. She didn't know the details of any assassination attempt, her father could simply deny the conversation took place. On top of that he was a powerful man. If he could plan the murder of the PM, she was pretty sure he could make her disappear without a trace.

Something he said struck her – her father was clearly worried about whatever this Contingency Planning Group was, and afraid of Rebecca Taylor. Emma concluded that she needed to speak to Rebecca Taylor. If her father was afraid of her, Emma needed to talk to her. She remembered her discussion with Dimitry, looked down at the secret papers referencing Taiwan and made the decision to head straight for the Chinese Embassy. She smiled to herself. Three years of studying Philosophy, Politics and Economics had not been entirely wasted.

She pulled out her smartphone and did some quick research. "Thank you Dylan," she said, as she walked past the bar. Dylan smiled, completely oblivious to the chain of events that would be set in motion by what Emma was about to do.

"Chinese Embassy, Portland Place please," Emma asked the cab driver who pulled over when she waved.

"You going on holiday love?" he asked.

"Yes," Emma responded, "need a visa." The cabbie spent the rest of the journey reciting a monologue about his ex-wife, who had been to China once but hadn't liked it. Emma wasn't really listening.

She was trembling as she walked into the Embassy. The lady at the reception desk did not smile at her as she looked up. "Yes?" she asked.

"I have something I'd like to sell you," said Emma, pulling the envelope with the copied documents out of her bag. She was deliberately hiding her face from the cameras which littered the lobby, as she had done outside as well.

The receptionist was highly trained, and knew better than to get her fingerprints on the envelope. "Would you like to open that for me and show me what you have?" she asked. Emma spread the documents over the reception desk. "One moment," said the receptionist. She made a phone call and shortly afterwards a serious looking man came down to the lobby. He too did not touch any of the papers either, but studied them closely. He barked something in Chinese and the receptionist handed him her phone. Another man arrived in the lobby and the two spoke briefly, although Emma sensed that a great deal of information had been exchanged. Emma recognised the second man as the Chinese Ambassador, whose picture was on the embassy's website.

Bizarrely, Ambassador Changchun spoke English with an American accent. "And what is the price for these documents, Miss...?" he let the question hang, and Emma filled the silence.

"Taylor," she answered. "Rebecca Taylor. And I want at least twenty thousand." Emma's heart was racing.

"Dollar?" asked the Ambassador.

"Don't be stupid," she responded. "Of course it's in Sterling."

The Ambassador slowly rubbed his chin. "I see," he said. "I'm afraid we cannot stretch to that. Thank you for your time. Please, to take your papers with you."

Emma had been banking on this response, and had planned her next move well. "Okay, but if you change your minds, just drop an ad in the personals of the Daily Herald. I'll be watching. These opportunities don't come up all the time you know." Emma gathered up the photocopied pages, stuffed them back in the envelope and put them back in her bag.

The Ambassador and his Defence Attache went straight to the secure communications room right in the heart of the building and the DA picked up the phone and called his official contact at MI5. "I have the Ambassador here. We would like to speak with the Director General immediately."

Robert Still was Head of the Call Centre at MI5 and had had a hard week already. This was the last thing he needed. His wife was eight months pregnant, hormonal and irritable, his boss was going through a messy divorce and his twin brother was fighting lung cancer. He recognised the voice immediately and knew that a request like this was not made lightly – there were only a handful of countries that could make demands like this, and China was one of them.

The conversation that followed involved a lot of shouting from the Chinese Ambassador, and a lot of note taking by the five analysts also listening to the call. When the conversation was finally over, Anne Tremaine hit the 'kill' button on the speakerphone and sank back in her chair. "Well," she sighed, "that was interesting. The Ambassador is never backwards in coming forwards."

"Do you want these typed up?" asked the senior analyst, gesturing to the team's notepads.

"Absolutely not," said Anne. "In fact I'd like them all please." It was not an unusual request and Anne personally shredded every page in front of her staff. "Everyone happy there's no record of this discussion?" she asked. There were general nods of assent. "Right then, off you go. Terrorists to find, plots to foil etcetera. Chop chop."

After the staff had left her office Anne turned to the window overlooking the Thames and took a very deep breath. She had to fight to maintain composure when she heard the name Rebecca Taylor come up. She needed to get hold of Will Richards, quickly, but as had been agreed by all members of the Contingency Planning Group, the name Rebecca Taylor was the trigger for non-electronic communication. No phones, no email, no texts. Anne stepped out of her office and asked her PA to get hold of the military's liaison officer, Colonel Charlie York.

* * *

Friday…

Emma woke early, as she always did, and went for a run. She enjoyed Chelsea in the early morning, no traffic and relatively little noise, just the delivery vans and the occasional dog walker. There was a newsagents at the corner of her street and she bought a copy of the Daily Herald, confused as to whether she did or didn't want to see anything in it.

She left the paper on the small dining table in the kitchen and deliberately went for a shower first before opening it. After dressing, she returned. She stared at it for several minutes before sitting down. This is ridiculous, she thought to herself, turning straight to the personal ads. She scoured them and saw nothing, poured herself a large glass of orange juice and repeated the process. "Nothing," she said out loud. "Absolutely bloody nothing."

Emma stood up and paced the living room. What am I missing? she asked herself repeatedly. After half an hour she sat down again. Whoever these people or this woman are, they're clever enough to be a step ahead of Dad. And like him or not, he's a shrewd individual. Maybe they're thinking a little bit differently. Maybe I have to think a little bit differently.

Emma spent another half an hour trying how to think differently and failed miserably. This was a world she didn't know or understand. Perhaps the Chinese hadn't passed the information on, perhaps no-one was remotely interested, perhaps her father had misheard the name. She looked out of the window and sighed. "This is going to be the death of me," she said out loud. And then, like a key in a lock after all the others had been tried, Emma suddenly thought of something. She started scanning the Births, Deaths and Marriages next to the Personal adverts.

One name jumped out at her – Becky Sower. It could not be a coincidence. Becky, Rebecca, Taylor, Sower, maiden name Portland and a reference to the Worshipful Company of Tailors. Becky got the number for the Daily Herald and called it, not quite sure how she was going to play this.

* * *

Will arrived at the Herald's offices just after nine o' clock. Hannah had pre-booked him in at reception with Jan and he went straight up to her office.

"Your sister's pretty good," she said as he walked in, referring to her band's performance the previous night.

"She is, isn't she?" he replied. "Just got a deal with Sony. Debut album out next month."

The office had only a skeleton staff. Being a Friday, most of the people who were in were working on the Sunday edition. "So what do we do now?" Hannah asked.

"We wait," Will replied.

"How exciting," said Hannah sarcastically, rolling her eyes. "I can't think of a better way to spend my morning."

"Ah," said Will, grinning, and holding up an index finger by way of a cautionary gesture. "I've already thought of that. Do you play cards?" he asked.

Hannah shrugged, "Yeah, from time to time," she said.

"Excellent. And do you like Star Wars?"

Hannah laughed, not knowing where this was going. "I've seen the films," she said cautiously.

"Then we are well matched," said Will, reaching into his inside pocket and bringing out a packet of cards. "Star Wars Top Trumps," he said, grinning broadly.

"Oh my God! How old are you?" she replied, covering her mouth with her hand.

Will replied without hesitation. "Nine," he said, and started dealing the cards.

Over the course of the next two hours Hannah discovered that Will played the guitar, and Will discovered that Hannah really wanted a cat. She was too discreet to ask him what it was he actually did for a living, and Will was kind enough to ask her what it was that brought her to England. Her explanation of European travel and living in the land of Shakespeare, Byron, Wordsworth and Coleridge intrigued Will.

"So you're a romantic?" he asked.

"Only on Tuesdays," she said. "Height?" she asked, looking at her card.

"You've got bloody Chewbacca again haven't you?" Will moaned.

"Yep, hand it over." Will handed her his card. "Ooh. The old wizardy guy! I think I'm going to win you know."

That was when the phone rang. Hannah picked it up – Will had already rigged a personal headset to the phone so that he could listen without having to pick up another receiver or set it to speakerphone where the few others in the office could have heard.

"Personals," said Hannah, cheerily. Will had asked her to respond as she would do on any other day.

"Hi, it's client services here, I have a lady on the line who wants to speak to you. She says she wants to get further details about a death announcement in today's edition. Her name is Rebecca Taylor. Are you happy to take it?"

"Of course, please put her through," said Hannah. Will had coached her on how to handle the call, to take as much information as possible and how to respond to any questions about the fictitious Becky Sower. There was a distinct click on the line as the call was transferred. "Hello. Daily Herald personals how can I help?" asked Hannah.

In her flat in Chelsea, Emma was shaking, cigarette in hand. She hadn't smoked since she was fifteen. "To whom am I speaking?" she asked.

"My name is Hannah, this is the personals desk at the Daily Herald. How can I assist you ma'am?" Will had asked her to continue using the American idiosyncracies and courtesies which she always had.

"I thought your name might be Rebecca Taylor," Emma asked.

"I'm afraid it isn't ma'am, but I have a friend of Rebecca's right here. Would you like to talk to him?"

Emma shook her head slowly and took a long drag on her cigarette. All or nothing, she thought. "Yeah, why not."

Will knew the name was blown and was quick to answer. "Rebecca Taylor here," he said. "How can I help you Miss...?" he was hoping for a name.

"If you're calling yourself Rebecca I'm not giving you my name," Emma replied.

"Would I be correct in thinking you're the young lady who walked into the Chinese Embassy yesterday?" he asked, quite straightforwardly. At this, Hannah stole a look at him, wide-eyed – she still had her receiver to her ear.

"Are you recording this? Do you have my number?" asked a nervous Emma. "I blocked my number, I bet you've got it haven't you? Do you know where I'm calling from?" she asked, clearly nervous.

Will's voice was steady. "I don't have your number, I don't know where you live," he said. "You've come through a commercial telephone exchange to an extension at a private business. We're not recording this and we can't find you." He paused. "Trust me?" he asked.

Emma wanted to say 'yes', because the voice she heard on the end of the phone sounded confident and trustworthy, but she couldn't get the word out.

"We should meet," said Will.

"Why can't I just talk to you on the phone?" asked Emma.

"Just because I'm not recording it doesn't mean someone else isn't," Will replied, thinking on his feet and trying to make sure he could actually get hold of this girl.

"Who would be?" asked Emma. "That American girl? Is she CIA or something?"

Will nodded to her. "I don't work for the CIA," said Hannah. "I'm a journalist."

Emma stubbed her cigarette out in a plant pot on her balcony. She had been pacing around her flat for the duration of the call. "Well, that's just bloody marvellous," she said. "My confidence in journalists is right up there with my respect for the CIA and that David Icke is right and the Queen is a blood sucking lizard!" she spat out. Emma recognised she was stressed, and lit another cigarette as a result.

Will was desperately trying to think of the best way to salvage the situation. He was still thinking when Hannah piped up. "You alright honey?" she asked. That was too much for Emma, she finally cracked, her back sliding down the wall until she was in a foetal position on the balcony, sobbing quietly.

Will nodded to Hannah, recognising that this American journalist who registered the births, deaths and marriages at the Daily Herald was doing a damn sight better job than him at calming whoever the hell it was on the end of the phone.

"I don't know what it is that you're involved in," said Hannah, and then trying to lighten the situation laughed a little bit, "and I suspect whatever it is you're up to your eyeballs in it." There was a choked chuckle on the end of the line. "But I tell you what, the man sitting next to me, 'Rebecca', as you apparently know him. I'd give him a chance." Hannah had no idea why she said what she said, she just felt it was the right thing to do.

"Okay," Emma said, holding back the tears.

Will then took the lead on the call. "Miss, my name is Will."

"I bet it isn't," came the instant response, as Emma laughed through the tears. Hannah looked up at him, eyebrows raised again.

"We can come to all of that later," he said. "I'd like to meet you. Is that okay?" he asked.

"Yeah, that's okay," said Emma. "Where?"

Will winced. "I need to be careful about this," he said. "Actually we both need to be careful about this."

"Why's that?" came the question straight at him. Will didn't answer her, once again wracking his brain about the best way forward. The possibility it was a set-up couldn't be dismissed. Will recognised that he wasn't necessarily the most sensitive communicator but he could put a plan together very quickly, as one of his bosses had once said, he was 'like ten men on speed'.

"And I want her there too," came the demand from Emma. Emma was afraid and emotionally vulnerable, the prospect of meeting this man on the end of the phone on his own was unpalatable. Will glanced across at Hannah, with a look of pleading that was impossible to resist.

"I can be there," she said.

"Where's it going to be then?" asked Emma.

Will's brain was working overdrive. Now he had to get three people in the same place at the same time and had to be absolutely confident no-one was watching or listening. The fact that he had no idea what this woman's intentions were did not help. Something was massively out of kilter, and it needed to be addressed. She could be a plant, a mole, a prostitute who overheard something in a bar, it didn't matter – this woman had not turned up in the Chinese Embassy by accident. He had to move.

"You in London?" he asked.

"Yes," came the curt response. "What makes you say that?"

"Wild guess," said Will, although he had heard the almost constant emergency service sirens while Emma was smoking on the balcony. It could have been any other conurbation in the UK but Will got lucky. "Are you a fan of Rembrandt?" he asked.

"No."

"Shame. Fantastic exhibition at the National Gallery at the moment. See you there at two."

"How will I know it's you?" asked Emma.

"I'll find you," Will replied, and ended the call.

Hannah stared at him open mouthed. "What are you doing?" she asked, incredulous. "I'm not getting into some secret agent crap just because you asked me. What the hell is going on?"

"Shush," said Will, taking her by the arm, "we need to move now, and this girl isn't going to talk to me without talking to you first."

"This is ridiculous," said Hannah.

"Yep. Wait until you see what happens next."

CHAPTER SEVENTEEN

The National Gallery...

Will and Hannah got out of the taxi at the southern side of Trafalgar Square, not having exchanged a word during the short journey from Wapping. After Will had paid the driver he turned to her with a big smile. "Exciting, isn't it?" he asked.

"That is hardly the word I would use," she replied. "What was all that stuff about the Chinese Embassy?"

"That," said Will, "is a very good question, and one which I intend to find the answer to."

"This is all weird," said Hannah, shaking her head. "Do you have any idea what you're doing?"

Will just smiled at her. "Like I said, exciting isn't it?" he grinned. "I have to make a call. Excuse me for a second." Will pulled his mobile from his pocket and speed dialled the number.

In an uninteresting looking industrial estate of warehouses in area known as Nine Elms, just south of the river Thames, the Duty Operations Officer's phone rang. "Boss," he said, recognising Will's phone number when he picked up.

"Ah, Q-man," he said, "I have a job for you."

"About bloody time," said Q-man. "There's only so much Playstation a grown man can put up with."

"Are the children irritating you?" Will asked.

"Every bloody day," Q-man said. "They're restless boss. Anyway, what's the job, what do you need?" came the question.

"Okay. I'm kind of making this up as I go along . Could I have," Will paused for moment. "Yes, right, could I have four cars, two bikes and I'd like a camera team as well please. Two-up in the cars, there's a need to debus and have a bit of a walk around."

Q-man was writing notes as he listened. "What's the target Boss?"

"Me," came the quick response.

Q-man's eyebrows raised. "You got company he asked?" warily.

"Yes, I already have and will have one more if all goes to plan."

"Friends or foes?"

"One friend," said Will, looking at Hannah, who was eyeing him suspiciously, "but I honestly can't call it right now on the new arrival."

"And the job?"

"I'm going to do a pick-up, debrief and drop-off. The pick-up is obvious, it's the last location we exercised when I was here before. You got my location?" he asked. Q-man did a quick triangulation on Will's phone.

"Are we celebrating 1805 again?" asked Q-man. "I take it your current friend is neither French nor Spanish, that would be culturally inappropriate," he said.

"No, she's one of the cousins," said Will, flashing a quick look at Nelson's Column and its commanding presence in Trafalgar Square. Then, looking confused, he asked, "since when did you know anything about British Naval history? Anyway," he shrugged, "I'll need front and rear cover for the pick-up and I would like the team to throw a surveillance box around us on exit. If this girl is being followed I want to know everything about who is doing it. Oh," he added as an afterthought, "I'll be needing one of your cabs as well."

"Roger that Boss." Q-man had continued to write notes throughout the call. "I'm thinking," he said, "you'll be wanting the full gunships?"

"Yes please."

"Right you are Boss, we'll see you on the target."

The half of the conversation that Hannah had heard left her even more baffled. "Q-man?" she asked quizzically. "Who is called Q-man for crying out loud?"

"Well," Will paused in thought for a moment. "Umm, Q-man. That's his name. That's why we call him that." He headed for the National Gallery when Hannah grabbed his arm and pulled him around.

The tone of her voice changed. "Will, seriously, what is going on here? Who are you people? Who is Rebecca Taylor and what is about to happen?"

He returned her intense gaze. Londoners and tourists swarmed around them in the square as they stood looking at each other. Will's thought process had to be rapid. This was one of those situations where he had to make a very quick decision, one of the many reasons he had been asked to set up the Contingency Planning Group. He frowned briefly. "Lots of questions," he said.

"Then give me lots of answers," came the response. "No answers, no Hannah," she dictated, "and I guess no Hannah means no Rebecca."

Will took her arm and gently led her to one of the unoccupied stone benches at the side of the square. "Have a seat," he said.

"Well thank you kindly," Hannah replied as she sat down.

"You've earned it," he teased. "And you've earned an explanation. It's only fair." He sat down next to her. "Yesterday the girl we are about to meet walked into the Chinese Embassy and attempted to sell them secret British government papers."

"Oh my God!"

"My thoughts entirely, although this is not as uncommon as you might think." Will's tone was neutral.

"Who is she?" asked Hannah, incredulous.

"That's where we get to the difficult part," said Will. "We don't know," he said slowly, turning to her. "And it is my job to find out. The reason it is my job to find out is because although we can't identify her, the name she used was a codeword for the organisation which I run."

"The Contingency Planning Group?"

"Yes, the Contingency Planning Group."

"And what is that exactly, it sounds like something you turn to when there's a hosepipe ban."

"That is entirely the point," explained Will. "The CPG, as we abbreviate it," he said unnecessarily, resulted in a smirk from Hannah. "The CPG," he continued, smiling, aware of his patronising tone, "is an umbrella group of capabilities, military, intelligence, police and anything else we need to protect the

United Kingdom. Its work is secret, its resources are secret, its budget is secret, its capabilities are secret."

"So what if I go off and tell someone about it?" Hannah asked.

"Well you can tell whoever you want," answered Will, "and I'll just change the name on Monday."

"Your name isn't Will is it?" she asked. Will didn't answer. "Am I in danger?"

Will couldn't lie to the woman who he had only met the day before. "You might be," he said, "but I'm a bloody good shot and the back-up team's already here."

"What back-up team?"

"See that cab on the rank with the guy with the big nose sitting behind the wheel reading the paper?"

Hannah looked across. "Yeah."

"That's the Q-man."

"I really need to find out why he's called that," she said.

"Me too," came the response.

"Is he it?" she asked, shocked. "He's the back-up team?"

"No, there are another four on foot, four cars parked up and two motorcyclists." He looked around, squinting into the winter sun. "Somewhere," he added.

"Well I can't see them," said Hannah.

"Me neither, pretty good aren't they," he grinned infectiously, taking a small pouch out of his pocket and putting a tiny flesh coloured earpiece into his left ear. "Now then, you walk on my left okay." He stood up and they started to walk across Trafalgar Square. "I'm going to hold your hand," he said, "do you mind?"

"Hell, I came here to have adventures," said Hannah. "May as well go along with this one. Don't suppose I've got much choice have I?"

"Not really," said Will, staring straight ahead.

Hannah thought of something. "You know when you said you were a 'bloody good shot'," she said, attempting to mimic his accent. "Does that mean?" she didn't finish the question.

Will didn't say anything, he just pulled her hand in close and pressed it to his hip. She could feel the handgrip of the pistol through his jacket. He turned to her and smiled. "Guess what?" he asked rhetorically. "There's another one on the other side."

"Is that it?" she asked, feigning disappointment as they climbed the steps on the north face of Trafalgar Square.

"Nope," said Will. "I've got another one under my left armpit."

"So where's your front and rear cover team?" she asked, remembering the phone call earlier.

"Well they're waiting for me to talk to them at the moment. Unsurprisingly the front cover team is already in the National Gallery and the rear cover team is about twenty feet behind us."

She looked at him. "How do you know that?" she asked.

"Q-man just told me," he answered. "Excuse me a sec." Will put his hand in his jacket pocket and pressed the send switch on the radio that was hidden under the armpit that wasn't sporting a pistol. "All call-signs this is the delivery boy. Keep tight on me. Acquisition is the blonde. She's blue on black, main steps, just killing the red dot now. Heading for the main entrance."

Hannah looked at him nervously, confused by what he was saying. He could feel the slight tremble in her hand. "Up there," he said, nodding in the direction of the entrance. And then Hannah understood. There was Emma, blonde haired and wearing an electric blue top and black jeans, stubbing out a cigarette. She twigged the 'red dot' reference.

"How do you know it's her?" she asked.

"Well I don't to be honest," he responded, "but she's been standing on these steps staring around like a rabbit caught in headlights and chain-smoking for Britain for the last twenty minutes. My guess is she's trying to look for us looking for her."

"How will you know?"

"Put it this way, if she goes straight up to Room 23 on the second floor, that's where the Rembrandts are by the way, I'll be pretty confident. If she spends three hours walking around all the galleries and just happens to walk through Room 23 I'll be less confident," he said.

"What would you do if it were you?" Hannah asked.

He squeezed her hand gently. "I'd spend three hours walking around all the galleries, checking who was behind me and not going near Room 23," he replied, "but then, the difference between her and me is that she wants to be found."

Emma had checked the gallery's website before leaving home and knew exactly where to go. She arrived half an hour earlier than she'd been instructed in order to watch the square and see if she could spot anyone looking for her. As she had nervously stubbed out her cigarette on the steps outside she concluded that she was probably not cut out for clandestine work. She had half-expected a dozen men in black suits and ties to be walking around with a finger pressed in one ear and talking into their hands. She decided that she needed to watch a lot less television.

* * *

Half an hour earlier…

When Q-man put the phone down he walked straight to the operational ready-room. A dozen people were sat on the sofas, reading magazines, watching television and playing assorted computer games. He stood in the doorway, waiting for their attention, which did not take long. As the magazines were put down and the computer games paused, Q-man smiled at them all. "Game on, children," he said. There was a very brief stunned silence.

"Gunships?" came a question from the back of the room.

"Gunships," he confirmed. Q-man's team looked at each other, smiling broadly, and a cheer went up, accompanied by applause. "Briefing in the Ops Room, two minutes. Be ready to go," he said.

Ten of the twelve men and women who were sitting in the ready room went straight to the vault at the centre of the warehouse, drawing Glock 26 pistols from the armoury before speed loading them with ammunition from the second armoury. In addition to the compact and easily carried pistols, Belgian FN P90 carbines were signed out which were then loaded and placed in sports bags. The team had practiced this at speed so often that it was second nature to them. The remaining two members went directly to the Operations Room and switched on their CCTV camera feeds.

One and a half minutes later, all of them were sitting in the Operations Room awaiting the briefing. "No mucking about," said Q-man, "this one's for real, and I don't have much time," he added while unfurling a map on the large table in the middle of the room. He used an old car aerial as a pointer. The map was covered in coloured spots with numbers on them. "The Boss is at Red 16," he said, pointing at Trafalgar Square. "I'm pretty confident he's going in the gallery. He has company, and he's going for a pick-up." He looked up at his team. "No reason why we shouldn't do this like we practiced. Mike, John, you're on the bikes. Phil and Sarah, lead cover please. Robbie, Jane, rear cover thank you." Q-man turned round to his CCTV operators. "You got him?" he asked.

"Yes," came the response, "west side of the square, sitting with a female on a bench."

"Let's see her," said Q-man. The operator brought up a still shot of Hannah looking skywards, clearly exasperated. "She's on his side," he added. "I'll be in the cab. We'll use Route Gold for the surveillance detection. Questions?"

There weren't any, and the team moved out to the garage area inside the warehouse and tested their radios. Moments later the convoy of four cars and two motorbikes pulled out of the warehouse and headed for Westminster, each taking a different route, but constantly communicating with each other. Just before Trafalgar Square the passenger in each car got out and the team now on foot paired up as couples. Shortly afterwards a registered London taxi pulled up at the rank just off the square, with absolutely no intention of taking any members of the public anywhere.

"We're complete in the entrance hall," said Sarah, from the lead cover team. "Looks clear."

"Roger that," said Q-man. "Robbie, you good to go?" he asked.

"Yep, we're on the wall right above him."

Q-man radioed Will. "Delivery boy you are cleared to collect the package."

Will and Hannah followed Emma into the entrance of the National Gallery. Emma was clearly nervous, looking around in an agitated fashion, but it was clear that she knew directly where she was going.

"Front cover, Room 23 please," said Will.

"Roger that." Phil and Sarah moved quickly to Room 23 ahead of Emma.

Will squeezed Hannah's hand and gently steered her in the opposite direction. "Where are we going?" she whispered.

"We're taking the long route," he answered, without elaborating further. "Rear cover check for baggage please."

"Roger." The rear cover team held back to see if there was anyone following Emma but found nothing. "Clean at the moment," came the response.

"Front cover?" Will asked while climbing a staircase on the other side of the hall.

"Just arrived on target, seems clean."

"Okay. Let's do this. We'll be in there in about one minute," said Will. He had specifically chosen Room 23 because it had no direct entrance from the corridor but could be accessed through two adjoining rooms, meaning that once in the room the cover team were perfectly placed to monitor who was coming in and out, and Will had a choice of more than one exit. He turned to Hannah, "Right then gorgeous," he said, "this is your moment to shine."

Hannah looked a little nervous. "What do you want me to do?" she asked.

"When we get in there, I want you to go up to her, introduce yourself, and tell her that I'm a top guy, and ask her if she's still happy to talk to me. If she says yes, I want you to run your fingers through your hair, and then I will come over."

"What if she says 'no' and bolts for the door?" Hannah asked.

"Then it gets tricky," said Will.

Hannah frowned. "Bundled into a car and disappeared forever kind of tricky?" she asked.

Will paused for a moment. "Potentially," he said. The fact that Will appeared to be being completely straight with her gave Hannah confidence in him. Will was being straight with her precisely because he wanted her to have confidence in him.

"Shall we?" he asked, before walking into the room and letting go of her hand.

Emma was sitting on the viewing bench in the middle of the room, clutching her handbag tightly. Will walked behind her and immediately noticed her right heel tapping frantically. Hannah took a seat next to her, and Will was impressed by how calm she was. Emma immediately looked across at her new companion, eyes wide.

"Hello," said Hannah quietly. Emma recognised her voice. "You must be Rebecca Taylor," she said. Emma just nodded, seemingly unable to speak. "Are you still happy to talk to Will?" she asked.

Emma looked at her feet. "I don't know who to trust," she said.

Hannah smiled comfortingly. "I think he's one of the good guys."

"How long have you known him?"

Hannah couldn't stifle a tiny laugh. Putting her hand on Emma's she rolled her eyes and said, "Oh, less than a day."

Emma smiled back. "Okay, I'll see him. Where is he?" she asked.

"Oh, he's here, somewhere," said Hannah, deliberately not looking around the room but brushing her long, dark hair behind her ear.

Will moved instantly. This was the time and he could not afford to have this girl change her mind. He walked across to the bench and sat down. "Self-portrait at the age of sixty-three," he said, nodding at the painting opposite. Emma looked startled. "From what I've read, he got a bit more expressive with his brushwork as he got older. You'd think he would've smiled a bit though," he added.

Emma didn't know how to take him. "Excuse me?" was all she could say.

"Then again, it was the last year of his life. Fair enough I suppose."

Emma looked across at Hannah. "It's alright," she said, "in the short time I've known him, this is about standard."

Will turned serious, but kept his voice low. "Ms Taylor, as I can only call you for now as I don't know your name, I am the man you spoke to earlier today. I work for the British government, and I think there is something you want to talk to someone like me about and I can give you my assurance that whatever it is, I can guarantee your safety."

Emma stared straight ahead, having heard what her father had said, the phrase, "I work for the British government," did not particularly inspire confidence. But then there was the American journalist, if she really was a journalist. She sighed and put her head in her hands.

Will put his hand on her elbow. "Come with me," he said quietly. Emma looked at him, clearly exhausted and mentally drained. He helped her up and they walked out of the room.

The cover teams saw what was happening and moved quickly again. Will heard several repeats of "Room clear," in his earpiece as they left the gallery and "Target clean," from the rear team.

"Where are we going?" asked Emma.

"Taxi ride," said Will. Q-man had moved from Trafalgar Square up to Charing Cross Station and was parked in the forecourt, still reading his paper. The team of four that had provided the cover teams returned to the cars that were parked up in the surrounding streets. Will held the taxi door open for Emma and Hannah as they climbed in. "One of ours," said Will, patting the door of the taxi, "nothing to worry about." He turned to the driver, "Good to go Q-man?" he asked.

Hannah simply shrugged when Emma looked at her, confused. "I need about thirty seconds," said Q-man, who was listening to the radio chatter of his team members. One of the motorbikes was already heading down Whitehall, calling the route clear. The two lead cars pulled into the forecourt of the station and Q-man pulled out behind them, the two rear cars were waiting in The Strand to follow them out. The second motorbike followed a short distance behind, with emergency medical kits and ammunition stored in the pannier.

Will had done this many times before, but still found it difficult to concentrate on a conversation when he had a stream of information coming through his earpiece, as each member of the team gave a near constant commentary on what they were doing. He slid the partition open to the driver's cabin and simply said, "Q-man, I'm going non-comms." He removed the tiny earpiece and put it back in the little pouch in his jacket pocket. "That's better," he smiled. "Now then, what can we do for you Rebecca?" he asked.

Emma was frightened and confused, and having no idea what to expect when she took the action she did, had planned for nothing. Who to trust was the major concern for her. One thing she did think was a good idea was to open her handbag and hand over the secret government papers she had stolen and stuffed into it and offered to the Chinese.

Will took them gently, folded them and put them in his jacket pocket. "Thank you," he said, and with a tone of voice that sounded completely non-judgemental, he asked, "Would you be good enough to tell me where you got these?"

"They were on my father's desk," said Emma, without elaborating. She seemed distracted, and looking out of the window realised that the taxi had done one full rotation of Parliament Square, had crossed the river southwards and northwards and was now heading back towards Trafalgar Square. "Where are we going?" she asked.

"Nowhere," came the simple response.

"Are we just going round in circles?"

"Pretty much."

"Why?" came the question.

"We just want to make sure you're alone," said Will.

Emma threw her head back in exasperation. "This is nuts," she whispered to herself.

Will remained calm. "May I ask what your father was doing with top secret documents on his desk?" he asked.

Emma composed herself. "Yes you may," she said matter of factly. "He is the Foreign Secretary."

"David Harris!" said Will, surprised at the turn of events. This was the first time that either Hannah or Emma had seen him looking surprised.

She leaned forward, extending her hand, "I'm Emma by the way," she said.

Will took it. "Will Richards," he replied. "I run something called the Contingency Planning Group." Emma's eyes widened. "You've heard of it?" he asked. Emma didn't respond. "I thought you might have done. We don't really advertise ourselves a lot but in this day and age it's almost impossible to keep a secret." He took a moment to look out of the window. The convoy of vehicles was now driving at a sedate pace along the Embankment. All the drivers were happy to keep one or two cars apart, and the motorbikes retained the freedom to move close or away as they pleased. "Would you mind if I asked how you heard of us?" said Will.

"I overheard my father talking about it," she replied.

Will knew that the Foreign Secretary was not privy to the name, capability or remit of the CPG – it was established as a domestic capability, and as such the Foreign Secretary had no requirement to know anything about it. He was also getting a little frustrated with what seemed to be Emma's deliberate decision to restrict her answers to the question he asked, without giving further detail. He checked himself, making an effort to think what it must be like for a person in her position. "Okay," he said slowly. Patting his jacket pocket he asked, "Would you mind telling me why you walked into the Chinese Embassy and attempted to sell these to them?"

Emma returned his gaze. "I had no intention of selling them to the Chinese and the full expectation that doing that would lead me to you," she answered.

"Interesting, would you care to explain why?"

"Someone told me that embassies are very suspicious of people who walk in the front door and basically sell themselves as spies."

Will cocked his head. "Really? That's quite true though," he acknowledged. "Who was the 'someone'?" Will wanted to explore every avenue of this story now.

"It was at a garden party at my parents' place," she said. "His name was Dimitry."

Will smiled and sat back in his seat. "Russian guy?" he asked.

Emma nodded. "You know him?" she asked.

"Yep, I know Dimitry. Defence Attache, former Spetznaz, that's Russian special forces," he explained, "career intelligence officer and a man who saved my life a long time ago in a galaxy far, far away called Kosovo."

"Is he a spy?"

"Difficult to define that word, but, as you would understand it, absolutely," said Will.

"Oh my God," said Emma, beginning to get tearful. Hannah put her arm around her, and glared at Will.

"Not a drama," he said quickly. "Really. There are two more questions I have though. First, why did you use the name Rebecca Taylor when you went into the embassy?"

"Because when I heard Dad and the Admiral talk about the Contingency Planning Group they said that apparently Rebecca Taylor is the woman to go to in the worst case scenario and they seemed concerned about who she was and what she could do."

Will made no show of his interest in the 'Admiral', and stored those questions for later. "And why was that do you think?" he asked gently.

Emma wiped the tears that were forming in her eyes and looked out of the window before turning back to Will. "Because they're planning to kill the Prime Minister," she said.

Hannah looked astonished. Emma burst into tears. Will handed her his handkerchief before turning back to Q-man. "Change of plan," he said, "we're going to Wiltshire." Q-man relayed the instruction to the rest of the team and the convoy started heading west out of central London.

"I'm not going to Wiltshire!" exclaimed Hannah. "I have a brunch with my neighbour tomorrow morning. I have never had brunch in England before and we have a table booked in Covent Garden!"

Will held his hands up in a gesture of surrender. "You can have brunch in Covent Garden tomorrow, don't worry," he said.

Hannah remained defiant. "I have no intention of going all the way to Wiltshire and back, that'll take hours," she said.

"It'll take about 20 minutes," said Will. "It's not the county, it's the name of the house." With that he held his hand to his chin and stared out the window, clearly thinking very, very intently.

CHAPTER EIGHTEEN

The Safe House...

The cars and the bikes turned into a quiet, leafy street, just off Holland Park. It was a private road and a security guard opened the barrier for them. Both Hannah and Emma were smart women and once they were out of the traffic realised they were, and had been the whole time, under escort. "Friends of yours?" Hannah asked. Will nodded assent. The lead motorcyclist indicated left towards a large Georgian house. As he approached the imposing iron gate it swung inwards, providing access to the oval gravel drive and double garage to the side of the main house – both garage doors opened simultaneously. The lead motorbike and the first two cover cars headed into the garage, the rear bike followed them in. Q-man's taxi and the remaining cars stopped in a holding position while the gates closed behind them.

"Won't be a minute," said Will. Once the gate was closed the other three cars drove in to the garage.

"What is this, the Tardis?" asked Hannah.

"Kind of," said Will. As they drove in they went down a curved ramp underneath the house. Neither Emma nor Hannah could believe what they were seeing. What they thought would be the underground carpark of a millionaire's house was a two hundred metre long warehouse of cars, assorted military equipment and stockpiles of things they could not even identify.

Emma pointed. "Is that a tank?" she asked.

"Yep."

She pulled his sleeve aggressively. "What the hell is going on?" she demanded. "I thought I could trust you. I thought you were taking me to a safe house or something."

"No," said Will, I haven't taken you to a safe house," he grinned, "I've brought you to the safest street in Britain."

Q-man parked the taxi. "What is that supposed to mean?" Hannah asked, exasperated.

Will remained calm. "This is my street," he said. "Every house is mine. How do you think I managed to get such a big garage? You can come in any one of the houses and leave by another. Both sides of the street. Quite handy isn't it?" he smiled.

This threw Emma, who was in the middle of a world she didn't understand. "And you!" she asked, spinning around at the driver. "What the hell does 'Q-man' mean? What's that all about?"

"I've gotta agree there," said Hannah. "Q-man? That's kinda weird."

Will joined in, with a puzzled expression. "Actually, that's a fair one. Why do we call you Q-man?" he asked. Q-man scratched the back of his neck and looked embarrassed. "Don't be shy," said Will.

"It's because I like queuing," he said, awkwardly.

"You like queuing?" spat Hannah.

"Yeah. It's orderly. It's like it should be. Like a library."

Emma and Hannah gave Will looks that could kill. "I didn't know that either," he said lightly. Perhaps we should go upstairs and get Mrs Hudson to fix us some tea," he added.

Hannah laughed with desperation as she got out of the car. "This is getting ridiculous," she said.

"Getting?" asked Emma.

Hannah continued, mocking with her best English accent, "Perhaps we should get Mrs Hudson to fix us some tea. What is this, the secret world of Arthur Conan Doyle?" She stopped in her tracks as the realisation struck her. Turning, she said to Will, "She's not actually called Mrs Hudson, is she?"

"This way," he said walking towards a small lift. Not looking back he added, "Mrs Hudson is the name I give to any kettle I use."

The door to the lift had a swipe card reader on it. Will put his card through and pulled the gate open, gesturing for Emma and Hannah to go first. He closed the gate behind him and after a very short journey, they emerged from a door which appeared to be the entrance to the under-stair cupboard of the house.

"Welcome to Wiltshire," said Will. "Right then, who wants a cuppa?" Hannah and Emma said "Me," at the same time and Will led them through to the kitchen.

"This place is amazing," said Hannah, as she walked through the hall, which was floored with black and white diamond-shaped tiles. The ceiling was double height and the marble staircase was the widest she had ever seen. A crystal chandelier hung at the top of the three-storey atrium. Hannah was too busy looking around to notice the man in civilian clothes carrying a machine gun standing in the kitchen.

"Jesus!" she shouted, when she saw him.

Will turned and put a reassuring hand on her arm. "This is Craig," he said. "Craig works for me."

Hannah shook her head. "Well, yes, of course he does."

Will made the tea and they went through to the drawing room, an elegant room with comfortable sofas covered in cushions, an open fire and mahogany shelves packed with old books.

"I wish my flat looked like this," said Hannah as she sat down. "What is this place?" she asked. Emma had been fairly quiet since she left the taxi and Will could see that her hands were shaking.

"This is Wiltshire," said Will, and turning and pointing out several of the other houses in the street he added, "and that is Derbyshire, and that is Yorkshire, and that is Ayrshire. The semi-detached ones over there are Fermanagh and Gwent. Each house in the street is named after a county in the United Kingdom. There are quite a few more that you can't see."

"And are they all like this?" asked Hannah.

"Nope," said Will in a matter-of-fact way. "This is the only nice one. This is where we bring guests. The others are all gutted and we use them for other things."

"Other things?" asked Hannah.

"Other things," Will repeated, and it was clear that he was not going to provide any further information. He turned to Emma and asked her to elaborate on everything she had said on the journey. Emma told him everything she had overheard the night her father and Admiral Dudgeon had been talking. Her recollection was extremely accurate, but then, her senses were highly alert at the time.

* * *

After listening to everything Emma had to say, Will walked to a small side table with a secure phone on it. "Tom, can you put a close protection team in here for the night please." Emma looked concerned, "Don't worry," he reassured her, "standard procedure." After two non-descript men arrived from the basement Will leaned backwards against the fireplace. "Well, I don't know about you two, but I fancy a drink. Nice pub around the corner, government's paying, been a pretty heavy day. What do you think?" he asked. "Incidentally, you're both staying here tonight, I have some thinking to do, so this is your last chance for fresh air this evening."

Hannah looked keen. "I'm up for it," she said. Emma shook her head and stared at the carpet and Hannah could see she was in a lonely place, "but I'll stay if you want me to?" she offered. There was already a bond between the two women, who had both experienced hugely unexpected events in a short space of time.

"No, you go," said Emma, "I'd rather just stay in and watch television."

Will opened a bureau next to the fireplace and pulled out an alphabetised folder of take-away menus. "These have all been tested by our boys and girls," he said, "and they have exacting standards. Just let Craig, the scary looking guy in the hallway, you know, the one with the machine gun, just let him know what you want, and he'll sort it. Alternatively, we have a small industrial kitchen and 24hr catering over there in Berkshire. You want a sandwich, snack, roast dinner, anything, they can sort that for you, okay." Emma looked up and smiled. "You sure you don't want to come for a drink?"

"I just want a hot bath, a duvet and I wish I had Gladstone, my teddy bear," came the tired response.

"Two of those we can manage," said Will. "Craig will show you to your room and where everything is."

Spontaneously, Hannah leaned across and hugged Emma. "It's going to be okay," she said, sounding confident but with absolutely no confidence at all.

As Will and Hannah walked back through the hallway he stopped in his tracks and turned to Craig, machine gun still cradled in his arms. "Get her a teddy bear," he whispered, "I don't care if you have to break down the fucking doors of Hamley's. Just make sure there's one in her room before she goes to sleep."

Craig had been on the receiving end of some very unusual instructions; this one topped them all. He couldn't help himself from smirking. Will turned to the door and spoke without looking back, "I shit you not Craig, if that doesn't happen, the look on your face will be very different when I shove that gun up your arse."

It was drizzling lightly as Will and Hannah walked the five minutes to The Red Lion. "Shouldn't you be on the phone or something, mobilising troops and speaking to the Prime Minister, at least calling the police for crying out loud?" she asked.

"Probably."

"You're not funny."

"Wasn't trying to be, I just need some time to think this through."

"What's to think? Her Dad wants to kill the Prime Minister."

"He might do," said Will. "But can he? There is a difference between intent and capability and I've not seen anything else to substantiate this. For all I know she's an attention seeking lunatic and my organisation will end up looking like idiots. She's safe, you're safe, I'll make some calls later and confirm that the PM's safe and no doubt in the morning I will wake up having slept on the whole thing and will have come up with a brilliant plan!" he beamed, holding open the door to the pub.

Hannah was not impressed with what she walked into. She was now familiar with the village-ness of London and despite the postcode she had so recently walked from she found herself in a dimly lit pub with a sticky carpet, unkempt customers and walls and a ceiling that looked like they hadn't been re-decorated since the war. She gave Will a long, hard look. "What a charming place to bring a lady," she said.

"One does one's best. For God's sake don't try to order a cocktail – we'll be murdered."

They sat in a corner booth with their drinks. "You're not really going to let me go to brunch tomorrow are you?" Hannah asked.

"Nope."

"So is this my last night of semi-freedom? You bringing me to the worst pub in London?"

"Yep."

"Could you be slightly more chatty? This isn't the best date I've ever had by the way," Hannah stopped herself mid-sentence, "not that I'm suggesting..." she trailed off.

"No, no, that's fine," said Will, awkwardly, "but you're right. Until we get this sorted I'm afraid you're in my gang for the moment."

"So, you genuinely have security-related issues that an American journalist has learned about a possible plot to murder the British Prime Minister. That's thin man," she said, laughing. The day had been so intense that Hannah's gin and tonic was quickly going to her head. "It could be worse," she added, "I could have found out about a secret underground bunker with a tank in it."

"Indeed you could, but I trust you," he added, sincerely. It was a sobering reply, but then Hannah noticed that Will's attention had moved and he was clearly looking over her right shoulder.

"What is it?" she asked.

He was quick to reassure her. "Nothing to do with us, or today or anything connected with it, but there is a chap over there playing cards who is about to go bananas."

Will had spotted the two tables of poker players as he came in, and although the stakes were, at least visibly low and legal, he knew that a one pound coin could represent a thousand pounds for the semi-professionals who played the leagues in the London pubs. "Standby," he said, "this is about to get ugly."

Will had been keeping a watching-eye on the tables since they'd come through the door, and sure enough the man he had thought was the most likely to do something stupid did so. He was one of the quieter players and hadn't smiled all evening but was going through pints of Guinness like they were water. He stood up and tipped the table over. Unsurprisingly, the pub went quiet and all eyes were fixed on the man. He was well over six feet tall, lean and fit looking, despite his fifty-odd years.

Hannah looked at Will for reassurance and he gently cautioned her with a slight raising of his hand. "It's alright for you," she whispered, "you can see the whole pub. I've got my back to this lunatic." Will was religious about making sure he could see at least one door and had an unobstructed view of any enclosed space he was in.

He also had a habit of immediately ascribing names to people he didn't know. The agitated card player was quickly christened "Noddy". Noddy was looking around the pub, arms at his sides with his clenched fists pointing forward, making him look a lot like a caveman. Several dozen people shrank from his gaze, attempting to make themselves look as small as possible. "Come and sit next to me," said Will quietly, taking Hannah's hand and pulling her on to the bench seat beside him.

"Shouldn't we leave?" she whispered.

"Why?" asked Will, matter of factly.

"He's a nutter," she said.

"Yep."

"Oh for God's sake, not that again," said Hannah under her breath. Will kept hold of her hand under the table.

"Do not move unless I tell you to move," he instructed her. "This is important." There was something about the tone of Will's voice which made it impossible not to do as he said.

And then something happened which Will had not expected at all. After mentally exercising several variations of how the situation could develop, most of which involved violence, Noddy turned to the barman and pointed an outstretched finger at him. "And what are you looking at, 'Charlie Big Potatoes'!" he shouted.

Hannah's head snapped sideways to look at Will, her face contorted with confusion. Will had nothing to offer in return, he was as confused as her. Someone behind Noddy giggled, whereupon Noddy spun on his heels again and shouted, "And what do you think's so funny, Charlie Big Potatoes?"

No-one in the pub had ever heard an insult like it, and looks of bewilderment abounded. "This is the weirdest thing I've ever seen," Hannah whispered in hushed tones to Will.

"I'm confident it'll get even better," Will replied.

"And you," shouted Noddy, pointing at a man in his thirties with a shaved head and a bulldog on a short leash. "You're not even worthy of being Charlie Big Potatoes!"

The surrealism of the situation seemed to have caught everyone off guard, for a brief moment Will included, right up to the point where Noddy grabbed an empty pint glass from the bar and smashed the top of it to make a stabbing weapon. "Oh shit," said Will, getting up from his seat.

"What are you doing?" hissed Hannah.

"Bedtime for Noddy," he replied, and Hannah had absolutely no idea what he was talking about.

Noddy saw him stand up. "You want some of this? Charlie Fucking Big Potatoes?" he asked, thrusting the broken pint glass in Will's direction. Will could not stop himself from laughing.

"Seriously mate, you have got to get something better than 'Charlie Big Potatoes'. It's laughable."

"Well, we'll see who has the last laugh when I push this in your face, Charlie Big Potatoes," said Noddy, waving the broken glass again.

Hannah, understandably, had been watching closely and saw Will smile the smile of a man who had been in situations like this before and seemed both tired of, and faintly amused by them.

Noddy rushed at him. Will turned his back, simultaneously sidestepping, dropping to the floor and extending his right leg. Noddy hit the floor face-first, but not before Will had grabbed the glass from his hand and put it in the empty bottles bin behind the bar. Noddy made it to his feet, enraged, and even groggier than he had been.

"Fuck you Charlie Big Potatoes!" he yelled, launching himself at Will, but this time he reached into his pocket and pulled out a butterfly knife. Will was trying not to laugh at the absurd insult when he saw the knife open and his focus sharpened. Will snapped Noddy's wrist backwards and twisted it, breaking it quickly as he turned him and smashed his nose into the bar, both of which broke a little bit. Turning him back again, Will kicked him so hard to the side of his knee that Noddy's leg bent in the middle. Will let go of him and let him slump to the floor.

It took Will only seconds to disable Noddy, while Hannah had watched open-mouthed. Will walked back to her, "Time to leave," he said. Hannah put her arm in his as they walked back to the safe house.

"You own a whole street full of secret houses, you have a basement with a tank in it, and you tell a man with a gun to buy a teddy bear for a grown woman." She paused. "Yesterday, I was just making sure I got the dates right when people died. And now you go and do a Superman routine in the most horrible pub I have ever been in."

Will smiled, "Well there might be some more of that to come."

Hannah hit him with her handbag.

"I like you too," he said, and laughing added. "And where were you when I needed you, Charlie Big Potatoes?"

* * *

Will made a number of calls that night, including to the Prime Minister's Close Protection Team, whose response, as he expected, basically outlined that threats like this were routine.

That evening Will also got a call from Jack Thompson, the Director of the UK Border Association.

"Jack, how you doing?" he asked.

"I'm nervous," was the reply.

"Then I'm listening," said Will.

"Are you still in charge of that Planning Group thing you told me about when we first met?" asked Jack. He had been sitting in his private study at home checking his work email account when he saw something that he thought Will should know about.

"Indeed I am. What's up?"

Jack was cautious, "Look, we could just be making things up as we go here but I've just seen an analyst's report that made me think perhaps we should contact you. Have you got something going on at the moment?"

Will was equally as cautious. "How do you mean?" he asked.

"I was just wondering if you were shipping people into the country you shouldn't be?"

Confused, Will said, "You've lost me there Jack. We talked about this. If I were bringing people in the whole point is that I would be talking to you first. That's the whole point of the Group." There was a silence on the end of the phone and Will started to realise where the conversation was going.

"Will, can I ask you a question? If these aren't your guys, could you please tell me that you know that someone or some people are going to try to do something really unpleasant? Because if you're not on this, you really need to be."

Jack was calling from an insecure phone and was clearly being careful not to say what he had found. "Can you send me a secure email from where you are?" asked Will.

"Of course, I'll give you what I've got straight after this. And Will, I enjoyed lunch with you when we met, you're a nice guy. I'm reading between the lines here a lot, and I'm getting bad vibes. I'd like to have lunch with you again sometime, stay safe. Take care on whatever the hell it is you're into."

"Thanks Jack". The line went dead and Will went into the drawing room and opened his CPG email account. Jack was as good as his word. Will opened the attached file and after a brief look at it stood straight back up, walked into the sitting room and poured himself a large Scotch. "Jesus. Fucking. Christ."

Will was now confident that Emma wasn't a fantasist and that his discussion with the Home Secretary wasn't unfounded. He went back to the drawing room and looked through the Border Agency report. It had been compiled by a junior analyst, which is why it had taken so long for it to reach him as it passed through her section supervisor, then department manager, was then reviewed by a senior analyst and was finally passed to one of the senior managers who passed it on to Jack, who had a thousand other things to do that day.

Will sat in the plush leather chair with his fingertips pressed together as he stared at the screen. Over the course of the last two days, one hundred and fifty eight people recognised as working for a 'Private Military Company', or 'mercenaries', as Will preferred to call them, had arrived in the UK. They had been clever, arriving at a variety of airports all over the country, as well as through the Channel Tunnel rail link from Paris and Brussels. Some had come through the big international ones, Heathrow, Gatwick, Manchester. Others had clearly taken several flights to get to the UK, landing at the more regional airports. It was most definitely not a coincidence. The passport control records showed that many were from Russia or former Soviet states. A large proportion also came from South Africa and there was a significant number of Americans.

"Shit", said Will to himself, untouched Scotch in his hand, just as Hannah tapped at the door. He looked around.

"Okay to disturb you?" she asked

"Crack on. Have a seat," he replied.

"These bathrobes are fantastic," said Hannah. "It's like a hotel in here."

"That really was the idea," Will replied.

"I popped in on Emma before I had a bath. Apparently there is no such thing as a replacement but the new bear is performing his duties adequately."

Will had just started to drink his scotch when Hannah said this, and he spat a mouthful out in the fireplace as he attempted to stop laughing.

"You're a funny one," she said, smiling and clutching a cushion from the settee.

"How so?" Will asked.

"Well, it's all Kung-Foo Karate Kid one minute and the next you're telling someone to buy a teddy bear."

"I don't like to be predictable," he smiled back.

"I figured that out already. So, tomorrow?" Hannah let the question hang.

There was a reason why Will had been staring at the fireplace so intently, he had been game-playing as many outcomes as he could think of. "Tomorrow," he said slowly, "tomorrow I ask Emma to do the bravest thing she's ever done."

"I'd tell you to take a hike," said Hannah.

"I know. But you are American, and Emma is English. We are more polite," he answered.

Hannah laughed. "And will you come to her rescue if it all goes wrong? Is it going to be all white horses and shining armour?" she asked.

Will's light-hearted tone became more serious, as did his countenance. "No horses, and no shining armour," he said. "Horse-power, yes. Black, not white though. Firepower, as in nasty bullet things. And due to budget constraints the only armour will be body armour." Will looked intently into the fireplace again and then turned to her, "Bedtime," he said.

"Excuse me!" Hannah responded.

Will laughed. "For you. Just you. I have some more things to think about."

"Do I get to play tomorrow? I am a journalist you know."

"Nope. You get to stay under the nicest house arrest in the UK. You might want to have a look at the movie collection," he said.

"Anything you'd recommend?"

"I'd suggest 'The Thomas Crowne Affair'."

"Why?" Will didn't answer the question, and Hannah could see that he wanted to be alone. She put an arm around his back and kissed him gently on the cheek. "Please try to get some sleep she said," as she went back upstairs.

Will got on the phone to his quartermaster. It was late, but there was no time for delay. Michael picked up the phone immediately, as he always did. "Yes Boss" he said.

"I need cars Mike, the black shiny ones."

"How many do you need?" came the question.

"All of them."

There was a seriousness in Will's voice which the quartermaster had not encountered before, but it didn't stop his surprised response, "All of them!"

"Yes, all of them, and I need each car fully bombed up and I want the crews two-up in every car."

"When do you need them?" asked Michael.

"Now."

"Shit."

"How many of the specials have we got in total?" Will asked.

"Hang on a sec Boss." Michael rolled out of his bed in the small underground flat he lived in under Wiltshire and walked the short distance to his office, where he looked at a gigantic whiteboard, criss-crossed with dividing lines and details of stocks of everything from ammunition to aircraft. "Okay, the black shiny ones," he said, "we've got twenty-four. They're not all here but we can get them here tonight. I assume it's here you need them."

"Can you split them up around the London bases please. We might be doing the bowler hat and briefcase operation."

Michael understood exactly what was being asked of him. "Your number plate?" he asked.

Will smiled. "I think it's time to give it an outing."

On the other end of the phone Michael was frowning as he thought of something. "Just one problem boss," he said, as he stared at the whiteboard. "You want all twenty four specials, and two-up in each one, that's forty-eight operators. I've got the guns, I've got the cars, I've got the garages. The problem is, you don't have the people."

"How many can you get tonight?" asked Will, recognising that he sounded snappy.

"There are twelve in on the standby night shift and twelve taking over at eight o' clock."

Will thought quickly. "Right, everyone gets to work a longer day. Leave the rest to me, I'll have the extra drivers and operators with you in the morning."

Will spent the next hour on the phone to guard and control rooms around the country speaking variously to eager young soldiers and old men nearing retirement who were wakened from their slumber. Night shifts were supposed to be quiet.

He called the Special Air Service, the Special Boat Service, the Special Reconnaissance Regiment and the Intelligence Corps, as well as New Scotland Yard and the Security Service. With one exception the calls were very similar. He would speak to a night guard, ask to be connected to the Operations Officer, and would then use the codeword "Night Owl", which they would then look up in dust covered folders which rarely saw the light of day, and he would then wait five minutes to get through.

The only exception was the Special Reconnaissance Regiment guard room. Will was anticipating the response, knowing that the number would be recognised. "Yes," came the simple and unexplanatory response as the call was taken.

"Major Richards here," said Will. "Could you put me through to the Ops Officer please?"

Will's voice was recognised. "This isn't a fucking telephone exchange."

"Corporal Gilbertson, if you don't get me the Ops Officer on the phone in under a minute I am going to send a very big man from Pentonville Prison to rape you."

Corporal Gilbertson laughed. "You're a very persuasive man Sir. Ops O coming right up."

Will's successor at the Special Reconnaissance Regiment was asleep when the call came through, having been on exercise for a week and having slept for approximately two hours a day. He was un-amused by the interruption.

"Will," he said as he was transferred. "We've just finished the Long Dragon exercise with the latest batch of recruits. I am bloody exhausted man. What the hell do you want?" he asked as he sat on the end of his bed in his tiny room in the officers' mess with one cupboard, a desk and a sink.

"I need hostile surveillance operators John," said Will.

"Don't we all," John replied.

"I need these ones tomorrow."

"How many?" asked John.

"What the hell is that noise?"

"I'm having a pee," said John, as he urinated in the sink.

"Jesus. Haven't you grown out of that yet?"

"Nope. Anyway, how many do you need?"

Will looked down at the rough chart he had put together. He had drawn aerial style pictures of four sets of six cars and put call-sign designations of the driver and co-driver on each car. Each set of cars had been bracketed with a colour, 'Gold', 'Silver' and 'Bronze', for the lead teams, and 'Red', 'White' and 'Blue' for the back ups.

He was six people short.

"You need kit as well or just the bodies?" asked John.

"We have the kit, just send me the best six you've got John, this is a serious business."

"I kind of figured that out when I got a call from you at this time of night. What's up?"

"It's bowler hat time, and we're playing for big stakes."

"In which case I will see you in the morning, with five of my best people with me."

Will laughed, "And why exactly would you be coming?" he asked.

"You asked for the six best people I have."

"Yeah, so why exactly would you be coming?" Will repeated.

"You can piss right off," said John as he ended the call and got dressed. He walked wearily to the guard room and Corporal Gilbertson handed him the contact folder with a raised eyebrow.

"You're up early Sir," he chirped sarcastically. The Operations Officer gave him a look that could have killed. "Coffee Sir?" he asked.

CHAPTER NINETEEN

A Question...

After she'd showered and got dressed Emma headed downstairs to the kitchen. "Thanks for the bear", she said when she saw Will at the kitchen table, flipping through a road atlas of London.

"You're welcome," he replied. "What's your kind of breakfast?"

"I normally just have a fried egg on toast," said Emma.

"Coming up." Will busied himself at the range cooker and then turned back to Emma. "I have to ask you to do something," he said.

Emma was cautious, "Which is?"

"I won't mess about here. I want you to bug your father's study."

He was surprised by the speed of her reply. "Okay," she said easily. Will looked up, "You don't have a problem with that?" he asked.

Emma shrugged. "In a perfect world, it wouldn't be my first choice of things to do today but hey, it's clearly not a perfect world." After breakfast they took a walk around the very well-kept garden. "This place must cost a fortune to run," she said.

"Yeah, it does, but if we let the gardens go to rack and ruin in an area like this the Russians and the Chinese would get very interested very quickly." Emma raised an eyebrow and Will simply pointed to the sky, "Everyone's always looking at everyone."

Emma smiled and nodded. "I see."

"What do you think of my rose?" he asked, gently guiding her to a sheltered corner of the garden under a Yew tree.

"Your rose?" she asked.

"Yep. My rose, I did the cross pollination and this is the only one of its type in the world. Andrew, the gardener, looks after her very well."

"It's beautiful, what's it called?" she asked.

"Sarah," he said simply. In response to Emma's questioning look he added, "Long story. All went wrong in a galaxy far, far away." Will saw the look on her face which betrayed her feeling of awkwardness. "Don't worry," he said, "it was a long time ago."

Emma decided to change the subject. "So what's all this about the bug then?" she asked. Will took her back inside and they returned to the underground complex. They arrived at a heavy steel door and Will pressed the button for the video entry-phone.

"Where'd you get the gorgeous blonde from?" came the youthful voice through the intercom. Emma blushed.

"I just bought her this morning at "Blonde's 'R' Us", will replied. "Would you let us in please Michael?"

"No. What's the magic word?"

Will turned to Emma and apologised. "He always does this," he explained, "he knows I can't say a certain word associated with plant life, so he picked it on purpose as my personal password."

"You need a password?" she asked, taken aback.

"Yes, when I'm with someone else, and he can see that, obviously," Will pointed to the camera. "If I'm under duress, I say "Hot Dog", except I'll have to change that now, because I've just told you, and he'll have to change my password as well."

Emma folded her arms and smirked at him. "I'm waiting for this."

Will frowned and pressed the intercom button. "Amenneny," he said.

The sound of digitised laughter came back through the system. "Well you ain't getting in. Try again."

"Anamennenee," he tried. "Shit this is irritating." The sound of laughter only grew. Will turned to Emma, "Help me out here," he asked, "can you just say the word."

"I don't know what it is," said Emma, trying hard not to smile.

"The plant thing, and there's a kind in the sea that looks like something off Star Trek."

"Try it again, one more time, and I'll see if I can help," she said, no longer able to disguise the smile.

Will had the good grace to try again. "Amannemeenee," he stammered.

Emma pressed the intercom. "I think he's trying to say 'anemone'", she said.

"Of course he is. I'm just playing with you. I know who you are, come in," said the voice on the other side of the intercom. The door buzzed open and Will led Emma into what looked like the reception desk at a dry cleaners, and was astonished to see a teenaged boy in a hooded top sitting behind the desk. He stood up as they approached the counter and extended his hand. "Hi, I'm Michael," he said, extending his hand.

Emma looked at Will, puzzled, and then shook hands with him, "Well of course you are."

"I'm the Quartermaster," he said.

"Why aren't you in school?" she asked, in the most school-mistress like voice she could summon up.

Michael was lively, and his cockney accent and beaming smile were infectious. "Because I was rubbish at that, and Will offered me a job here, and I get to play with guns and everything." Emma shot Will a withering look. "No, don't worry Miss, I'm responsible now."

"Now?"

Michael looked embarrassed. "I tried to rob him once. It wasn't the best idea I ever had, but the scars are healing nicely now."

Emma put her elbows on the counter and her face in her hands. "Jesus Christ who are you people?" she asked, with no expectation of an answer.

Will turned to Michael. "I need one of the special lightbulbs and a rapid response trigger please."

"Yes Sir," said Michael and disappeared down the long lines of industrial shelving.

Emma stood up straight. "He tried to rob you?" she asked.

Will shrugged. "Stupidest decision of his criminal life but the best thing that could have happened to him really. He's a good kid, he's practically invisible on the streets and whatever new weapon is out there he can tell me about it. He's a lot smarter than he thinks he is. I like him." Will turned to her and grinned.

"And this?" she asked, indicating the storage area.

"If Michael wasn't a street criminal, or working here, he'd be a librarian, or spreadsheet designer. He likes order, he knows where everything is."

"He's a child!" exclaimed Emma.

"Yep. And all children need order and rules." And at that moment Michael returned with two small boxes. He opened them and handed Will a lightbulb and a pair of ear-rings.

Will turned to Emma. "Right then, serious time," he said, and then explained that the lightbulb was a listening device that she should swap for one on her father's desk or as close as she could get to it. The ear-rings were also transmitters, though with a much smaller battery lifetime, less than 24 hours, and these were her lifelines. Smash either of them, he told her, and the cavalry would come running. "These aren't here to do anything else than let us know you need help," he said. "We've been doing some maths. If you smash one of these, we can be there in just under a minute. All you need to do is stand on it."

"Great," said Emma, without enthusiasm.

Hannah came down the stairs as Emma was leaving to get in one of the mini-cabs the CPG ran. The two hugged, in recognition of the seriousness of the situation, but no words were exchanged.

* * *

It was normal for Emma to return home from university from time to time and so it was no surprise to her parents when she arrived unannounced. The idea of bugging her own father's study seemed ridiculous, but nothing had seemed faintly normal since she had overheard him talking about assassinating the Prime Minister. It was eleven o' clock in the morning and her mother had already hit the gin; her father was out playing a round of golf and so Emma decided to act quickly.

She unpacked the bag that Will had handed her containing spare clothes and toiletries and carefully took out the lightbulb. She was already wearing the ear-rings. Creeping into her father's study, pulse racing, she walked to his desk, carrying the bulb in her cardigan pocket. She unscrewed the bulb from the lamp and took the replacement out from her pocket.

It was then that Emma realised she had a problem. Her father's desk lamp had a screw thread – the lightbulb Will had given her had a bayonet fitting. "Shit," she said under her breath, quickly replacing the original bulb. She looked around the room, desperate for an alternative. Every light fitting she tried was the same, there was no hope of planting the bug. Her heart thumped in her chest as she desperately tried to figure out what to do next.

Emma was a bright young woman though and could think on her feet. On her way to the garage she called to her mother through the kitchen window. "Alright if I take the little Peugeot?" she asked, "I need to get something from town." Her mother simply waved assent and Emma drove the short distance into Wendown, a small market town with a plethora of antique shops on its high street full of overpriced bric-a-brac. As she pulled out of her parents' impressive drive the surveillance box folded. Emma's hands were slipping on the steering wheel as she sweated profusely.

"Got her," came the call over the radio network. "No duress signal."

Will turned to Rachel, who he had specifically chosen as his driver that day. "Right then, we're on," he said. In under a minute four cars had put a protective box around an unaware Emma as she drove to the Witches' Cupboard, where it took her less than ten minutes to find a lamp with a bayonet fitting. She didn't bother haggling with the old man at the till and drove straight back home, missing the gear changes as her arm trembled.

Emma found an unused socket fairly close to her father's desk and was plugging the lamp in just as he came into the room. "Hello darling," he said, "What are you up to?"

Emma didn't miss a beat. "I was in town and I saw this in the window and I thought it would fit nicely. My treat," she said smiling.

Her father kissed her. "Thank you princess, that's very sweet."

"I've just got to put the car back in the garage," she said, and left the study. The Foreign Secretary's garage was in fact a converted barn, and so many tradespeople visited the estate that the sight of a van on the driveway or a catering company setting up in the orchard garden was not unusual. What was unusual was watching a group of men unloading automatic weapons from the back of a Ford Transit van, which was precisely what Emma saw through the window of the main staircase as she went to park the car. Who these people were or what they were doing Emma had no idea. What she did know was that they weren't any of the Diplomatic Protection Group officers she had come to know. She took a deep breath and thought for a moment, deliberately trying to calm herself. Will had told her that her adrenaline would be flowing and that sometime's a quick pause could be beneficial. It took her less than ten seconds to remove both earrings and stamp on them. Emma wanted help and she wanted it quickly.

Will had transferred to a different Audi from the one he shared with Rachel as they waited outside. Michael had driven it down to the village especially. "Get a bus, get a taxi, get a train," said Will, as Michael handed him the keys. "Just get away." Michael could tell he was serious.

When the signals from the earrings disappeared Will put the car in gear and raced for the wooden gates. "All call signs, all call signs, break, break, break!" he called over the radio. "Gold Two you come with me!" he shouted.

Rachel dropped in behind him as Will took the car up to 80mph, splintering the wooden gates of the mansion as he shot into the oblique drive. There were only inches between the two cars as they raced up the gravel. The destruction of the gates immediately set off the intruder alarm and an ear-splitting wail screeched around the house and grounds. The men unloading weapons from the van were briefly taken by surprise, and then quickly started loading them with ammunition and looking for the threat. They found it soon enough when Will and Rachel came into view, screaming up the driveway and causing both cars to go airborne as they ignored the speed bumps on the approach to the grand house.

Will was planning on nothing more elaborate than grabbing Emma and speeding her away, right up to the point where he saw two men with automatic rifles shooting at him. He grabbed the handbrake and ripped the car into a sideways spin, spewing gravel at them and causing them to turn away. Rachel couldn't stop in time and slammed into Will's car. Quickly throwing the gear into reverse, she pulled back and turned the car sideways on to the shooters. Will was running for the front door of the house, pistol drawn. "Guns!" he shouted as he barged into the reception hall.

Rachel had already crawled across to the passenger side of the car and pulled a light machine gun from her ready-bag. She opened the passenger door, crouched behind the engine block and started returning fire.

Will found himself pointing his pistol at a bewildered Foreign Secretary on the landing who had come running from his study, and screaming at Emma, who was still on the staircase. "With me, now!" he shouted. Emma and her father looked at each other for a moment, neither knowing what was going on. But Emma ran down the stairs.

"Blow the front car!" Will shouted once he'd got Emma's hand in his and they ran across the driveway. Rachel fired a last volley of shots and crawled back into her car, remotely detonating Will's unoccupied Audi and throwing her own into reverse, the tyres spitting gravel onto the lawn this time, which would subsequently upset the head gardener.

'Red 23', as she'd been known, erupted in a cloud of smoke and a blinding flash – the mercenaries could see nothing through it. Will opened the passenger door as Rachel was still spinning the car through a J-turn and pushed Emma in.

"Stay down!" he shouted.

"We're away," said Rachel calmly as the car accelerated towards the decimated gates. Rather than hammer the car's suspension on the speed bumps she steered off the drive and onto the grass, causing the back end of the car to slide a little.

"I thought these were supposed to be four wheel drive," shouted Will from the back seat.

"They are," retorted Rachel, "I'm just having fun with it." She couldn't stop grinning. "I knew there was a reason why I applied for this job."

Back at the house, the Foreign Secretary was on the phone to the Diplomatic Protection Service telling them his daughter had been kidnapped at gunpoint. His private security detail had already pulled up still pictures from the CCTV of Will in the reception area, and a picture of Rachel's Audi as she fired across the bonnet. The registration was clear, "X23 MTM". As they emailed the pictures to the control room in Downing Street, the duty supervisor was already on the phone to the duty controller of traffic at the Metropolitan Police Service.

Emma was crying as Will held her down on the rear seat. He squeezed her hand, "Don't worry," he said, and clambered through to the front passenger seat. It was only then that he saw the bullet hole in the left hand side of his jacket. Pulling it aside he saw the remains of his radio under his arm.

"Fuck's sake, I've been shot," he said to Rachel.

Rachel briefly looked across. "No you have not you big baby. You're just going to have use the car radio, that's all."

"I thought women were supposed to be sympathetic," he responded.

"Not at 90 miles an hour," she said, skilfully turning the car onto a slip road for the M25.

Will hit the transmit button in the glove box and spoke to his hastily assembled team, some of whom were already on the motorway and some of whom had hung back. "All teams, all teams, this is the Milk Tray Man. It's time for bowler hats and briefcases."

A quarter of a mile behind Rachel three more highly polished, black Audi S5s were in convoy. They slipped quietly on to the motorway and formed a rolling wall behind the callsign they knew as 'The Milk Tray Man.'

Back in the Central Traffic Control Room in New Scotland Yard, Inspector Williams was starting to shout at people. "It's the Foreign Secretary's wife, she's been kidnapped! Find that bloody car!" The truth had, unsurprisingly, become distorted as the Chinese Whispers phone calls were passed along.

The Foreign Secretary's wife was, in fact, staring out the window at the foreign looking men on her drive who looked very angry and appeared to be assembling guns. She found her husband's job confusing and poured herself another gin and turned the page of that month's 'Horse and Hound', assuming that all the commotion must have been yet another police exercise. Her husband never told her anything anyway.

The traffic police on the M25 were under the impression that a foreign diplomat had been kidnapped by Islamic extremists and that there was a possibility the car was going to be used as a bomb, which is why they had called the Army Bomb Squad and asked for armed backup.

The Diplomatic Protection Group didn't give a shit what anyone else was thinking or doing and just went hell for leather to the nearest junction to get on the M25.

And all of them were looking for X23 MTM.

"Got him," called one of the operators at Scotland Yard. She was checking the automatic number plate readers and the registration had hit. "Clockwise at Junction 15".

"Send all available teams," said Inspector Culling, conscious that his annual appraisal was due.

In addition to the legitimate law enforcement agencies of the United Kingdom chasing Will, Rachel and Emma, the Foreign Secretary's personal army were also on the case, having scrambled hurriedly and commandeered every car in his garage.

Will was on the phone when the first police car's lights and sirens erupted. "Oh shit," he said, "I was hoping to avoid this." He turned to Rachel, "I was just trying to get through to them and now this happens. I was hoping they'd give us an escort, not attract attention."

"What do you want me to do?" asked Rachel.

"Drive the car," said Will, without humour. He looked at his watch. "I will think for sixty seconds and then give you an answer," he added.

"You better."

The sixty seconds were up. "What the fuck was that?" shouted Rachel, as the rear window blew to pieces.

"Whose closest to us?" Will asked over the radio.

An exceptionally calm southern Irish voice responded. "This is Gold Three. You have one marked and one un-marked police car behind you. There is also a blue BMW M3 shooting at you."

Rachel didn't need to ask a question. She smashed her foot on the accelerator and pressed her own transmit button. "Everyone on the circle. Everyone. Team leaders call in when you're here."

Elaine was the first to respond. "MTM Escort this is Gold Leader, we are complete and on target."

"Blue Leader, we're right behind you."

"Bronze Leader, we're two junctions ahead."

"White Van Man here," we're going the opposite way as requested.

All the team leaders called in, and then Will transmitted again. "Rainbow team, rainbow team, this is the Milk Tray Man. I have an unwanted party guest here and it's serious. I would like the people who can't hear you to start hearing you, and I'd like the people who can't see you to start seeing you. We're going round the circular blue river like particles round an atom right now and I need some space."

The drivers of all twenty four Audi S5s switched their air-conditioning to off. That switched off the current to the electro-magnets holding the fake number plates on. As cars across the M25 swerved to avoid falling number plates, the Traffic Control Centre screens lit up. The target known as 'X23 MTM' was now being followed by plate recognition systems all around the beltway. There were twenty four of them, and Inspector Culling didn't know what to do.

The police and Diplomatic Protection Group, being fed information from Central Control, had no idea where to focus their attention, and put as many resources as they could wherever they could.

And then the dance began.

Will had spent a lot of time perfecting this, often late into the night, with toy cars. The six teams of four cars started waltzing with each other, switching lanes and circling each other as they progressed. Those following completely lost track of who was who. Same cars, same registrations. Marked police, unmarked police and the Foreign Secretary's mercenaries all seemed lost.

And then all twenty-four switched off the encryption on their radios and started talking to each other. They talked exclusively about music.

"Bronze Two this is Blue Four, what you got?"

"Van Halen," came the abrupt answer. "You?"

"ZZ Top."

Silver three broke in, "You people are Philistines, how can you do this without Strauss? This is Strictly Come Driving."

As the cars spun around the motorway the BMW following Will and Rachel somehow caught up with them. A burst of gunfire hit the rear of their car. "You just lost your right light cluster," said Elaine calmly, in the closest car to Will's.

Emma, hearing everything, made the decision to look out the back window. "Shit, that's my Dad's car," she said when she saw the BMW.

"Gold Leader, who's driving?" asked Will to the nearest escort to him.

"I am," said Gerry.

"Thank fuck for that, you can't shoot for shit. Elaine, get to the back and pop the boot." At 90 mph on a busy motorway Elaine grabbed the weapons bag from the footwell, took her seatbelt off and crawled to the rear seats, where she dropped one of them and took up her position in the boot of the car.

Gerry tore up the motorway and pulled in inches from the BMW. "Good to go?" he shouted to Elaine. "Good to go!" she shouted back and Gerry pulled the boot release lever and she started firing at the car. With the driver dead, it swerved into the central reservation causing a pile up behind it that would take several hours to clear. It allowed Rachel to get off the motorway and Will to take stock of the situation.

It was only then that he realised Emma had been shot through the neck. She had said nothing as Will pushed her to the floor of the car. He grabbed the first aid kit from under the seat and ripped a bandage to put pressure on both the entry and exit wounds.

"No dramas," he said, "We'll get you patched up."

"Not today you won't," whispered Emma, clearly struggling for breath. "The Sound of Silence," she added. "The Sound of Silence. That's what I always wanted played at my funeral."

Will held her as she took her last breaths.

CHAPTER TWENTY

The Funeral and the Palace...

"No-one can know she's dead," said Will as he led Hannah to the crematorium at Fort Harvest, a secure facility on the south coast normally used as a training centre for covert operations, but with a long history, and some innovations from World War Two which still remained. "This is where we normally bury the guys who do things governments don't like to talk about. She'll be in good company."

They walked through a beautifully tended garden with dozens of plaques on the lawn, each of which told a story in itself. "Some of your countrymen over there," said Will, pointing to an area backed by a stunning rose bush.

"Roses," she said, gasping for breath and clutching her hand to her chest. She was emotional enough already without this.

"Yeah. We thought it was appropriate, national flower and all that."

"What did they do?" she asked.

"I don't really know. What I do know is they died fighting, or they wouldn't be here, and they would have been helping us out big time. A guy from the CIA comes over every year on the Fourth of July. He kind of acts as a representative for all the units and agencies who have people here."

"What happens?" she asked.

"Well, it usually rains, and then we take him to the bar, and he doesn't get to buy a drink all night. Everyone gets drunk and tells the same stories as they did the year before, mostly about the bravest dead guys they've ever known, or the near misses they've all had. If you think about it properly, it really sucks. If it weren't for the beer, most people would probably be weeping."

They were approaching the door of the chapel cum crematorium. "Here we go," said Will, "you okay?" he asked.

She squeezed his arm. "Are you?" she answered.

"Oh yeah, I'm fine, I just love funerals. I've got used to them."

Emma was cremated at the Fort for two reasons. The first was the requirement to keep her death secret, the second was because she was considered by all those whose opinions mattered to have died in the service of her country on a covert operation. None of the CPG steering committee voiced an objection when Will requested that a memorial plaque be added in the garden.

Will and Hannah quietly took their seats, alongside almost all of the drivers who had been on duty that day. Will leant forward and shook hands with Gerry and Elaine, both of whom were trying hard not to let their emotions show. "This sucks," said Gerry, his gentle Kilkenny accent softening the anger of his words.

"Don't I know it," said Will.

Elaine turned to him, with eyes so concentrated and a face so fierce that Hannah sat back in her chair. She had never seen a woman so angry before. "Wherever this ends up going, you better keep us in. Right to the end."

"I promise you," said Will, kissing her on the cheek.

The service was short, and as he promised, Will had arranged for "The Sound of Silence" to be played as Emma's coffin passed through the curtains. Those who attended stood around outside the chapel trying to talk about anything other than what had happened. Few people could look each other in the eye. For the members of the Contingency Planning Group, this was one of the worst possible outcomes for their first real time operation, and no-one felt it more heavily than Will. He couldn't stand the small talk and walked off into the memorial garden. Hannah followed him.

A bell rang loudly and repeatedly from another building in the Fort. "The bar is open!" came a shout from an open window. As was customary, all those present started applauding, recognising Emma's sacrifice.

As people drifted to the bar, Hannah said to Will, "You not going?"

"No," he replied, "And I've got to get you back to the house anyway." For the first time, Hannah sensed a vulnerability in him. His eyes were glassy, and it was clear that he had been working hard to stop himself from crying. They walked back to the car in silence and Will opened the passenger door for her, and then slammed his own door shut with such violence that Hannah jumped.

She hadn't anticipated the sudden change in his demeanour. "Hey," she said, touching him on the shoulder. He turned with a look on his face which worried her.

"I am going to get these fucking people," he said as he turned the ignition. "I am going to find them and I am going to fucking kill them. Every fucking one of them. I am going to pour down the equivalent of a fucking waterfall of liquid fire on them." Despite his evident enormous anger, Will quietly put the car into gear and slowly drew away, gently tapping the radio buttons and tuning into a classical channel. He was no music specialist, but as he listened to Strauss an idea formed in his head.

Hannah was too frightened to speak for the entire journey back to London.

* * *

Will had spent the night in his office running worst case scenarios and ran out of the Defence Intelligence Staff using the front door of the building for the first time in his life whilst simultaneously calling the Operations desk at the Directorate of Special Forces. "How may I help?" came the polite but non-specific answer. The civilian administrator staffing the Directorate always enjoyed the feeling she was being enigmatic.

"Will Richards here, can I speak to the Operations Officer, the Intelligence Officer, or failing that, the Director please?" he asked. "Actually, scrub that, is the Director available?" Will was pushing tourists aside on his way to Buckingham Palace.

Judy knew that a call from Will Richards was to be treated as high priority, she had a post-it note on her desk with the names of VIP callers. On the list as well as Will were the Commanding Officers of the three Special Forces units and the Prime Minister. "Hold please," she said.

General Green picked up his phone. "Yes Judy," he said in his usual terse fashion.

"Will Richards for you Sir, would you like to take the call?"

"Yes."

Will could tell by the click on the line that he'd been put through and didn't even bother to introduce himself. "Sir, I need everyone you have available today and I need them in London this afternoon. Sorry for the short notice."

Having seen an extraordinary variety of events throughout his military career the General's response was typically straightforward. "What's going on?" he asked.

"Possible coup d'etat Sir."

"Which country?"

"Ours Sir. The United Kingdom."

The General remained passive. "When?"

"Probably today."

"Are you okay Will, you sound out of breath?"

"I'm running down Whitehall, I'm on my way to the Palace," Will gasped.

General Green looked up at the disposition charts in his office, which outlined the deployments of his troops. "How sure are you?" he asked, with a hint of suspicion in his voice.

"Not mucking about Sir," rasped Will as he turned through Horseguards Parade and sprinted for Buckingham Palace.

The Director of Special Forces was now out of his seat, scouring the charts on his wall. He lowered the phone and shouted through to the adjoining offices. "Jim, Andy, get in here!" The Intelligence Officer and Operations Officer came running through, knowing that when the boss shouted, it was serious. General Green was normally exceptionally soft-spoken. "CPG on the phone," he said quickly – there was no need to elaborate. "How many people can we get in to the Alpha site this afternoon?"

"Maybe a squadron's worth," said the Operations Officer.

The General put the phone back to his ear. "I can get you a squadron Will."

"Not good enough Sir, this is really, really serious, this is the whole point we were set up for." General Green could barely make out what Will was saying through the gasping breaths as he sprinted past the tourists in St. James's Park.

"I can't do any more without committing the reserve Major Richards."

Will stopped running as he approached the gates of Buckingham Palace. "Sir, I know the theory, but today is the day to commit the reserve, believe me, we need it. Can I explain when I see you?"

General Jim Green trusted Will Richards, and knew he wouldn't make a request like that unless he meant it. He put the phone down and looked up at his Operations and Intelligence Officers. "Gents, get me everyone you can, at the Alpha site, as fast as you can. I don't care if they're on leave or on top of a mountain in Wales. Get the RAF on the phone, tell them we need helicopter transport, tell anyone who can't make it to Poole or Hereford to take a taxi if they need to. If they haven't got the cash tell them to steal a car."

"What's going on?" asked Laura, his PA, walking into the inner office.

The Director of Special Forces smiled. "I haven't got a bloody clue!" he said. "Fun. Isn't it!"

* * *

As he walked across the inner courtyard of Buckingham Palace Will made his next call, to the office of the Right Honourable Sir William Moore, the Private Secretary to the Queen, who recognised Will's number as he walked past his own secretary's desk on the way to the stationary cupboard. Moore picked up the ringing phone from his secretary's desk before she could get to it as he frequently did. Suzanne gave him her usual look of indignation as Moore put his fingers to his lips to silence her.

"Will, how the devil?" he asked, his home county public school accent not remotely dented by years of living in London.

Despite the gravity of the emerging situation, Will remained cheerful. "I'm well Sir, thank you. May I assume you're still wearing that tatty Saville Row tweed jacket which really needs to have a visit to the dry cleaners?"

Moore smiled broadly. "Of course I am, but as I think I've told you before, it's like a wok, it should never be washed. Anyway, what can I do for you?" he asked.

Will's tone became more serious. "I need the Palace Sir," he said quickly, now walking briskly through the State Rooms and into the White Drawing Room.

"What, all of it!" came the incredulous response.

Will paused briefly, "No, just the basement, the kitchens."

"What the hell is going on?" asked Moore.

"Long story, not enough time right now though. It'll be great for your memoirs I'm sure."

"Is Her Majesty in any danger?" Moore asked.

"Possibly, yes. Where is she? Is she in London?"

"No, she's in Windsor, at the castle."

Suzanne was looking up at her boss with wide eyes. She had never overheard a conversation like this before and never seen the colour drain from the Private Secretary's face in quite the way it was.

Will was giving orders now. "She doesn't move Bill, she doesn't move until I say she can. Get her and the family into the strong room. Tell whoever is in charge of the guard that their alert state has just gone to critical."

"Seriously?"

"I'm not fucking about Bill and I've no ambitions to be a comedian. Get them to safety."

"Where are you?"

Will ended the call as he entered the Private Secretary's office at the rear of Buckingham Palace, smacking the door open against the wall as he did so. He was slightly breathless. "Bill, we need to move fast, get on the line to Windsor please." He turned to Suzanne. "Suzy, in about thirty minutes, several hundred scary men," he paused, smiling wryly, "and some even scarier women if truth be told, are going to start arriving here. Most will arrive in helicopters in the back garden. Some will arrive at the gates in unmarked cars. I am about to replace the policemen on the gates with my own people. The Commissioner of the Metropolitan Police knows this, but whether that's reached his coppers on the ground yet is debatable. Please get hold of the detachment commander and tell him what's about to happen. If he's got any issues he can call me." Will turned on his heels and went for the door, then was caught with an afterthought. "Tell him as well, that as much as I love the Police Service, his guys really need to give way to mine. No-one's going to show up without ID, but if someone even points a gun at them there will be hell to pay. These guys will be seriously racked up."

CHAPTER TWENTY ONE

The telephone intercept that morning...

When the Director of the Government Communication Headquarters rang Will's mobile, he was not slow to answer. "Will, how are you?"

"Sweating."

"Well then, now's the time to spray the deodorant, I'm going to give you some very bad news." Simon Wilkinson was sitting in his office in Cheltenham, in the impressive new building almost universally referred to by everyone who worked there as "The Doughnut" as a result of its round shape and central garden. Will had called the organisation earlier and told them about his concerns. Due to the nature of them, they had been escalated as far as the Director, who insisted that he should be informed of any related reports. A somewhat breathless young man from the intercept department had knocked on his door a few minutes earlier.

Wilkinson took the folder from him and read it in silence. He looked up slowly, removing his spectacles. "How many people have seen this?" he asked gently, pointing at the folder.

"Two Sir. I wrote it; you read it, that's it."

"And how many people contributed to the collection, analysis and conclusions of this intelligence?" he asked.

"There are seven of us working on this at the moment."

The Director of GCHQ nodded slowly and then said, "Everyone who has worked on this needs to be here in this office in the next two minutes. Here, use my phone," he said, passing the handset to the graduate trainee.

It was five minutes after they had arrived and Wilkinson had received confirmation that the entire team was in agreement about the conclusions that he called Will.

"Will, I have every member of the team that is working on this in front of me and there is no dissent. We put an Echelon trace on the obvious words following your concerns. I am about to read you a direct transcript from an email sent from a smartphone this morning."

Will groaned, "Oh Christ, this is not going to be good is it?"

Wilkinson read slowly and deliberately. The intercept and analysis team in his office looked at each other nervously, some biting their lips, others their nails – their average age was twenty eight. "Have secured vehicle. Driver disposed. Will pick up PM as discussed."

"Well what the fuck is that supposed to mean?" asked Will.

"Keep listening," said Wilkinson. "Package installed under rear passenger seat. Our replacement driver unaware. Scheduled for pick-up for lunch appointment this afternoon."

Will was, unusually for him, losing his patience. "Simon, I don't have the faintest fucking idea what all that means and I don't have time to fuck about playing verbal Sudoku right now. What do your people with their giant fucking heads and really bad dress sense actually think that means."

Simon Wilkinson paused and smiled. "We're on speakerphone Will, and they're all here."

"You're not making my day any better," said Will, shaking his head at his own stupidity. This was GCHQ after all, where everybody listened in. "Sorry everyone," said Will with a sigh, "but I bet at least one of you is wearing a tank top." Debbie West, the youngest member of the team only one year out of a mathematics degree at University College London stared at the floor in embarrassment.

Wilkinson continued. "Firstly, I think you've just ruined your chances of a date with young Debbie, who is, granted, clearly wearing something her Grandmother knitted her for Christmas," he looked up, "and is now giggling and nodding. But secondly, these guys have done some homework. The PM is due to head for lunch at the American Embassy this afternoon, in about thirty minutes actually, and we triangulated the phone to within three hundred metres of Whitehall. Thirdly, we're fairly confident the recipient was your old friend Paul Gilmour."

"Okay, and…" Will let the question hang.

Simon Wilkinson shook his head, "I thought they gave you this job because you were smart."

"Nope, it's because I'm cheap. Speak to me in English Simon."

"It is our assessment that somehow, method unknown, someone has taken custody of the Prime Minister's car, killed the driver and disposed of the body, put a bomb under the back seat and is about to send another driver, who is unaware of what is going on, to pick him up. Imminently. Can I make it any clearer?"

Will was out of his seat and running. "No, that's pretty good, thank you. Just one question, please don't tell me this was sent in clear?"

"No, it's been encrypted very cleverly."

"So how the hell do you guys know about it?"

"Because we un-encrypted it," said Wilkinson, "and we did it even more cleverly than them."

As the Director of GCHQ ended the call he looked up at the team who had brought him the information. "Right then, looks like it's going to be a long day. Who's for pizza?" he asked, opening his top draw and pulling out a menu.

Debbie held her hand up like a schoolgirl. "Sir, it's book-swap night tonight at the library, I really have to go."

Wilkinson didn't even bother to look at her as he dialled the number for the local pizza delivery company. "Sit down Tank-Top. There's a war on. And not one of you will leave this room until it's over and we've won."

Will had used the underground tunnels from the Palace to get into Downing Street – he had to run and he was breathless. He caught the Prime Minister just as he was in the black and white tiled entrance hall, ready to leave for the lunch at the American Embassy. "Sir," he said, grabbing the PM's arm, "hang on a sec." He'd spoken to the Head of Government Transport before his subterranean sprint and was confident that what he'd asked for was in place.

The PM looked at his close protection officer, who knew Will well, and held his hands up in a gesture indicating that there was no danger. "What is it Will?" he asked.

"Slight change of plan Sir. I'll be escorting you today."

"What the hell's going on?"

"I'll explain on the way." Will turned to the policeman assigned to lead the close protection team for the PM that day. "You okay with this Pete?" he asked.

"No. I'm coming too. Whatever you're up to, there's a Range Rover full of tooled up cops behind you, and they won't react quietly to the unexpected. What's going on?" he asked.

"Van switch," said Will.

"Where?"

"St James's."

Policeman Pete raised an eyebrow sceptically. "Okay, I'll tell the boys."

As they left, the Prime Minister waved to the cameras in Downing Street before stepping into the car. Will closed the door after him and climbed into the front passenger seat. Pete spoke briefly through the window to his deputy team leader in the Range Rover behind the PM's Jaguar, advising him of the revised circumstances and to listen closely to his instructions over the radio.

As Pete got into the back of the PM's car, Will turned from the front seat and from the look on his face it was clear that neither the PM or Pete should utter a word, let alone ask a question about what was going on.

"I thought Andrew was rostered today," he said to the driver, who didn't return his gaze.

"His kid got sick. Had to pick him up from school," came the response.

The Jaguar and following Range Rover pulled out into Horse Guards Road and made their way up to The Mall. At the junction with The Mall they turned right and cut up through Marlborough Road onto Pall Mall and followed the turn into St. James's.

Billy and his team, parked up just north of St. James's, were following Will by the GPS tracker he had clipped to his belt. "That's it, let's go," he said, and a lead car and a white van with details for a small building firm painted on it drew into the road.

Will was beginning to sweat slightly, knowing that time was against them. As the PM's Jaguar approached one of the zebra crossings on St. James's, a woman pushing a pram walked across the road, cued by Billy over the radio; there was no baby in the pram, but underneath the doll was a submachine gun. Dressed as a Norland nanny, no-one would have thought that Jenny was ready to open fire if things didn't go according to the hastily drawn up plan.

The PM's driver didn't notice the transit van heading in the opposite direction as he stopped the car. Will pulled a silenced Beretta pistol from his belt and shot him in the temple. "Time to go," he said, as the mercenary slumped back in his seat.

The Prime Minister was speechless as Pete hauled him from the car and into the van which was now alongside, with its side loading door flung open. Will got out of the car, running around the back and jumping into the van. Despite, or perhaps because of the busyness of the road and pavements, very few people actually noticed, and those that did barely registered that something unusual was going on.

"Follow us," Pete instructed the close protection team over the radio. The sheer size of the following Range Rover meant that the cars backed up behind it had no view of what was going on. The driver switched on the hidden lights behind the radiator grill and the siren started to wail. As the van headed back down St. James's towards the Mall, the Range Rover pulled a U-turn and slipped in behind it.

Sitting on the floor of the van, David Marshall looked up at Will. "What the hell is going on?" he demanded. He was shaken but still very much in control of his thinking.

"A coup," came the very stiff response.

The Prime Minister shook his head. "Of all the people. Jesus Christ Will, we put the safety of the country in your hands. How could you do this?" Will laughed. "You think it's funny?" he asked, incredulous.

Will shook his head, "No, I don't think it's funny, you just don't understand, that's all." And at that moment an explosion ripped through one of London's most exclusive streets. The Prime Minister's Jaguar was lifted three feet off the road as the PE4 explosive under the driver's seat detonated. The explosion was mostly contained by the car's armour but the shockwave smashed dozens of windows, including those of several of the most exclusive gentlemen's clubs in London.

In the private gentlemen's club Boodle's, the Seventh Earl of Hertfordshire was startled into wakefulness by the noise. Asleep in his chair with a copy of The Times on his lap, he awoke to find himself covered in broken glass, but mercifully spared from laceration. One of the club's staff, who had not been so fortunate, came running into the smoking room dripping in blood. "Are you alright Sir?" he asked, genuinely.

The Earl looked at him in disbelief. "Arthur, you are bleeding man! Bleeding!" he stammered. "Get thee to a hospital, immediately!" The Earl stood up and walked to what was left of the window, peering at the now flaming wreck of the Prime Minister's car. "Well that's not going to help the traffic," he said.

Back in the van Prime Minister David Marshall was beginning to figure things out for himself. "Where are we going?" he asked.

"The Palace," said Will, quickly.

"They are never going to let us in the Palace in a builders van!" the PM said, in a slightly alarmed tone.

"Technically Sir, 'They', is actually now, 'Us'. They're all my people," Will reassured the PM. The van and its Range Rover Escort drove in through the Mews entrance and came to a stop in one of the carriage houses. "This way Sir," said Will, as he threw open the van's door and then led him down a steep staircase into the kitchens. The Prime Minister was not prepared for what he saw. The dozens of stainless steel tables normally used for preparing state banquets were not attended by chefs and assistants in kitchen whites. Instead, under the vaulted brick ceilings of the palace, a force of just under two hundred, including twenty six women, dressed head to toe in black, were cleaning an assortment of weapons the Prime Minister didn't even know existed.

"Jesus Christ," he said, his mouth open as he stared at the sight before him.

Will looked at him. "Not quite, but we are in the miracle business," he smiled. "Come with me, we have things to talk about, and we don't have a lot of time." Will dragged the PM into an area which had been hastily converted into a briefing room.

CHAPTER TWENTY-TWO

Preparations...

As he stood on the bridge of the HMS Dauntless, moored in the Thames, Captain Simon Jones remembered how this had all begun. He had not been particularly surprised to receive the invitation to lunch at the Naval and Military Club in St James's Square. When the Chief of the Naval Staff's office had called him to ask if he was available he responded immediately that he was and then cleared his own diary, despite the fact that it meant cancelling lunch with his sister, Emily, for the fourth consecutive time. Emily was understanding. Jones had flown through the ranks in his naval career, unlike his father, and Emily was pleased for him. This was the third time that Admiral Dudgeon had invited him for lunch in two years and opportunities like this were not to be missed.

Dudgeon was waiting for him in the formal Long Bar overlooking Grosvenor square. "Good afternoon, Simon," he said, smiling broadly as Simon approached.

"Sir," Simon replied, returning the smile. "Good to see you."

Dudgeon handed him the gin and tonic which had been waiting for him on the bar. Simon lifted it to the window to let the sun shine through the glass. "You cheeky bastard Jones," laughed the Admiral, "of course it's bloody Bombay Sapphire."

"Just checking Sir."

"Right, shall we go through for a spot of lunch?" Dudgeon asked.

Simon thought for a moment. "Is this going to be a good lunch or a bad lunch Sir?" he asked. "It's just that your office was terribly evasive about the purpose of the invitation."

Dudgeon put his arm around Simon's shoulders as he escorted him to the dining room, known as always in that part of

London as the Coffee Room. He sucked air through his teeth before saying slowly, "That, is a very good question."

The Admiral ordered a bottle of the Club Chardonnay, "Bloody good stuff you know, even though it's the house wine," he said.

"I enjoyed it very much last time," said Simon.

The Admiral laughed. "You remembered! Well done you." As the wine waiter came forward Dudgeon pointed his finger into his glass and said, "just pour Alberto, you know I can't taste for shit."

"Of course Sir," said Alberto smiling, with full and frank experience that the Admiral really did not know his wines.

The elegant dining room with its impressive chandelier, white linen tablecloths and crystal glasses, as well as the giant portraits of significant military leaders from years gone by seemed to have an effect on Dudgeon, who leaned back in his seat and sipped his wine. He turned to Simon. "Why aren't you a member here Simon?" he asked, and without waiting for an answer added, "I'd propose you."

Simon's eyes narrowed. "Sir, as you are well aware, I'm currently posted to Portsmouth with the Type 45 Destroyers." He grinned cheekily. "Unlike the Whitehall Warriors such as yourself I think the expense of membership here would be a bit extravagant – it's not like I can just pop up for lunch." He buttered a warm bread roll and looked up, adding, "not that that wouldn't be nice." Simon was beginning to wonder if this meeting was going to be about a possible posting to London, to the Admiralty or to Whitehall, and rather than play games he came straight out with it. "Sir, why am I here?"

They were briefly interrupted by Marie, the Portuguese head of service who brought them their starters. Marie insisted on serving the Admiral personally, having known him for over a decade, initially when she was a new starter and he was the Director of the Club.

"Thank you Marie," he said, and she smiled and nodded at him. Turning to Simon he said, "I have a job for you." Simon looked up, curious. "It's not what you're thinking. It's not a post here in London, it's much, much more important than that." Simon had never seen Dudgeon look so serious.

"Is this a covert operation?" he asked quietly.

Dudgeon smiled wrily. "You could say that," he said. "Simon, you're the fastest promoted man from your intake at Dartmouth Naval College. You're a clever, capable and astute young man." Simon raised his eyebrows and was about to speak when Dudgeon held his hand up to stop him. "No, no need to be modest. But what I do want you to do now is be honest, because I am going out on a limb here. You remember when I was commanding the Fleet off Somalia?"

"Of course Sir."

"And you went after that pirate mothership and sank it?"

Simon rested his cutlery on the plate and looked to the ornate ceiling. "Oh Christ Sir, where is this going?" he sighed.

"I ordered you not to do that. I ordered you," the Admiral said quietly, "and yet you still did it."

"Is this coming back to bite me?" Simon asked.

The Admiral paused. "Not in the way you might think. I wanted you to sink that ship more than anything. Those murderous bastards deserved everything they got. You may have noticed that nothing has ever been mentioned about that incident, officially or unofficially."

"I had noticed that Sir, yes." Simon was becoming nervous about where the discussion was going and started scratching his ears.

"You're a good man Simon, and a damned good Naval Officer. I kept something quiet for you because I thought you did the right thing, despite what our political masters may have dictated. Now I am going to ask you some questions, and if you don't like them, I want you to do the same thing for me, keep quiet about them. But I think I'm doing the right thing."

Simon looked the Admiral straight in the eyes. "I think I'm rapidly going off lunch," he said.

"How many men does it take to run the bridge on a Type 45?" Dudgeon asked directly.

"Twelve if it's moving, eight if it isn't."

"In which case I need you to find seven men who will help you," said the Admiral.

"Help me do what Sir?" Simon was both suspicious and curious.

The Admiral dabbed his mouth with his napkin and rested in his chair. "I bet you hate this government don't you?" he asked. Simon said nothing. "I have a plan to change it. Find seven officers you can trust, put HMS Dauntless where I want it, when I want it, and you'll be following me to the Admiralty. It won't be pretty, but it's the right thing to do."

Captain Simon Jones thought for a moment. "I'm in," he said, and the deal was sealed.

* * *

Mr Gilmour had not been sloppy with his planning, and the coup was timed to coincide with the Defence and Security Event International's expo at the Excel exhibition centre in London's Docklands area. The expo was the largest of its type in the world, and that was how Jones had ensured the Type 45 frigate, HMS Dauntless, was moored up as close to the heart of London as she needed to be. In addition, as an arms dealer and with his status as an exhibitor he had loaded the exhibition centre with everything he felt necessary to secure the targets he had identified.

Three four tonne trucks drove out of the rented warehouse in East London and headed for Excel. Gilmour had no difficulties getting the convoy through the security control, having the highest level accreditation and, due to the size of his business and investment, being treated like a VIP everywhere he went on the site.

"Good afternoon Mr Gilmour," said the security guard as he opened the roller-shutters to the loading bays. Gilmour simply smiled through the open window. He had a team of twelve with him, and they quickly went about the business of transferring the contents of the "Gilmour Ltd" ISO containers into the back of the three trucks. More than two hundred assault rifles were carried in first, all immaculate in their wooden crates. Fifty night-sights came in next, handled delicately by Gilmour's couriers to ensure the lenses weren't damaged. Metal boxes carrying twelve grenades each were added. Gilmour wanted a minimum of six grenades per man, which took up significant space in the second truck to be loaded. The final truck was filled with thousands of rounds of ammunition and the heavy machine guns which Gilmour expected to be pivotal in the event that a counter-attack was launched – an eventuality which he thought would be unlikely considering the planning that had been done. Last out of the ISO container were the two pallets of uniforms – exact matches of British Army combat fatigues and London's Metropolitan Police Service.

The guards looked surprised when they heard the roar of the diesel engines of two German-made Boxer armoured personnel carriers as they powered up. As they were leaving, Gilmour waved cheerily to the security guards from the commander's turret of the lead carrier, and this very unlikely convoy drove back to the cavernous warehouse in Wapping, where the first dozen of his force had started massing. The trucks were unloaded and soon the place resembled a giant storeroom. On trestle tables in the middle of the floor were the different areas for clothing, ammunition, weapons, first aid kits and a variety of other assorted pieces of military paraphernalia. There were smiles all round as the mercenaries saw how well equipped they were going to be – often on previous jobs they felt they had had to do the work on a minimal budget. It was clear that no expense had been spared on this occasion. Many had served together before and there were handshakes and laughter in many quarters. The Russians pulled out their hip flasks and the Americans handed out chewing gum. The South Africans were mostly trying to grab as much explosives and firepower as they could.

A small field kitchen had been assembled in one corner and after they had shared a meal of piping hot stew Paul Gilmour walked onto a small stage and called for attention. There was a giant plasma screen behind him and he began his briefing. Despite the number of men in the warehouse there was no need for a microphone, the acoustics were such that every man could hear him clearly. "Right, this is how it's going to happen," he started, and the men listened intently as he outlined the plan. There were some details which he left out, but he assured them that they would meet no resistance initially, although there may be some small issues later on. This was the best paying operation most of them had ever been on, and the notion that they might be able to finish it without firing a shot added a mood of confidence.

An hour later, after they'd changed clothes and looked like policemen and soldiers, they boarded coaches, and led by the two armoured personnel carriers drove out of the warehouse and headed west for Whitehall, the Houses of Parliament and Downing Street. The two armoured vehicles turned the heads of almost every member of the public they passed, but most people actually smiled, some even waving and giving thumbs-up signs of approval, assuming there was going to be a military parade of some sort. Paul Gilmour couldn't stop himself from smirking as he received what appeared to be approval from members of the public whose government he intended to overthrow.

The Foreign Secretary had already put a call in to the Head of Security in Parliament advising him of the imminent arrival of troops and police reinforcements. He was to co-operate with them fully and inform his officers immediately. He dutifully did so, and as the impersonators piled out of their coaches in Parliament Square they were welcomed by a security force which looked grave and concerned.

What none of them had any reason to notice was Becky Wills, the Foreign Secretary's PA, sprinting out of the Foreign Office with a rucksack containing her boss's laptop computer, every post-it note and scrap of paper she could find on his desk and three mobile phones which she'd found in a cupboard. Earlier she'd had a personal visit from the Home Secretary, at Will's request. Becky knew she was never going to win Mastermind, but she'd kept fit since school, and that talent which was so tragically unrecognised then now got her out of harm's way at the last safe moment. Becky didn't stop running until she got to the address she had been told to memorise, and as she rang the bell at the Directorate of Special Forces, no less than the Director himself was there to meet her. "Bloody good work Becky," he said genuinely. "One way or another, we've probably got the bastards now eh?" Becky was too breathless to answer. "This way," said the General, gently putting his arm around her shoulder. He did not underestimate the pressure she must have felt.

As the public in Westminster and Whitehall were cleared from the area, the coaches were steered across the approach roads forming makeshift roadblocks. One of the Boxer vehicles took up a position at the junction of Whitehall and Trafalgar Square, the other remained in Parliament Square, the statues of Winston Churchill and Abraham Lincoln staring down on it as it drove slowly around the area.

Those in the team who had been identified as managing the closest impersonation of an English accent had been picked to play the part of the police, and it was they who cleared the public and spoke to the genuine police in the street. But Gilmour took the lead on two tasks personally. Firstly, he identified the senior officer at Parliament and ordered him to move all his men inside to secure the building, and that he would secure the exterior perimeter. That day the number of armed police officers on duty was six. The revolutionaries had timed the strike thoughtfully, although it was a lucky coincidence for them that Parliament was in recess at the same time that Gilmour could access his arsenal from the Defence Expo in East London. Not only were the security team operating on a skeletal staff, so was the whole building.

As Gilmour stood in the Grand Central Lobby of the building, the dozen members of the first mercenaries inside pointed their weapons at the police. "Put them down on the ground, no-one gets hurt," he said, gesturing at their own weapons. "I have a mandate from the acting Prime Minister, we can't be sure who to trust," he lied. The police officers who minutes earlier had been chatting with lost tourists looked stunned, but nevertheless complied, with the exception of Police Constable "Milky" Allen, a former soldier who thought something was out of kilter.

He quietly moved the index finger of his right hand from the trigger guard of his MP5 rifle to the trigger itself and asked, "What's going on?"

Gilmour tried to bluff him, "I don't have time for this, it's a national security scenario."

"Really, so why's a copper in charge of a load of squaddies?" he asked pointedly.

Gilmour was becoming irritated, "There is still Police Primacy," he bluffed again, "the army is merely providing something called Military Assistance to the Civil Powers."

Yeah, I know what that is, but this isn't it," said Milky dismissively. He raised his weapon and pointed it back at the men facing him. A Russian called Oleg took exception to that and fired five rounds into Milky's head and chest.

"Don't!" shouted Gilmour as the other police officers reached for the weapons they had earlier placed on the highly polished marble floor. They all followed suit when the senior officer stood back up slowly, realising the futility of attempting to win a firefight while so helplessly outnumbered. They were herded into an upstairs office and handcuffed with their own cuffs.

Elvira Konjic was one of seven Polish contract cleaners working in the empty public galleries above the chambers when she heard the shots. She screamed involuntarily, and it was at that point that another one of Gilmour's teams ran up the staircase and seized her and her colleagues. "Evacuate, evacuate," they shouted, leading them down to street level and directing them away from the building. The last thing Gilmour wanted was hostages who could tell the story of what happened after the event. The shooting of the policeman in the Central Lobby had been unfortunate. As his men cleared the rest of the building, Gilmour took a small detachment to where he thought any counter-attack might be launched, Westminster Underground Station. Only metres from their stronghold, he needed to empty it and secure it against a possible subterranean infiltration. The station manager was resistant at first, arguing that for safety reasons trained staff would have to remain in one of London's newest, and deepest stations. Gilmour told him he would arrest him under counter-terrorist legislation if he didn't stop all train movement on the entire line and evacuate his entire staff. It took several minutes to do it. For the Londoners on the last train through the station who wanted to get off at Westminster, it was no surprise when the driver announced that for safety reasons the train would not be stopping there. For the tourists, it was a disappointment. Both groups were somewhat taken aback as the train trundled through at reduced speed and through the windows they clearly saw what looked to them like British soldiers, armed to the teeth, setting up a heavy machine gun position.

CHAPTER TWENTY THREE

The Briefing...

"You're up Boss," said the RSM of 22 SAS as he walked in. Will looked up from the notebook he had been scribbling in frantically for the last thirty minutes.

The RSM had spent the same time talking with the officers and SNCOs as they rapidly put together the strike teams with the resources available to them.

"They all set then?" Will asked.

The RSM gave him the direct look which only a seasoned veteran could give the man in charge. "They will be when they know the plan." His voice was flat. Will found it hard to return his stare. The RSM was a large man and his physical presence alone was intimidating. It was clear he had doubts. "You got one? Plan that is?" he asked.

Will held up his notebook and tapped it with his index finger, smiling.

"Major Richards Sir, I've known you long enough to know that I can see in your eyes that we're in Indiana Jones territory here. You're making this up as you go along."

Will couldn't lie to a man for whom he had such respect. "RSM," he said, looking at the orders notebook in his hand, "I know officers aren't supposed to talk like this, but the phrase 'back of a fag packet' doesn't do justice to what I've come up with here." He paused. "You know Kate Moss?"

"Sadly not in a religious sense."

"Well this is thinner than her."

"Best I go and tell the strike team leaders that it's the best plan I've ever seen then," said the RSM, as he turned and left the room.

Will sucked air through his teeth as the RSM poked his head back through the door. "What is the plan Sir?" he asked.

"Mostly shooting," said Will. He lost the levity and added, "Good men are going to die tonight."

"It's nearly always like this Boss." The RSM paused briefly, then looked carefully around the storeroom. "I've seen some weird shit in my life but never have I seen a man plan counter-revolutionary warfare surrounded by hundreds of tins of dried milk powder."

Will smiled, fully aware that the RSM had just done exactly what he was there to do. Will's anxiety had left him.

The RSM walked into the main kitchen, which had been hastily rearranged into an operations room. Signals technicians and specialists from GCHQ had hurriedly set up radio, telephone and CCTV intercepts. The strike team leaders were studying the screens with the intensity of doctors carrying out keyhole surgery.

Most of the troops were looking at the numerous floor plans of Parliament and Downing Street, attempting to memorise every corridor, every room, every staircase. There was a little joviality, as there always was in intense situations, but among those with the greatest experience there was a sense that this time was different.

One of the younger troopers was eager to see the CCTV feeds. His eyes narrowed as he tried to interpret what he was seeing on the roof of Parliament. "What's that?" he asked, pointing at movement on the screen.

Captain Dave Peterson, leader of Strike Team Foxtrot didn't turn around as he spoke. "They're setting up air defence on the roof." He checked his notes quickly. "We've spotted one portable radar system, at least half a dozen rocket propelled grenade sites and four heavy machine guns".

The trooper couldn't suppress his surprise. "Bloody Hell!"

"No,"Captain Peterson corrected him, " the 'Bloody Hell' moment young man is the SAM-7 on the terrace. Have a look," he said, pointing to another screen.

Sure enough, there on what was once where the Members of Parliament took afternoon tea was a team with a Russian-built surface to air missile system.

"Where the fuck did they get that?"

The RSM had walked up behind them. "Wouldn't we all like to know sunshine? Wouldn't we all like to know?" His voice, as always, was measured but resonant. His nickname among the troops was Plumbum, not just because he looked like was made of lead; it had long been agreed that if lead could talk, it would sound like the RSM.

He looked around the kitchen and his voice echoed off the spotless tiles as he called for attention. "Strike Team Leaders to the briefing area, Boss is on his way. The rest of you, keep the fucking noise down. I am getting a headache, which is something I don't like when I am about to kill lots of people. I much prefer to do it with a clear head." He paused. "Get Away!"

The room emptied just as Will walked in. While he'd been planning the RSM had broken the troops they had into eight strike teams. The eight team commanders sat in the briefing area by the CCTV intercepts. All of them were smirking, some hiding it less well than others. Will was puzzled. "What? Seriously, what could be funny right now?"

Some of them glanced across at the RSM, who was also trying hard not smile. Will spotted this instantly and looked to the RSM, raising his eyebrows as if to ask "What?" again.

"Sir, troops to task as requested. May I present, from left to right, the commanders of strike team Foxtrot, Uniform, Charlie and Kilo. And behind them the commanders of Tango, Hotel, India and Sierra."

It took Will a moment to understand and then he sighed, smirking a little. "Very good, very good. And if you think that's funny, wait 'til you hear this. It's what I've called, for the sake of clarity, 'The Plan'."

The RSM stepped forward, staring intently at the strike team commanders, "I've seen it, and it's bloody brilliant," he lied.

Back at the Directorate of Special Forces, the Director turned to the Commanding Officers of the SAS, SBS and the SRR as they watched the briefing through a webcam. "That means it's just like everything else we normally do, doesn't it?" He stood up from his desk and opened a walnut cabinet. "Gentlemen, we're going to be watching this like we're at the cinema, so I think a drink would be appropriate. Sorry about the size of the screen though," he added, gesturing to his computer monitor. At which point Becky went to the outer office and returned shortly afterwards carrying a digital projector. "How the bloody hell did you find that?" he asked.

Becky smiled proudly. "I'm a P.A. That's what we do."

DSF turned to the others, "Gentlemen, we're creatures of a rapidly diminishing age. Get that picture of Wellington off the wall will you and we can watch this properly." As the Special Forces Commanders removed a full length portrait from the wall, the Director turned to Becky and thanked her. "The country is in crisis," he said quietly, as she plugged the cabling into his PC. "And you have helped to fix it. So you will sit with us and watch as once again, British fighting spirit prevails. So would you like a sherry, a brandy or a glass of port?" he asked.

Becky looked around nervously. As an East End girl who rarely had a drink outside her local pub, and for whom a white wine spritzer was an exotic drink, she didn't know how to respond. As the others in the room laid the painting of Wellington against a fireplace she whispered to the General, "I've never had any of them, I don't know what they taste like." The etiquette of the moment temporarily subdued her terror at everything that had happened.

The General recognised her predicament and responded immediately. "In which case," he said, his voice low, "I think both of us should try one of each. What do you think?" She beamed back at him and he squeezed her hand gently. "Don't you worry," he said calmly, "everything'll be alright. I believe it was Bob Marley who came up with that one. Now you fix up that projector and point it at that wall and I'll get the drinks sorted."

Back in the palace kitchens Will stood in the briefing area, well aware that he was about to give the speech, and the military orders, of his life. The RSM took him by the arm, "Just wanted to check something on this blueprint Sir," he said, and guided him to a table at the back of the room. "You were in the drama club when you were at university weren't you?"

Will was stunned. "How the hell did you know that?" he asked, looking at him quizzically. He raised his eyebrows in acknowledgment, "Stupid question. Why are you asking me now?"

The RSM spoke quietly. "Sir, right now is the time to get your BAFTA, your Oscar, your Tony award, or one of those other things those actor pansies get for pretending. Do not, do not, let them think you're not confident about this. These men and women will follow you to hell and back, but do them the courtesy of letting them think that at least some of them will live. They're hard as nails and they're the best trained troops in the world but between them they've still got wives, husbands, and children. Suicide missions never go down well with people as well trained as these."

For the first time Will had the confidence to be confident. He took the RSM's hand and shook it, and with an unusual breach of protocol, used his first name. "I know John," he said, "I'm one of them."

The RSM smiled at him. "Will, you're a once in a lifetime fucking lunatic. And I'll be covering your back."

"Don't miss. There'll be people watching on telly and everything."

The two men gripped hands for a few seconds more and then turned back to the Strike Team Commanders. "Curtain's up Boss," said the RSM.

Will walked back to the front of the briefing area and looked at the seven men and one woman sat in front of him. Behind them the signals specialists had set up the communication links to the DSF, GCHQ and the Metropolitan Police, all of whom were watching intensely. He had prepared military orders, not a speech, and he certainly didn't feel Churchillian, but somehow words just came to him. He worked as hard as possible to ensure his voice didn't tremble.

"I'll be traditional, and start with 'Situation – Enemy Threat'. We don't have much time. The enemy has seized Downing Street, the Houses of Parliament and potentially control elements of our communications networks. There are armoured personnel carriers at each end of Whitehall. We have reason to believe they are also in control of a Type 45 Destroyer moored in the Thames. They have placed air defence systems on the roof of the House of Commons. Despite what you may have heard though, the Prime Minister remains well and truly with us. I know this because I personally threw him in a van just over an hour ago. We plan to get that out to the public shortly. The BBC is broadcasting that Islamic terrorists have assassinated the PM and advising the public to stay away from central London. That is almost certainly a line fed to them by the enemy which is led by traitors and manned by mercenaries. This is going to be a difficult night."

As Will paused for breath a few of the Strike Team Commanders looked at each other. There had been rumours, of course, but this was all getting a lot more complex than most of them had expected.

"This is not an embassy siege," Will continued. "This is not a hostage crisis. This is a coup d' etat, right here in the United Kingdom. I am embarrassed to say that it involves senior members of the Government of the United Kingdom and also its senior military commanders."

There was a collective intake of breath and the Strike Team Commander of Tango couldn't help himself. "Bollocks! Seriously?" he asked.

"Do I look like I'm auditioning for Comedy X Factor? Yes of course it's fucking 'seriously' Dave," said Will. He took another deep breath, remembering what the RSM had said. "Gentlemen, and Lucy," he continued, acknowledging the only female Strike Team Commander amongst the group, "tonight we will be fighting for what this country stands for, and what it doesn't stand for is a bunch of fucking hired guns from other countries taking over our Parliament, or a handful of arrogant, powerful men from our country paying them for it."

Lucy put her hand in the air. "You don't have to hold your hand up Lucy," said Will. "What's your question?" he asked.

"Who does what?"

"Good point. I want five of you to take Parliament. There is a small squad currently ripping to shit what some traitorous wanker in GCHQ did as I speak – that's another story. I need another team to take Downing Street, and I want two in reserve. And trust me folks, tonight means that being the reserve means you will definitely see action." Will looked around the room and thought for a moment. "Right then, King Arthur's Round Table time, who wants to go where?"

The phrase was well known to the Strike Commanders. Within a minute they had decided between them which team was going where. The RSM watched quietly from the back as they discussed the order of battle. Will wrote their response down in his notebook. "I'm going to skip a few bits now," he said, "because time is against us and you know what we're up against, but I'm not being funny, these people are among the best in the world. They wouldn't be here if they weren't, they'd be in some crappy job in Angola or Sudan. But," he said, pausing for emphasis, "they're not defending their countries, they're defending their bank balances. They haven't had a long time to dig-in, and they're not expecting us, not at all. I know it sounds odd considering what's going on, but we will have the element of surprise. I've just got off the phone with Air Command, and we have two Apaches on their way to deal with these tossers in Whitehall in the APCs, and we can have a Typhoon air patrol over London if required."

There were smiles all round. "But don't let me fool you folks, we're going to take some hits tonight. You make your own judgement on what you pass on to your own teams, but there will be blood on the various carpets before this is all over." He turned to the maps hung on the wall, paused, and turned back to the team commanders. "There is something else you need to know if you don't already. Every single one of them is dressed in British Military Uniform or as a Metropolitan Police Officer. Make sure all of your people are in black kit if they're not already. Everything's backwards. And, here's the difficult bit," he continued, "and I'm not talking about the actual attack."

Will looked toward the RSM who nodded his assent, and after a pause, continued. "It's possible, entirely possible, that you will encounter members of the police who don't know what's going on, standing on duty as usual. If you have the option, and that's a big 'if', restrain them. If you do not have time and you feel that lives are in danger you are authorised to kill. Those are the rules of engagement and they have been signed by the Prime Minister."

Nobody said anything immediately but there was a definite shift in the collective mood.

"Holy Shit," said the Strike Commander of Team Uniform.

Will's voice was deadpan. "Yep."

After he'd completed the briefing there was complete silence. Will surveyed a room where eight people were staring back at him. "We don't have time for questions so if you didn't get it the first time you'll need to phone a friend or ask the audience." No-one smiled, including Will. "Okay, boys and girls, let's get out there and dance like no-one's watching."

Lieutenant Commander Lucy Jones, Commander of Team Kilo, piped up. "Anyone fancy some pizza, I'm starving."

Yeoman of Signals Eric Milne checked all his screens in astonishment and then turned to Will. "Sorry to bother you Boss but every mobile signal in London has just been cut. Landlines are going down quickly as well."

Will watched as the strings of light illustrating telephonic connectivity on Eric's map of London slowly faded into darkness. "What about our systems?" he asked

"We'll be fine for the moment, we're off the main grid, but someone really needs to do something about that ship."

"Ship?" asked Will.

"It's the Dauntless, it's the only thing I can think of with the capability to jam these networks."

CHAPTER TWENTY FOUR

Counter-strike…

David Harris's aides had explained to the policemen at 10 Downing Street that the Prime Minister had been killed in a car bomb attack, most likely carried out by Islamic terrorists. He was hustled into the Drawing Room where he immediately called the Head of News at the BBC. Twenty minutes later two vans arrived at the famous black door and a camera and broadcast crew joined him.

"This is an emergency broadcast," he said. "This needs to go out live and introduced as a newsflash." The BBC engineers were quick to move, their egos massaged by the thoughts of the stories they could tell afterwards about the 'moment of history' they were involved in.

In the subterranean kitchens of Buckingham Palace, Will looked up as he finished his orders. The television tuned into the BBC News Channel had just jumped picture and it caught his eye. The immaculately made-up newsreader attempted to maintain her composure but was clearly looking around the studio for direction and listening intently to the voice in her earpiece.

"My apologies," she said, "we are now going live to Downing Street. This is a newsflash and announcement by the government."

"Turn that up," said Will, pointing at a young technician sitting by the screen. As he did so, the picture switched to a solemn looking Foreign Secretary, sitting behind a desk in Number 10.

"Jesus Christ," said Will, sighing, "I want that twat taken alive. You can shoot him, but don't kill him. I want to see him in court. Dinner at Claridge's for whoever takes him."

The Foreign Secretary stared intently into the camera lens, trying to look and sound as statesman-like as he could. "My fellow Britons," he started.

"Oh, for fuck's sake," was the response from more than one of the Strike Team Commanders.

"This is not the United States of Britain," said Charlie Bishop, Commander of Strike Team Tango, expressing what everybody in the room felt. "Tosser."

The Foreign Secretary, unmoved by sentiments he couldn't hear, and unknowing of the small force gathering to counter him, continued. He thought he sounded statesmanlike as he paused for effect. "Our great nation has suffered a devastating blow. I would not be speaking to you now if it were not for a matter of grave national importance. Just after four o' clock this afternoon our Prime Minister was killed in an explosion which we believe was a car bomb, almost certainly planted by an Islamic terror group. It is too early to name it at this time, and I urge all of you not to exact reprisals on the Muslim communities in these isles. However shocking this news may be, it is vital that we retain our British values of decency, morality and courtesy." He looked down at his desk and took a deep breath before continuing. "As a result of these circumstances, and in my position as Deputy Prime Minister, I have taken the executive decision to assume interim governance of the United Kingdom, and I have taken measures to secure the Houses of Parliament and Whitehall, which contain the great offices of state. Our nation has served as the Mother of Parliaments, and we have a long and proud tradition of freedom and the rule of law, but sadly, temporarily, I have imposed martial law in Westminster. We do not yet know what attacks may be directed against us. Please, stay in your homes, do not attempt to come here out of curiosity. The Police and the Army will be robust in their response." Looking directly into the camera he added, "We shall prevail. Terrorism will not be rewarded. Democracy will rule the day."

The broadcast was cut and the Test Card, an image not seen for years, came up on the screen. Will grabbed his phone. Looking up at the strike team leaders he apologised. "I've gotta go guys," he said. "Do what you need to do."

BBC Director General Mike Adams had been watching the same broadcast in his office in White City when Will's call came through. "Will," he said as he picked up, "what the hell is going on?"

"Long story, not what it seems," Will replied. "Do you remember last year when I spoke to you about the emergency broadcast system?" Mike remembered the conversation perfectly clearly and Will didn't wait for an answer. "I need you to get it up and running immediately."

"What's the script?" asked Mike.

Will looked at the ceiling for inspiration. "He'll make it up as he goes," he answered.

Mike was confused. "Who will?"

"The Prime Minister."

"But he's…"

Will cut him off. "No he's not. I'm sending him to the site now." He turned to Captain Sadie Byron, head of the signals intercept team and standing at the back of the room. Sadie was pretty, with a short blonde bob and the body of an Olympic athlete. Will and Sadie had first met in St James's Park where her dog, Arnhem, jumped up at Will, pushing him to the ground and devouring the remaining half of the hot-dog he had bought from one of the nearby concession stands. Sadie was terribly apologetic and scolded Arnhem extensively. It was two days later when they met again – Will was giving a lunchtime lecture in the Ministry of Defence about the importance of expecting the unexpected. Luckily, Sadie was sitting in the back row, and nobody noticed as she strained to conceal her giggling.

Will fixed his gaze. "Sadie, take a troop of sixteen. You are the Close Protection detail for the Prime Minister as of now. Anyone you or he don't recognise comes near him, shoot them. This includes anyone in uniform; police, army, traffic warden, I don't give a shit."

Will and Sadie's second meeting was at a drinks reception at Clarence House, where she again apologised profusely for Arnhem's behaviour. "Why 'Arnhem'?" he had asked.

At the time Sadie had only just passed Special Forces selection and the straightforward question was a welcome distraction from the royal drinks party, which un-nerved her. Her grandfather was killed at Arnhem, after single-handedly charging a machine-gun nest. "In my family we do whatever needs to be done," she said, "even if that involves knocking people over and eating their hot dogs."

"Do what needs to be done," said Will, and she smiled as she remembered their conversation.

"Where is he and where are we going?" she asked.

There was no need for Will to answer as the Prime Minister strode in at the back of the room, his leather shoes grating on the rough concrete floor. "I'm here and we're going to Kent," he said. "I know the way."

Sadie looked to Will and he nodded. "Yes Sir," she said as she stood up. Less than five minutes later David Marshall was lying in the boot of a Range Rover under a blanket. Will chose a road move rather than a helicopter flight because of their proximity to the sophisticated air defence systems they were facing.

"This smells of dog," was his first comment as he was unceremoniously thrown in the boot. He was also profoundly unimpressed with the other three cars in the convoy, all of which looked like they'd spent far too much time in Tesco car parks having trolleys thrown at them.

Sadie tired of his complaints. "My dog is gorgeous," she instructed as she hurtled through the Dartford Tunnel at just over 100mph. "As for the rest of the cars in this convoy, they look that way for a reason. You want to get where we're going or you want to look like you're the President of North Korea."

The Prime Minister couldn't help but smile under the blanket. "When am I allowed out?" came his muffled question.

Sadie was quick to answer. "When we're on the motorway." She checked the mirror to confirm the two cover cars behind her were still in convoy. The lead car, a Skoda with a BMW engine under the bonnet was cutting through the late evening traffic with no problems. Fifteen men and one woman were heading south-east with precious cargo hiding under a doggy-smelling blanket. "I have a question for you," Sadie asked, realising that things were moving a little bit quickly.

"Fire away," came the shout from the boot. "Question that is. Not guns."

"Where are we going?"

"You ever catch a ferry from Dover before?"

"Yep."

"Head that way. You know the castle?"

"No."

On the back seat Jamie Jones, who was relishing his first real-life close protection job, turned around. "I know the castle," he said, grinning, "I grew up in Dover."

The Prime Minister raised his head above the seat rest. "Brilliant. You tell her how to get there, and get Will Richards to make sure they've opened the doors." The PM slipped back down under his blanket and Jamie leant forward to speak to Sadie.

"Who's Will Richards?" Jamie asked.

"Don't you worry about that," said Sadie. "I'll get the doors open, you just make sure we're in front of the right doors."

As they raced down the M2 Sadie made a brief call to Will. "I think I know where we're going. Apparently I need to check with you that the doors'll be open."

"They're open," said Will.

As Sadie and her colleagues approached the drawbridge of Dover Castle the giant wooden doors opened, and standing in the courtyard was BBC Director General Mike Adams, spotlit by the floodlights illuminating inside the castle. Mike's helicopter was parked just outside the immense stone walls. His shadow, projected on the turret behind him made him look like a giant as he walked forwards. The PM climbed out of the boot, where he had been happy to remain despite being given clearance to remove himself from under the blanket. He extended his hand to the BBC Director General, who shook it warmly. "Odd day," he said.

"Yes, isn't it?" was the reply. "Shall we?" he asked and led the Prime Minister into the Keep. Sadie took four men with her and instructed the remainder to secure the entrance and the courtyard. In the main hall they passed a number of armoured statues, swords and pikes in hand. Mike Adams turned to Sadie and nodded at the pistol she was carrying. "Times and weapons change, but people don't do they?" he grinned.

"Nation shall speak peace unto nation," she responded without hesitation, quoting the BBC's motto.

Adams took a large key from his pocket and opened the door to a flight of steps which seemed to descend forever. Lit only by bare lightbulbs on a single wire, the stone steps were cold, and there was a dank smell. "What the hell is this?" asked Sadie.

Despite the seriousness of the circumstances, the Prime Minister turned to her and responded. "Seventh level of hell," he said, "or perhaps more accurately, the BBC Emergency Broadcast System." After several minutes of descent and progress through another three doors they found themselves in a small, round room. On the walls were posters from the 1960s depicting the nuclear threat from the Soviet Union. A single chest of drawers was the only piece of furniture save for a table and chair in the middle of the room. On the desk was a microphone, attached to a laptop computer which was plugged into what looked like a car battery. A solitary cable from the side of the laptop disappeared into a hole in the ceiling.

Sadie was looking at Mike Adams through lowered eyelids. In a staccato voice she asked, "This is it?"

"Yep."

"It's shit," she replied.

"It works," he answered. "Stand alone power system," he said, indicating the car battery, "no internet connectivity, therefore no viruses, and the most powerful transmitter in the developed world."

"And that would be..?" asked Sadie.

"That would be something we don't talk about, a bit like Bletchley Park used to be," said Mike. He rolled the chest of drawers away from the dank wall, revealing two simple switches, both of which he flicked. "Won't be a sec," he said, disappearing out the door. He came back with a camera, tripod and a plain white linen bedsheet. "Give us a hand will you?" he said to the Prime Minister's protection detail, and they hung the sheet behind him. Mike connected the camera to the laptop and started running the emergency protocol software. "When you're ready Sir," he said to the PM.

As the Prime Minister took his seat in front of the sheet, Mike Adams turned the laptop towards himself and corrected the camera angle. "Right Sir. When I hit this button, every TV and radio broadcast channel in the UK will cut straight to us. You ready, or do you want a moment, maybe write something down?"

Sadie bit her lip as she stood at the sidelines watching. She liked to think she'd had an interesting life, but this was beyond expectation.

"Do it," said the Prime Minister.

Mike tapped the keyboard and counted him in. He'd started at the BBC as a cameraman and made his way up into management. He wondered if he would finish as a cameraman as well. Gesturing with his fingers he also called the first three numbers. "Five, Four, Three…" and then counting the Prime Minister in just with the fingers on his hand Mike Adams, Director General of the British Broadcasting Corporation, effectively became the Executive Producer of the biggest show of his life.

Across the country, television screens flickered and radio stations turned to static. On the televisions, a poorly lit image of the Prime Minister appeared. Unlike what people were used to, there was no microphone attached to his lapel. With the microphone on the desk in front of him he looked like a bingo caller in a cheap Blackpool nightclub, but he was calm and poised at the same time as projecting a fierceness the public hadn't seen before. He had never made a speech like it, and he never would again. He never thought that he would have had to. It was not prepared, it was not rehearsed and it had not been checked by advisors. He thought of some of it on the journey down from London, but mostly, he was making it up as he went along.

He managed to remove his thumb and forefinger from the bridge of his nose just as the broadcast went live.

"Good evening," he smiled. "I suspect some of you may be surprised to see me. Clearly, I am not as dead as you may have heard. I have not been blown up by Muslim terrorists. My survival will come as a surprise to the small number of people who would like you to think that I was, but I assure you an even bigger surprise is coming their way. And that is happening right now." The Prime Minister's face grew sterner. "There is no martial law in the United Kingdom, there are no no-go areas for our citizens. As I speak there are Special Forces units re-taking those areas of Westminster which have been hijacked by foreign mercenaries and tiny elements of the government which you elected, and the civil servants and some in the military whom we appointed. For that I can only apologise. I will be announcing a General Election shortly after these events have been concluded. I will not pretend to you that this is an easy thing. It is not. People will die tonight. Good people will die tonight. They have husbands and wives and children, just like you do. They have parents. They have gardens, football clubs, holidays booked, just like you do. When this is finished, remember them." David Marshall looked down at the desk briefly. "This is the United Kingdom of Great Britain and Northern Ireland. Her Majesty remains the Head of State. The most professional soldiers this country has ever seen are currently retaking those buildings occupied by the mercenaries. Have you ever seen an angry soldier? They scare the living hell out of me. This is only going one way, and there is only one outcome, victory. And when it is finished, I will be back here to let you know. "

Mike Adams knew exactly when the speech was finished and when to cut the broadcast.

CHAPTER TWENTY FIVE

Attack...

Captain Charlie Newton, the leader of Strike Team Foxtrot had volunteered to go for the tunnels. They took the route from Buckingham Palace under St James's Park in the sure and certain knowledge that they were likely to encounter resistance and boobytraps. The first setback came just as they were passing under Downing Street. A young trooper named Billy Phelps was the first to reach a steel door in the dimly lit passage. It had a wheel on it like a naval vessel and Billy, who had never been in the tunnels before, reacted instinctively. He span the wheel as fast as he could to unlock the door and heaved it open, setting off the explosives attached to a trip wire behind it. Billy died instantly and bits of his shattered body flew back through the tunnel.

Charlie was the closest to him as the explosive wave ripped down the enclosed space, knocking him on his back. He wiped the blood from his face and quickly threw a smoke grenade down the passage, adding to the fog of debris and brickdust which had engulfed the narrow tunnel. "Get your eyes on!" he shouted back to his team. The remaining fifteen troops quickly snapped their night vision goggles into place – newly issued, these had the benefit of thermal imaging as well as an enhanced low light capability. Charlie saw the outline of two armed men about fifty metres from him. The second grenade he pulled from his jacket was designed to kill rather than confuse. The levels of adrenaline he was experiencing caused the second setback of Foxtrot's progress that night. Charlie was left-handed, and following the shock of the explosion, and watching young Billy effectively disintegrate in front of him, he had pulled the pin of the grenade with his left hand, leaving him to throw it with his right. "Bollocks," he said to himself. Followed quickly by, "Fuck it," and he bowled the best cricket ball of his life. The grenade hurtled through the smoke, unseen and unheard by the two South African mercenaries at the other end of the tunnel. Neither were killed but both suffered serious shrapnel wounds.

It was at this point that Charlie and the rest of the Foxtrot team wished they had ear protection. Between the explosion at the door and the grenade, the noise in the tunnel, which had a low ceiling and was barely wide enough for two people to pass, left them all with ringing in their ears and unable to hear each other. It was hand signals only for the rest of the approach under Parliament. Charlie knew the tunnel would be difficult, and had expected the unexpected, but he hadn't worked on the basis that he would be one man down with a team that was to all intents and purposes deaf before they even reached their assault position. The very experienced Corporal behind him despatched both of the mercenaries with two single shots to the head.

In the tube tunnel under Whitehall, Sergeant Nick Allen held his hand up to halt the men of Task Force Charlie, a call-sign to which the recently deafened Captain Charlie Newton had earlier argued could be confusing, to which Nick had replied, "only to officers". They were approaching the southbound platform of Westminster Underground station and Nick had spotted six men defending the platform, all heavily armed. He ushered the first five of his own troops forward and huddled with them. "Set to single shot only", he whispered. "We're going for one each, left to right." The fire team stepped gingerly across the railway line, six abreast in the darkness, each squinting through their rifle sights. The mercenaries on the platform heard nothing as they moved into position. Nick shouted, "Go!" and six shots rang out in the tunnel, each one hitting its target. Because of the close range, four of the team had opted for head shots, the other two for a bullet in the chest. They ran forward quickly and the remainder of the strike team were close behind them when the distinctive sound of a heavy machine gun opening fire drummed through the tunnel. They all dropped below the platform's edge.

"This is fucking outrageous!" shouted one of the team. "This is London, not fucking Tripoli!" He poked his head over the platform and saw what Nick had not, the gunner with the heavy machine gun hidden by the escalator. Nick looked round to see the trooper pull the rocket system from his back.

"No!" he screamed, "What the fuck are you thinking?" The rounds from the heavy machine gun were thudding into the curved wall of the station behind him, shattering the tiles. Nevertheless, the trooper extended the portable missile launcher and looked through the sights, only the top of his head visible above the platform.

He saw an advert in the middle of the platform. "Bugger me, kids go free at Thorpe Park this month. I've got to take the wife and kids to that."

Nick was unamused. "Put that thing away! You're going to get us all killed. That's an anti-structures missile you doughnut!" he screamed. "In case you hadn't noticed, we're under a structure! About a hundred feet under a structure, and it's made of concrete and steel!"

Trooper Chris Hume was having none of it. Over the repetitive thuds of the machine gun he shouted back, "Technically Boss, it's a Light anti-structures missile, so we might be alright." The noise of gunfire which had echoed around the tube platform suddenly stopped, and there was the tell-tale sound of a click, and the moving parts of a gun forced forward onto a chamber with no round in it. Trooper Hume didn't waste a second, popping up from the protection of the sunken rails and firing straight at the gunner. The rocket took the man's head off and buried itself in the wall behind him before exploding. Chris turned to the Strike Team Leader and grinned infectiously. "Told you it'd work," he said.

There was a brief moment of silence and then tiles started to fall from the roof as the impact of the blast and shockwave affected the Underground station. "Move!" screamed Nick, and the team heaved themselves up onto the platform and ran for the escalator, which unsurprisingly had stopped, while the tunnel collapsed behind them.

When they got to the top Nick surveyed the scene. "Holy Jesus!" was all he could bring himself to say, as he looked at the collapsed floor behind him.

Trooper Chris Hume couldn't stop laughing. "I've always hated this station," he said, "reminds me of the Death Star. Which kind of makes me Luke Skywalker, doesn't it?" he beamed.

"No," said Nick, "it kind of makes you an insurance liability." As the strike team moved into an all-round defence posture, Nick looked at the exit signs. "Anyone familiar with this station, what's left of it that is?" he asked.

Trooper Hume stepped up to the plate again. "You want to come out the Parliament side," he said, pointing, "that's the way to go." There was an escalator which, extraordinarily, was still in operation. The strike team sprinted across the lobby and started running up the escalator stairs. At the front of the charge, Nick turned around and stopped his team. He put a finger to his mouth to shush them and the look in his eye made it clear he meant it. Many of the team looked at him in amazement. Any attempt at a quiet entry had long been blown, and several of them held their arms up questioningly. But Nick's background was with the Special Boat Service, and for him, silence was always a weapon. The sixteen troopers of Strike Team Charlie felt somewhat incongruous as they stood silently, weapons in hand, dressed head to toe in black combat fatigues, inexorably progressing towards street level. Several were shaking their heads in disbelief.

As they reached the top of the escalator Nick crouched down, and they all followed him. As it levelled out, he saw two of the mercenaries talking to each other and shot them both as the machinery pushed him onto the polished floor of the station. Within seconds the ticket office area erupted in a storm of gunfire. Strike Team Charlie charged up the few remaining stairs and cleared the area, killing another eight mercenaries. At that point in the evening, the only casualty for Team Charlie was Trooper Chris Hume, who took a round to the left shoulder, an injury which would lose him the use of his left arm and hand. As the round flew through him and he was spun on his feet, the only thing that the men standing next to him could remember were the words, "Oh bollocks, and I wanted to learn the saxophone."

He took a field dressing out and started looking after himself. "Would you piss off," he said to the two who came to help him, "I'm fine. Don't you people know there's a fucking war on?"

Strike Team Charlie regrouped by the station exit to Parliament Square, unaware that Foxtrot were experiencing serious difficulties in the tunnels under Downing Street. Nick heard an almighty explosion and then over his radio came the confirmation that both the enemy armoured personnel carriers had been destroyed and that there were no targets left in Whitehall. He could hear the unmistakable sound of the rotor blades of Merlin helicopters, ready to drop Kilo, Tango and Hotel into the courtyards of Parliament. Turning to his troops he shouted, "Right guys, do or die."

While Strike Team Charlie had been fighting their way through the Underground Station, above them the two Apache helicopter gunships which Will had asked for had flown low and fast from Wiltshire, but didn't have a full picture of what was happening, receiving intermittent radio briefings along the way. They were aware there was a surface-based air threat but were unaware of exactly what it was they faced. As they approached Parliament they immediately picked up the men on the roof. "Engage," called Major Harry Canning, lead pilot and commander of the air sortie. The weapons officers of both helicopters opened fire on the roof with their deadly machine guns. A rocket propelled grenade flew up at him and his quick reactions saved them as he dodged the aircraft to the left. "Close," he said. "Let's deal with those armoured personnel carriers, I'll take the one in Trafalgar Square, you can have this one," he said to his fellow pilot who could seen him through the window as he pointed down at the vehicle below him in Parliament Square. Major Harry Canning flew over the Cenotaph memorial in Whitehall, not unaware of the irony of the situation, and opened fire with Hellfire missiles on the Boxer vehicle which he considered to be arrogantly and blatantly disrespecting Nelson's triumph over previous adversaries. As he spun the machine through a hundred and eighty degrees it struck him that when he woke that morning he never thought he'd be flying a helicopter gunship through the heart of Britain's governmental power.

His wingman had despatched the other armoured vehicle in a similar way and decided to fly over the Houses of Parliament to get a look from the Thames-side view, to see if there was any assistance he could provide the troops who he knew were now flooding through the underground tunnels. It was then that his onboard systems started alarming, and Captain Tony "Buck" Rogers was engaged by the surface-to-air missile system which had been set up on the terrace.

* * *

As Nick Allen's Strike Team Charlie sprinted from Westminster Underground Station across Parliament Square to the St Stephen's Entrance of Parliament, a missile burst into the fading sky from the terrace of the building. Turning slowly and almost gracefully it raced back and hit the Apache, that had made their job so much easier, destroying the tail rotor. Somehow the pilot managed to ditch it in the Thames, saving the lives of those who otherwise would have perished.

While Foxtrot and Charlie had taken the subterranean route, Kilo, Tango and Hotel had rushed to the beautifully administered gardens at the back of Buckingham Palace, where six Merlin helicopters awaited them. A lot of work had been done behind the scenes. These strike teams were twice the size of the others, as they would be the main assault force, and each had split into two teams. Sixteen troops boarded each helicopter, and the flight time was less than a minute as they sped towards the Houses of Parliament.

Major Harry Canning had taken the loss of his friends personally, and had repeatedly strafed the terrace from where the SAM-7 had been launched – hoping he had neutralised the threat to anything in the sky. The Merlin helicopters approached confidently. They flew in an extended line formation over the building, lurching as they stopped to hover over the six courtyards Will had selected as assault points. Working on the basis that the mercenaries would attempt to defend from the outside in, rather than the inside out, Will's plan was for Strike Teams Foxtrot and Charlie to set-up a diversion at St Stephen's Entrance and create whatever mayhem they could coming up through the tunnel in the Queen's Robing Room. A secondary diversion would be instigated by Uniform rushing the Sovereign's Entrance having come the long way, at first in the back of a minibus as far as Lambeth Bridge, and then on foot, with an approach through The Victoria Tower Gardens.

The Commander of Strike Team Uniform, James Jackson, would never tire of telling the story of the look of surprise on the young mother's face as, completely unaware of the situation, sixteen men dressed in black and highly armed piled out of the back of the bus. Her response was to pull the hood of her child's pushchair down. Strike Team Uniform rushed through the park, past the innocence of the swings and the roundabout, preparing to assault the southern entrance.

Ropes dropped from the helicopters and the forces loyal to the Crown sped down them, eight on each side. But not without casualties. After the Apache attack Gilmour knew there was going to be a fight, despite what he had been led to believe, and anticipated an aerial assault, although he was not expecting it to be this audacious. Gilmour had taken a small fire team from the outer perimeter and based it in the House of Commons Chamber, where they had taken up positions next to the interior windows. As the first wave of Lucy Jones's Strike Team Kilo touched the ground, they were struck down in a volley of gunfire. The helicopter pilot pulled up and away, despite the two troopers still hanging from the ropes, with nothing but the strength of their grip to keep them alive.

"I'll put you down in the next one," came the radio message from the pilot. As the two men hanging on for dear life swung past the Big Ben Clock Tower, one of them checked his watch and grinned. Silhouetted against the gleaming clockface he was happy to know that his watch was accurate.

His friend couldn't hear him over the din of the rotor blades. And then suddenly, as quickly as they'd risen, they lowered again, and the bottom of the rope was touching the ground. Without hesitation they loosened their grip and slid down the ropes. Seconds later the entire assault team was on the ground.

"Where the fuck is this?" shouted Lucy to Kilo's Deputy Strike Team Commander.

"I think it's London," was the sarcastic response. "I've seen films about this place on the television. They like breaking windows here."

Lucy smiled. "When in Rome…"

"Shall we?" he asked.

Strike Teams Tango and Hotel swept down the ropes into the inner courtyards without opposition, primarily because of

Strike Team Charlie's sprint over the open ground from Westminster Underground Station to the St Stephen's Entrance, which had diverted the merceneries' attention, as planned. Two had been caught in the crossfire.

Nick knew they had fallen but was not about to stop. "Keep going!" he screamed, throwing an empty magazine to the ground and sprinting at a pace he hadn't managed since he was a student. As Nick and Strike Team Charlie assaulted the St Stephen's entrance, firing a rocket propelled grenade in the process, James Jackson and Strike Team Uniform were taking the Sovereign's Entrance. The minibus which had dropped them off earlier had easily driven around the improvised roadblock of the coach, reversing at high speed into the giant wooden doors as James and his team approached on foot.

Having cleared the tunnel approach under Parliament, Charlie Newton and his troops emerged under the trap door in the Queen's Robing Room, unopposed. "Cool" said Charlie, his hearing returning as he heard the muffled sound of a firefight to his left. The first few out of the trapdoor took up defensive positions while the remainder of the team climbed out, and then swarmed in the direction of the firing they could hear. Strike Team Uniform was taking severe injuries, with four men already out of action. What the mercenaries weren't expecting, was Captain Charlie Newton's Strike Team Foxtrot approaching from their rear through the Royal Gallery. Newton ducked back behind the door and explained what was happening. The Uniform Team attack had stalled at the gates and needed assistance. He had seen at least twenty men holding their position inside the building. He looked at his troops, who were nervous and exhilarated. "Maximum force," he said, "that's all I can give you right now. They're everywhere."

Strike Team Foxtrot exploded through the doorway in four teams of four. The first turned right, the second left. The third team simply launched itself forward and the last walked backwards through the gap, scanning the balconies above them. In total, thirty-eight rounds were fired. Twenty-seven mercenaries were shot.

James Jackson's team sprinted into the lobby.

"You're welcome," said a somewhat breathless Charlie Newton, grinning like a child.

"Always a pleasure to see you Charlie," said James. "Now let's get the rest of these pricks."

Strike Teams Foxtrot and Charlie became as one, and then they burst into the House of Lords.

In the tunnels behind Charlie Newton's team, Strike Force India, led by the Canadian-born Chris Savage, diverted from the route to Parliament and found themselves standing by a lift which could only take four people, and even then it was intimate.

One of Chris's team stared at him. "This is a really fucking bad idea."

Chris remained steadfast. "If this lift never comes back down, then I will agree with you. But if it does, then you will come up and join me."

Chris went first and three more of his task force joined him. As the lift rose one of them started singing, "Do you know the way to San Jose?"

All of them laughed. And then the singer asked the obvious question. "Where, exactly, does this come out?"

Chris smiled to himself. His eight year old daughter had just started reading the books. "You familiar with Harry Potter?" he asked. He received nothing but an inquisitive look. "Well, this would be the cupboard under the stairs." Chris opened the protective gate as they slowed and reached street level. As he slowly opened the door in front of them and then stepped out with no sign of mercenary presence, Chris beckoned the others out.

"Shit," mouthed the singing star of the lift. Chris pointed his index finger down, indicating to return the lift. The doors were closed and it descended. The four men formed a square with their backs to each other and prepared for a fight.

Three minutes later the four men had turned into sixteen and Strike Team India was ready to take 10 Downing Street back. None of them had ever expected to take a lift from works tunnels under Westminster to the cupboard under the stairs of the house with the most famous door in the world.

David Harris, Foreign Secretary, Deputy Prime Minister, self-appointed Acting Prime Minister, had no idea it was there as he sat in an office upstairs watching Sky News. He'd heard a few explosions, and they had concerned him, but he couldn't get Gilmour on the phone and he suspected they might even be theatrics.

Chris Savage's team had found no-one on the ground floor, and slowly started the ascent up the main staircase, past all the portraits of previous Prime Ministers. The first floor balconies had sentries posted, but they were lazy and inattentive. Chris and the four men behind them fitted silencers to their weapons and eight muffled shots dealt with the problem.

Half of the team continued up the stairs but Chris held the other half back when he heard the television. "One chance," he mouthed as they stood outside the door to the Prime Minister's Private Office. He was never quite sure how all eight of them got in the room as quickly as they did. Six of the mercenaries lay dead on the floor when the shooting stopped – two of the troopers were changing magazines at the time but it didn't matter. Vases and statues lay in pieces and the windows were shot out in the course of the firefight. Chris smiled – David Harris sat in front of him, alive and alone and looking terrified. Upstairs there was more gunfire, and then a call came down from the remainder of Strike Team India. "Building clear!"

Chris Savage got on the radio to Will, who had remained in the kitchens at Buckingham Palace, moving hastily commandeered Connect 4 pieces around printed out floorplans of Parliament and Downing Street. The Royal toybox had been raided to use tokens to represent the attacking and defending forces. The loudspeaker on the table relayed the words he had been waiting for.

"Black Door secured. Eighteen enemy dead. Primary target alive." There was a pause, and then Chris Savage smiled. There were eight weapons pointed at David Harris, six dead men on the floor around him, blood splatters over much of the furniture and the walls, and he had nowhere to go.

"Bet you thought this day was going to turn out different, didn't you?" he asked.

The colour had completely drained from Harris's face and it was clear that he was terrified. "Who, who are you?" he stammered. Savage looked to his colleagues and then back at

Harris. The contrast in the demeanour of the two men could not have been more noticeable. Savage was calm, Harris was breathless. "I am the Prime Minister of the United Kingdom, you will not get away with this," he said, his voice obviously tremulous.

"No you're not and yes we will," said Chris. "Besides, you're the one about to not get away with this."

"What are you going to do to me?" Harris asked.

Chris's eyes narrowed. "Well first, we're going to tie you up, then we're going to take you out of this office, which isn't yours by the way. You may find on the way out that due to the shock of these events you're a little disoriented. This could involve you accidentally bumping into the doorframe or even tripping down the stairs. Do be careful."

"Are you going to kill me?" asked Harris.

"Probably not, it depends on how many of the rest of us die tonight. And I'm keeping count. You might get a bit bruised though." Harris's wrists were plasticuffed behind his back. "Feeling Prime Ministerial?" Chris asked as he stood behind the man who had attempted to assassinate the elected Prime Minister. All he got in response was a scowl of indignation. "Shame," said Chris, smashing his hand into the back of Harris's head, shoving it straight into the beautiful mahogany table he was sitting behind. The thud of his head on the desk masked the sound of his breaking nose. Harris could taste the blood in his mouth as he was wrenched from the chair and dragged to the door, where his captors studiously mis-timed his exit and his forehead slammed into the doorframe. His descent down the stairs to the ground floor was equally uncomfortable.

***

It was just then that the Regimental Sergeant Major of the Special Air Service put his hand on Will's shoulder. Will looked up quickly. The RSM was staring intently at the patched in monitors to Parliament's CCTV system. "What is it?" he asked.

"It's stalling," was the simple reply.

Despite the emotion and pressure of the day, Will smirked as he picked up his rifle. "Best we un-stall it then." He turned to Hannah, "You stay here, do not move." She had insisted on staying with him, and he felt it was the least he could do after all he'd put her through.

Sure enough, in the Central Lobby of Parliament, Strike Teams Kilo, Tango and Hotel were having a hard time of it. Having fought their way into the main building, they found themselves attempting an assault into the House of Commons, where Gilmour had pulled his men back to.

Gilmour had never expected an assault as ferocious as this. Gunfire ripped down the corridor between the Members' Lobby and the Central Lobby. Priceless stained glass and several statues had no defence against the volleys of fire which ricocheted off the walls. As the marble legs of a Victorian politician Lucy Jones didn't recognise fell away, she briefly thought about doing a proper tour of the place when it was quieter.

Twenty feet below her, Will and the RSM were sprinting down the tunnel which led to the Queen's Robing Room. As they emerged through the trap door they could hear the sound of automatic gunfire only a few dozen metres away. Will turned to his most experienced advisor. "Suggestions?" he asked.

"I'm thinking," said the RSM, as they ran past the red leather benches of the House of Lords. "This is fucking surreal," he added, as they stopped just outside the Central Lobby. Even in their relatively well protected position, pieces of plasterwork and stone were snapping past their heads and falling at their feet. An occasional round found its way into the benches, blowing the leather open like a burst pillow.

Will grinned. "I have an idea," he said.

"Fucking Hell," said the RSM as he fired down the central corridor and changed magazines. "And it would be?"

"Swarm attack," Will shouted back, trying hard to be heard over the noise of the firefight. The RSM rolled his eyes.

"Brilliant, the last bastion of the clueless."

"But I've got to make another call first," he said, grabbing his radio. Will was still worried about what the HMS Dauntless was doing, but hadn't had time to address his concerns, so he used his radio-phone to make the call to RAF Northholt, just outside central London. In the operations room the duty administrator picked up the phone. After the BBC broadcast everyone knew that it was an odd day. "RAF Northholt, how can I help you?"

Will was struggling to be heard over the sound of the gunfire around him as he slowly moved forward. "This is the Milk Tray Man. I need an air defence patrol over Westminster please." The calm sound of his voice did not reflect how he was feeling. He ducked as a round came over his head, smashing into the stone pillar in front of him and showering him in debris. "Fucking hell!" he said, his composure breaking for a moment.

Senior Aircraftman Sheila Phillips looked up at the Station Commander, who had already put the standby flight crews on high alert. Earlier that day she had joked with them while they ate lunch at the picnic benches close to the runway. "You've got the worst job in the RAF Sir," she said to one of the pilots on high readiness. "You sit here all day dressed up in that kit and you don't get to go anywhere. If I were you, I'd transfer to tankers."

The Station Commander was watching her intently as she thumbed through the folder on her desk. The moniker "Milk Tray Man" was listed as the Commanding Officer of the Contingency Planning Group. "Please authenticate," she asked quickly.

Will was now crawling under a bench as the incoming rounds turned from single shots to automatic fire. His ears were ringing and he was struggling to hear. This was not the best time to be having a conversation. "What?" he shouted.

"Authenticate," said Sheila, dropping the pleasantries.

Will still couldn't hear her. "Get me a fucking air patrol over Westminster, right now."

Three feet away Paddy Hardy yelled, "Grenade!", and bravely stood up despite the incoming fire and lobbed it in the direction of the mercenary gunner. When it exploded it blew the adjacent windows to pieces, covering anyone who hadn't taken cover in pieces of stained glass.

Sheila's ears rang with the sound of the explosion, but she was still focussed. "Milk Tray Man I need authentication," she persisted.

Will finally heard her. "This is the Milk Tray Man. I authenticate twenty-three, fifty-seven, eighteen. Now get me some fucking aeroplanes and put the pilots on the line." Sheila looked down at her folder and the numbers matched the call-sign.

The Station Commander had already anticipated Sheila's nod of confirmation as he hit the red 'Scramble' button on the wall of the Operations Room. Flight Lieutenant Dave Parsons and Squadron Commander Carl Hancock ran from the ready room to the two Typhoon Eurofighters already out of the hangar and ready to taxi. The jets, with their distinctive triangular wings, already had the ascent steps wheeled up to the cockpits. Once inside, both men plugged their headsets into the communications system as they taxied in parallel to the runway.

Northholt's Station Commander had taken Sheila's headset and asked two questions, one of which was simple, the other one not quite so much. "Milk Tray Man, are you still there?" he asked, hearing the gunfire in the background.

"Yep," said Will, as he rolled to avoid yet another falling statue toppling towards him. "You the boss?" he asked

The response was clear, "Yes, and the drivers are now patched in. What do you need?"

"Loads of fucking bombs." A bullet whistled past his left ear and took a small chunk out of the wall behind him. "For fuck's sake," said Will as he tried to get even lower, not realising he'd actually taken shrapnel to his left arm.

The Station Commander watched through the large windows of the Operations Room as the two Typhoons opened up their throttles and slowly started rolling down the runway. The slowness lasted only a few seconds before the jets tore up the tarmac and after housing their landing gear climbed for altitude almost vertically.

"Milk Tray Man, this is Base One", said the Station Commander. "You have two Typhoons airborne over north-west London. I'm assuming you're busy right now, so I'll hand you right over."

Carl Hancock pressed his transmit button. "This is Zulu One," he said, his voice detached as it came over the radio. "Situation?" he asked, as he levelled out over north London.

Having noticed that Will was on the radio and busy, four of his men had gathered around him and were firing almost constantly across the Central Lobby at the mercenaries. Two of them were shot as Will's new-found bodyguards dragged him back behind a wall in St Stephen's Hall.

"Situation is there's something out there which can take out an Apache. I don't know what it is or where it is. They had stuff on the roof of Parliament but we've taken care of that. Can you boys find it? We're kind of busy right now."

The Typhoons raced towards central London. "We'll be there in under a minute."

"Cheers guys. Can I leave you to have your fight while I have mine?"

"Deal," said Carl, before switching to the air-to-air channel. "Dave, you picking anything up?"

On HMS Dauntless, Captain Staunton and his crew of eight had been watching their screens as the two jet fighters took off. He looked to his radar operator, "What's that?" he asked, pointing at the single blip on the screen.

"It's transponder is identifying it as a British Airways flight, BA 1033 to Malaga."

Staunton didn't miss a beat, "Challenge it," he said, turning to his Communications Officer.

Lieutenant Commander Andrew Jones pressed his transmit button. "BA flight 1033 this is the HMS Dauntless. You are on a course which will take you over government restricted airspace which is currently under the protection of the Royal Navy. Divert from central London or you will be fired upon."

In the cockpit of his Typhoon, Carl Hancock smiled and put on his best civilian airline Captain voice. "Good evening HMS Dauntless of the Royal Navy. I have had no such instruction from the tower at Heathrow. Do not fire, repeat, do not fire. This is a civilian aircraft with 228 passengers on board, and eight crew. We will get out of your way as soon as we can."

The radar operator's eyes widened as it dawned on him what was happening. The two fighter jets had been flying so close together that they only appeared as one target. In the seconds it had taken during the radio exchange they had come close enough to be distinguished as two separate aircraft. And at that point his schoolboy error of not thinking about the speed of the approach of a passenger aircraft compared to a fighter jet hit him. He spun in his chair. "Sir, it's not a British Airways flight, it's two fighters."

In the skies above Central London the rapidly approaching Squadron Leader Hancock switched channels and asked his wingman, "Do you think they bought it?"

"Not a chance," was the response, as the two Typhoons hurtled towards the River Thames.

On the HMS Dauntless Captain Staunton was not slow to respond. He turned to his Weapons Officer. "Engage," he ordered.

"Yes Sir." And with the press of a mouse button a Sea Viper missile erupted from the deck of the destroyer.

Both pilots reacted immediately to the warnings in their headsets, pulling straight up and turning to the right, still in formation. Dave Parsons was first on the radio. "You getting that?" he asked. "My system's telling me that's blue-on-blue."

"Snap."

"What the...?"

Carl had run his systems quicker. "I have a firing solution. It's coming off something on the river, Docklands way." He paused. "Decision time. Seven seconds to impact."

Flight Lieutenant Dave Parsons took eight seconds to think and was blown from the sky. On HMS Dauntless there was no celebration. "Fire again," instructed the Captain.

Hancock saw his fellow-pilot and friend incinerated in the skies over London, and then immediately responded to the second missile lock-on alarm he'd heard that evening. Twisting the aircraft onto its back he plunged for the relative safety of ground level. And then he saw on his flight-computer what the target was.

"Milk Tray Man, Milk Tray Man, this is Zulu One, over."

Will was halfway up a staircase outside the Members' Dining Room when the communication came through. "How you getting on?" he asked, ducking beneath the balustrade as more rounds came his way.

"It's not going well to be honest. Zulu Two is out of the game and I've got a massive missile about to hit me up the arse. And its come from a Royal Navy boat on the Thames."

Will smiled at the calmness of the voice on the other end of the radio. "Okay, reality time. You have authorisation to take out the boat. Or 'Ship' as the Navy likes to call them."

"Yeah, well that's great but I've rather gone off them at the moment," said Carl, pulling the stick back and levelling his fighter out, missing the smokestacks on Battersea Power Station by inches.

"Plan?" asked Will.

Carl smiled. "Yeah, I've got one, and it involves everyone who fired this thing at me having a really shitty day."

"Good man." Will changed magazines and offered covering fire to the four men climbing the stairs behind him. "I always thought you lot were a bunch of posers, but if you fancy a pint on Monday I'm buying."

Carl was flying low over the Thames, the river almost boiling in the wake of the jet's engine. The roar was deafening. "Will you still be alive on Monday?" he asked, as he passed Parliament and saw the flashes of gunfire through the windows on his left-hand side.

There was a momentary pause in the shooting as both sides listened to the scream of the Typhoon's engine. Will saw the jet momentarily, just as it pulled up over Westminster Bridge and then disappeared behind it as it lowered altitude. Seconds later there was another roar.

"Zulu One, you have a missile following you."

Squadron Leader Carl Hancock wasn't smiling anymore. Flying at six feet above sea level was something he'd done as a young pilot, when the instructors weren't watching. As he followed the river and turned east at Waterloo Bridge, he recognised he had only seconds to get this right.

Annie Radford was having a glass of Pinot Grigio on the balcony of her flat near St Katherine's Dock when she first heard the sound. Carl Hancock pulled a barrel roll through the gap on Tower Bridge between the pedestrian crossing at the top and the bascules that formed the road. As the Typhoon jet twisted through the bridge her jaw dropped. She dropped her glass when she saw the Sea Viper missile chasing it, ripping up the Thames and going under the bridge.

Carl Hancock was fairly confident his time was up. "Missile with my name on it," he said to himself, as he flew the Typhoon straight at HMS Dauntless. "May as well make it count." He fired his anti-missile chaff and at the last second his targeting computer stopped giving him a lock-on warning and all the red lights in the cockpit turned green. "Oh yeah!" he shouted as he pulled back on the stick. "Good evening HMS Dauntless, this is BA 1033, also known as the Royal Air Force, and you can fuck off!" The Typhoon responded effortlessly and soared skyward as the Sea Viper missile smashed into the ship's bridge, killing all eight men on board.

On the staircase where Will and his team were vastly outnumbered, a grenade rolled down the stairs, its pin still intact in the detonator. "Fucking idiots," said Will, pulling the pin and throwing it onto the balcony above. "Zulu One, this is the Milk Tray Man, how you doing?" he shouted as the detonation of the grenade temporarily deafened him again.

As Carl Hancock pulled the nose of the Typhoon around in a gut-wrenching turn he replied with a smile, "Well they're all in bobbins. You want me to hang around for a bit in case anything else comes up?"

"Yes please."

* * *

When they heard what had happened the reserve unit of the Sierra Team headed straight for HMS Dauntless. In the van on the way there a very quick discussion was held. Inspector Alex Williams turned to his troops, many of whom he had not met before they assembled that afternoon. As a police officer on attachment to the Special Forces Support Group he recognised his lack of expertise for the environment they were about to assault. He took a breath. "Right then, boats, who knows anything about them?"

As they careered down Fleet Street towards the Dauntless, Sergeant James Durup of the Special Boat Service kept his head low but raised his eyes in a look of sheer contempt.

"What?" asked Williams innocently.

"You're doing this on purpose aren't you?"

"I have no idea what you're talking about."

"It's a ship. A ship! It's not a fucking boat!" yelled Durup.

Inspector Williams kept a straight face but his eyes betrayed him. "You guys get really wound up about that don't you?" he asked rhetorically. Durup gave him a stare that could have killed. "Anyway. Sounds like you're our man. Can you get us to the bridge?" he asked as they passed the Tower of London.

"Of course," was the curt reply.

"I don't mean this one," said Williams, pointing out the window at Tower Bridge. "I mean the one on the boat."

Durup shook his head in mock disbelief. "You unspeakable bastard," he said. "Yeah, I can take us to the bridge, but I might throw you out the fucking window when we get there."

Minutes later the un-prepossessing white van pulled up alongside HMS Dauntless in the Docklands area of London. The unarmed civilian security guards manning the gangway were still in shock from the events of a few minutes earlier and were thrown to the floor, gagged and bound in seconds. On close to the minimum wage and having absolutely no security training whatsoever they were happy to be left alone on the riverside dock as Durup led the team into the superstructure of the ship.

The damage to the front of the bridge was evident as they had approached, but the ship's fire suppression systems had taken care of the aftermath. HMS Dauntless looked like it had a bloody nose but it looked considerably less than beaten. Strike Team Sierra moved through the hatches with caution; Durup was keen to get them to the bridge but knew that there could be unpleasant surprises on the way there. Wendy Jones, the only female in Strike Team Sierra was right behind Durup as they climbed the final stairs to the centre of operations of Dauntless. It turned out there was nothing to fear. What was left of the eight officers on board was largely unrecognisable.

Inspector Williams smiled as he entered the bridge and saw what had happened. He turned to Sergeant Durup, "Nice work," he said. "How much does one of these cost?"

"They're about a billion quid each."

Williams couldn't stop laughing. The nervous tension on their approach, having fully expected an opposed boarding finally broke out. He was not the only one. Without a shot fired they had control of the ship. "We should really check out the rest of this boat," he said.

"I never want to work with you again, Sir," said Durup, as he turned for the bulkhead. As he walked behind Wendy Jones a radar systems control panel which had been quietly overheating after the missile impact reached the point where it exploded from the operations desk. Wendy took the full force of the impact, shielding Durup from the blast.

* * *

Back at the Houses of Parliament Will had returned to the Central Lobby. "Coming through!" he screamed, "Follow me!" And with that he charged the House of Commons, with RSM John Valimaki right behind him. The rest of the assault team watched open-mouthed as the two men sprinted through the lobby, seemingly bullet-proof. They both threw smoke grenades and then opened fire at the balconies above the green leather benches, where they suspected most of the mercenaries would be based. Behind them, what was left of three assault troops came howling into the Chamber.

Nick Allen, who had made such a spirited attack on Westminster Station was the first man from Strike Team Charlie to make it into the House of Commons. He took a gunshot to the knee which severed his leg. He took cover behind a bench and shot two mercenaries before losing consciousness. Because of the speed of the attack his hiding place went un-noticed by his comrades, and Nick Allen died of catastrophic blood loss.

As the sixty-nine surviving members of the Contingency Planning Group, outnumbered and lacking the benefit of the high ground, battled their way up staircases and through the complex corridors of the building, the RSM suffering from a stoppage on his weapon pulled the ceremonial mace from its mountings and ran screaming at a Russian who took the full force of it in his face as the RSM took cover to fix the problem.

"Good work," said Will, emptying a magazine into the western balcony.

In the Palace kitchens, watching the silent CCTV feeds, Hannah didn't need lip-reading lessons to know what he said.

And then Will saw him. "I know that fucker," he said, and for the first time in his life Will threw a grenade that hit its target. The journalists' balcony took a direct hit. Mr Gilmour saw the grenade arcing towards him, as if in slow motion, and saw Will Richards, survivor of torture in Venezuela, at the hands of the men Gilmour had trained, laughing at him.

The firefights continued for another seven minutes as the men and women of the Contingency Planning Group systematically cleared the building. Many of the mercenaries surrendered; those who did not were killed. Parliament looked like a housing estate after a riot. The decadence of the building's fabric was shredded. The police team which had been captured earlier were discovered sitting cross legged on the floor with their hands in the air. The troopers who found them looked confused. "Handcuffed us with our own handcuffs," said one of them. "Schoolboy error. We've all got keys to them, we just figured we wouldn't be much use without any guns so stayed put."

When the sound of gunfire stopped, the RSM turned to Will. "Well this was an interesting day," he said.

"Wasn't it," said Will, sadly.

They had been listening to the reports over the radio – twenty eight members of the Contingency Planning Group were confirmed dead at that point. "One more has to die," said the RSM.

"I know."

The RSM nodded. Lucy Jones changed magazines and from the western balcony of the House of Commons fired a single shot between the shoulders of Major Will Richards' back. He slumped to the floor.

At the palace, Hannah clapped her hand to her mouth. "He's not dead!" she screamed, "He can't be dead!"

The CPG technicians cut the feed to the cameras and started packing up. "It happens," said a man that Hannah vaguely recognised. She was confident he had driven her at some point during this insane few days. As he left the room she noticed he had something that looked like a hearing aid in his right ear and he appeared to be talking to himself.

* * *

Admiral Dudgeon was sitting in his grace and favour flat in Mayfair watching events unfold on all the rolling news channels he could access. As usual, a large scotch was on the occasional table next to his wingbacked leather armchair. Outside his front door, Inspector Andy Marlborough of the Metropolitan Police's SO15 counter-terrorist unit turned around to his six man team, having inserted a miniature camera through the keyhole and taken a picture. It was there for all to see on the screen of the tablet he had produced from his small backpack. Using only hand signals, Marlborough beckoned forward the forced entry team, both of whom took off the door hinges with battering rams in seconds. The remainder of the team rushed in and surrounded the Admiral, weapons pointed at him.

Dudgeon was a man who took risks, but he wasn't stupid, and he knew instantly what had happened. "Game over, isn't it?" he asked.

Inspector Andy Marlborough was not slow to respond. "For you, yes. And may I add, I don't like you very much." Dudgeon's glass of whisky flew across the room as the policeman behind him kicked his chair from behind and the Admiral landed face down on the thick carpet. He was quickly restrained.

CHAPTER TWENTY SIX

Aftermath...

For the third time that night there was a BBC Newsflash. Prime Minister David Marshall was brief.

"Ladies and Gentlemen, an attempted coup has been thwarted by the magnificent efforts of our Special Forces. As I'm sure you will appreciate, I am not at liberty to comment on what they did or how they did it. Many of them died in the process of securing our freedom, and liberty, including their commander, Major William Richards, whose name is the only one which will be released by Her Majesty's Government. We are in the process of re-establishing normality. This may take us a day or two. Please bare with us as we do so, remain resolute in your confidence in the police, armed forces and government and remain assured that there is a capability in this country which will take on any adversary which seeks to undermine the will of the people of the United Kingdom. I cannot tell you what they are called, but rest assured, whilst we sleep, they are watching over us."

The broadcast cut to stock footage of the Royal Standard flying over Buckingham Palace and the sound of the National Anthem.

The Prime Minster turned to the man sat in the corner of the room. "And what about you?" he asked.

"What about me?" was the deadpan reply.

"Well, you're sort of dead, aren't you?"

"No. I'm absolutely dead," the man said as he attempted to rise from his chair, clearly struggling from wounds and the exhaustion of the previous few days. "I used to be the Milk Tray Man. Now you may call me the Last Chocolate in the Box."

"Are you taking the piss?"

"Yes Sir."

"There's a lot of glory for you in this," said the Prime Minister.

As he tried to stand Will's left knee gave way, a combination of the injuries from the glass he knelt on that night and the recurring weakness of the tendons from his time in Venezuela. "I don't give a shit," he said, "Do you guys have a bar?"

Will and the Prime Minister enjoyed a large scotch together. "I don't get why you have to be dead," he said, puzzled.

Will looked him in the eye. "People know my name now, they know my face, the whole idea of the Contingency Planning Group is now out in the open. Those arseholes we faced tonight," he paused, "well the ones that are alive are really pissed off, and they'll still be pissed off when they get out of prison, and the ones that are dead, well they've got brothers and cousins and friends who do things just like them. If I'm already dead, and I got this hugely insightful assessment from a friend of mine in the Intelligence Corps, it's less likely that people will come looking to kill me." He looked at the carpet, "Bloody clever those Int Corps guys, don't know how we'd get by without them."

When the Prime Minister had stopped chuckling he asked, "And so how did you do it? Someone showed me the footage. You got shot, and I saw your vest get holed and blood come out of you."

"Yeah, neat, isn't it?" said Will with a gleeful smile. He took his body armour off slowly, the genuine wounds he got in both arms restricting his movement. He handed it to the PM who examined it.

"Yeah, look, I was right," he said sticking his finger through the hole in the back of the vest.

"When you put that Marxist-Leninist Union championing lunatic David Johnson in front of the Intelligence and Security Committee, you made a good move Boss." Will felt he'd earned the right to be a little less formal for a bit.

Not for the first time that day David Marshall, newly restored Prime Minister of his own country looked confused. He simply raised his eyebrows.

"Think of everything was what he said to me. Anything and everything. Have you seen the latest production of Les Miserables?" he asked. Now the Prime Minister was really confused. He nodded his assent. "Well, my best friend from school is the special effects director on that, and in that scene where they're on the barricades at the end and all those French chappies die, he's the one who figured out how to make it look a bit better than a primary school play. Small explosive charge placed in the vest, little bag of red food dye – not rocket science to be honest with you."

"But I saw the CCTV footage, someone shot you, everybody still standing looks up at the balcony at the same time."

"I bet they do. That's when Lucy shot me," he said, reaching into his left pocket, "with this," he added, producing an empty case with red paint on its base. "Blank round. Lucy gave it to me as a souvenir." He yawned. "Excuse me."

The PM smiled. "Fair enough, long day, guest room's free if you want it."

Will climbed the stairs wearily and sat on the side of the bed, amused by the bullet holes that the Downing Street strike team were responsible for. He got as far as taking off his top before collapsing into the soft pillows and welcome sheets. The housekeeper was unimpressed the next morning when she discovered the bootprints and bloodstains on the expensive Egyptian cotton linen.

CHAPTER TWENTY SEVEN

One year later...

Susie Jones left the Docklands Light Railway at Limehouse after a horrible day at the department store where she worked in Oxford Street. It was the run-up to Christmas and the store had been heaving and the customers rude, as always, the ones that could speak English that was. All she wanted to do was get home, get her heels off and sit down with a glass of wine. She looked at her watch. She'd had an early shift so it was just coming up to seven. Then, without thinking, she glanced at the date. "Oh my God!" she said to herself, but out loud. She hurried down the steps and onto the street. She was out of breath when she made it to her tiny flat just off the Commercial Road. Susie almost burst the door in, threw her coat on the kitchen table, swapped her heels for flats and went straight back out. She knocked on the door opposite.

There was no immediate answer. "Hannah? Hannah it's me." Susie's voice sounded urgent.

"Alright, coming you headcase," came the call from within. Hannah opened the door, glass of wine in hand.

"I'm so sorry, if I'd realised the date I would have got back quicker. I'm so sorry." Susie looked genuinely upset.

"Muppet. I'm okay," Hannah replied, although Susie was pretty sure she'd been crying.

"Come on, let's go for a drink."

"Well get a coat on then for God's sake, it's freezing out there," Hannah said.

Susie held up a finger. "Good point." She turned like a whirlwind back to her own flat and retrieved her coat from the kitchen table. Susie had always been a bit impulsive. After they'd left the block they walked arm-in-arm to the Barley Mow, the pub by the river where Hannah had a drink with Will the first day she met him and where Susie was first introduced to him.

"You sure you're happy to go here?" Susie asked. She was, understandably, worried about the memories it could bring up.

"I've been coming here all year Susie, and it's the only pub round here with an open fire." She shrugged, and smiled. "If there's one thing you Brits do do well, it's pub fires."

"Have you been thinking about it a lot?"

"Yeah. Pretty much constantly. I'm a dates person. I don't even have a list of my family's birthdays and anniversarys. Got 'em all tucked away in here." She pointed to her head, and then laughing, added, "Probably why I got the job I did." She paused. "I took the day off today. My boss was pretty good about it. He said I didn't need to put it down as annual leave."

"Did you go back?" asked Susie, looking up at her friend.

"I did. I actually did. I didn't think I was going to but I did."

"You've never been back before have you?"

"No. No, I haven't. I didn't even know I was going to when I woke up this morning but something drew me there. I can't describe it Susie. It's weird."

It was beginning to spit with rain now. "Great, that's all we need," said Susie as she started to walk faster.

"I kind of like it," Hannah replied. She smiled again, "They say never wish your life away, but maybe it'll wash away some of the memories." She laughed, "I'm joking of course."

"What was it like? Going back I mean."

"Well," and this time Hannah smiled down at her diminutive neighbour, "they've cleaned it up pretty well." Susie laughed.

"No bullet holes then?"

"Well, I'm not kidding, but they've actually left some on purpose. Just to remind everyone I suppose. You know that door that they hit with the stick when they open Parliament?"

"You mean 'Black Rod'?" Susie offered.

Hannah laughed again. "Yeah, sorry, I keep forgetting the name which is amazing because I think it's the funniest thing ever."

"What's funny about 'Black Rod'?"

Hannah looked incredulous. "Are you serious? Honey, you need to watch more late night television."

Susie jabbed her in the ribs. "Shush. Anyway, what about Black Rod?"

"Well the door's almost smashed in where they hit it. They don't paint it, they don't varnish it. It's years and years of history. And I think they're doing the same with the bullet holes. Just to make sure no-one forgets."

"How'd you get in? I thought you had to book months ahead."

Hannah threw her head back and swallowed hard. She turned to Susie, her eyes welling up. "Well they didn't last time!" They both laughed. "No, seriously though, I was just standing outside looking up at Big Ben and remembering. I was just with all the other tourists and everyone else and this guy came up to me. It was kind of weird really, but I've kind of gotten use to that after everything that happened. He was a well-dressed guy in a suit and he just lightly put his hand on my shoulder, you know, not in a scary way, and he said, "Ma'am, I think I know who you are. Would you like to go inside?" I just stared at him. Then he put his hand in his pocket and he pulled out a, like a leather wallet thing, and it..."

They were at the door of the pub. Hannah stopped talking and they walked to the bar. Susie ordered a bottle of, for her, a very expensive red wine. As Hannah went for her purse Susie stopped her. "No. My treat. You've earned it. Anyway, I want to know more about this mysterious man and his wallet."

Hannah spotted an empty table close enough to the fire to enjoy it but not so close that they would feel uncomfortably hot. "Let's go there." As they walked across Susie remarked on the slightly raised small stage by the window. It being a Friday, it was set up for live music. The members of the band were doing the final checks to their amps and instruments. It was a tiny stage for a five piece band.

"Ace. Music."

"Well done Einstein." Hannah poured them both a glass of wine. Surprisingly, neither of them recognised the keyboard player.

"So, anyway, wallet man..?" Susie asked.

"Yeah, wallet man. Now this is gonna sound kind of weird, and, like all the other stuff Susie, you can't tell anyone." Hannah looked her straight in the eye.

"You're doing your serious face again. I've told you about that. Have I ever, ever, even squeaked about this stuff?" she asked, with a slightly hurt look.

"No, you haven't." Hannah touched Susie's knee. "Sorry, but you know, it's just the whole thing was so...so...so," Hannah was stumbling for the words.

"Weird?" Susie prompted.

Hannah laughed as she spoke. "Yeah, weird, and scary and ridiculous." She sighed. "God, I don't know. None of it made any sense and he told me never to talk about it. And I trusted him on that. I don't think it's a good idea to talk about it really."

"Yeah, I get that, but I WANT TO KNOW ABOUT WALLET-MAN!" Susie asked, raising her voice more than she intended to and bouncing up and down in her chair. Hannah looked around warily.

"Okay, so this guy's come up to me and asked if I want to go inside, and while I was looking at him, he just pulled out this wallet thing with an insignia of an owl with a Roman sword over it."

Susie frowned. "What the hell is that? That's just weirdsville central."

"It gets weirder," Hannah replied. "Underneath there was a scroll, you know like British heraldic stuff? It just said 'Contingency', and under that was another scroll, and I paid close attention to that. One of the things about my job is that I look at words every day and I have to make sure they're right or people get very, very upset. So I know I remembered this right. 'Semper Vigilantes, Semper Audiendo'. That's what it said."

Susie frowned again. "'H', I'm completely lost. I just sell perfume. What the hell does that mean?"

Hannah looked serious, drank her wine and looked out of the window. "I had no idea Susie. This guy just took me through one of the doors, gave me a pass to hang around my neck and said I could go wherever I wanted. He never told me his name, he wasn't asked for ID by the policemen at the barrier. We just walked straight in. He didn't leave me, he was always about six feet from me but he just let me wander around. Anyway, when I got home I looked it up."

"And?" Susie leaned forward in anticipation.

Hannah looked resigned. "'Always watching. Always listening.' Says it all really."

"What was it like when you got inside?"

"I've just told you. It was weird."

"And you didn't ask him who he was or what was going on?" Susie was incredulous.

"No, I didn't. I suppose I was in a kind of shock. A lot weirder has happened that I didn't ask about." Then they were interrupted.

The woman at the keyboard tapped her microphone and the distinctive sound of hand on mic filled the pub. Most people stopped their conversations or at least lowered them. "Good evening everyone. I'm Lucy Milton and these are, as they hate to be called, the Miltonette's." Lucy raised her arm in the direction of the band.

A round of applause went up in the pub. Susie turned to Hannah. "Isn't she..?"

"God, yes!"

"We haven't been back for a very long time. A very long time. So hopefully we can make some new friends as well as saying hello to some old ones. We'll be trying some new stuff as well as the old stuff. Hope you have a great night!"

Susie looked across at Hannah. "Bloody hell. You alright?"

"Yes honey, fine."

"This one's been specially requested," said Lucy. She counted the band in and they started with a cover of Sam and Dave's 'You Don't Know What You Mean to Me'. Hannah looked up to the ceiling and then down at the floor. She turned to Susie.

"They have got to be kidding. This can't be happening!" she said, tears in her eyes, but still smiling at her friend.

"They aren't and it is honey." Susie put her arm around Hannah as she leant her head back and tried to stop the tears.

"Dear God, will it ever end?"

The band had started with a flourish and now Lucy was singing with a belting voice, "Baby don't you worry, about your man. He'll be coming home just as soon as he can."

"Oh for the love of... Today, of all days, they have to play that?" Hannah said, turning to her friend with tears quietly streaming down her face, half laughing, half choking.

"Do you want to go home 'H'? We can put a film on." Susie asked.

Hannah reached into her pocket and pulled out a tissue. "No. I am not going to be defined by all that stuff forever. No. It's Friday night. It's nearly Christmas. He won, that's why we get to be able to do this. I will not be a miserable asshole."

Lucy was really getting into the opening number now. "You don't know, what you mean to me," she was ricocheting off the ceiling.

Hannah turned. "Actually, I am going to be a miserable asshole. Hold me." Susie put her arms around her friend as she sobbed so frantically that she shook.

* * *

Half an hour earlier...

"This way boss," came the instruction. The man dressed in black trousers, black jumper, black jacket and a black overcoat stepped into the black car that was parked in the secure underground carpark just off Holland Park.

"We got confirmation Billy?" asked the passenger.

"Not yet boss. Should be just a couple of minutes though." The driver had an east-end accent and looked to be in his sixties. "Nice pub this one. At least it used to be. Not been down there for a couple of years."

"You know the roads then?" came the question.

"Course I bloody do boss."

"Excellent." The 'Boss' didn't say another word for the remainder of the journey.

* * *

Lucy was still singing her heart out, and Hannah thought it was time to give Susie a break. "You'll have to wash that now," Hannah said as she pointlessly attempted to wipe tears off the shoulder of Susie's cardigan.

"I think you've pretty much washed it already," she laughed.

"Oh God. What a mess I am," Hannah volunteered.

"I think you're doing pretty well, considering," said Susie. "Do you miss him?"

"This'll sound odd but I don't know. I only actually knew him for a few days. But I think about him all the time. Almost constantly."

Hannah looked up, and as she did so she saw two black Audis drive past the window. She shook her head. "Can't be," she said out loud, without realising.

"Can't be what?" asked Susie.

"Nothing. I'm imagining things."

Both cars turned into the carpark, reversing into adjacent spaces. One had two occupants and the other a single driver. There were two entrances to the Barley Mow, one on the roadside and one by the river. The pair walked in by the riverside entrance, the single man through the main door.

Perhaps more alert than she normally would have been by what she'd seen out the window, Hannah noticed their entrance. "Something's not right here," she whispered to Susie.

"What?"

"Something's not right. I learnt enough from Will to know that. We should go." As she was collecting her things one of the men who'd come in the back door paused as he walked past their table. He turned and smiled at her.

"Good evening Ms Roberts," he said. It was the same man who had escorted her into the Houses of Parliament.

"Who the hell are you?" asked Hannah. She had her hand on the wine bottle and was ready to smash it over his head if she needed to.

"I'm a friend Hannah. Actually, I'm a friend of a friend. Actually, we're all friends. You remember Duncan?" he asked, gently indicating a man standing at the bar. Hannah looked across the room and saw someone she recognised. "You will have known him as Paul. Paul is still the best driver in the team."

Hannah gasped. Paul turned his head from his stool at the bar and raised an eyebrow. He appeared to be engrossed in the

Evening Standard crossword and was the driver of the second car.

Hannah put a restraining hand on Susie's wrist because she knew Susie was about to get cross.

"Would you care to explain what is going on?" she asked. "Are you about to take me somewhere?"

The man she'd met earlier that day outside the Houses of Parliament looked grave. "On the contrary Ms Roberts, I'm about to show you something. But you must never talk of it again. Never." He turned to Susie. "And you Ms Jones? We don't have much time. Would you like to work for a large and powerful organisation?"

"I already do," said Susie, as confidently as she could muster. She was absolutely terrified and hoped that this strange man couldn't see her knees shaking. Hannah and Susie were gripping each other's hands now.

"One like this..?" The man reached into his pocket and pulled out a small wallet. He opened it. All Susie could see were the words, 'Semper Vigilantes, Semper Audiendo'. He turned to Hannah, "Our business cards have got a bit more sophisticated since the first one you saw." Hannah remembered back to the first time she met Will in the lobby of the Daily Herald.

Susie looked across at Hannah. "Jesus!" was all she could say. She looked up at the man. "What the bloody hell have I done?" she asked.

"We understand you can keep secrets," was the only answer she got. The man walked to the bar, got himself a drink and sat down facing the band. There were now three of them within eight or nine feet of Susie and Hannah.

Susie turned to her friend. "I think we should go. This is nuts."

"I agree," Hannah replied, and then she saw another black Audi drive past the window. "Oh Christ, this is not happening by accident." One of the new arrivals looked like he was talking to himself. "Oh God, he's talking to someone," Hannah said.

The band finished their song and everyone left the tiny stage except for Lucy. The pub erupted in applause. "Now the last one was a special request," she smouldered into the mic. "This one is a very special request."

As the last Audi pulled into the carpark the driver hit his send button and said, "Roger that. Clear to go. We're complete at Red Five. The Milk Tray Man is inbound."

The passenger opened the car door. "Thanks man," he said.

"Legendary pleasure," replied the driver. "I can't ever tell anyone about this can I?"

"You never told anyone about Churchill..."

"No I did not. But then you're not a fat man with a cigar wearing your bathrobe."

"That is true. And I'm not him. It's not about me though, is it?"

"It most certainly isn't Boss." Billy paused. "Holding pattern?"

"Yes please Billy." The passenger closed the door and Billy reversed out of the car park.

Upstairs in the pub Lucy was adjusting the volume on her amp and microphone. There was a horrible amount of feedback. "Sorry. Sorry!" she said as it ripped through the pub. She corrected it and carried on. "Right then, like I said, very special request."

Hannah was wide-eyed and flicking her head around trying to figure out what was going on. "There's at least three of them," she said.

"How do you know?" Susie asked.

"When you know what to look for it's obvious. Well, we already know two of them don't we? And then there's the guy by the window pretending to read the paper. Three single blokes, Friday night, drinks hardly touched, all wearing jackets inside. Guess what's under them?" she asked.

Lucy started to play. It was a gentle arpeggio. The pub hushed to almost silence.

"I heard that you're settled down." Her voice was captivating. Hannah was feeling frantic but trying to look as composed as possible. While she was looking across at the stage she didn't see the door from the street open and a man dressed in black take a seat at the L-shaped bar. He quietly ordered a drink.

"Old friend, why are you so shy," Lucy sang, "Ain't like you to hold back or hide from the light..."

Hannah's gaze moved across to the bar. She grabbed Susie's hand and nearly broke her wrist.

"What's wrong!" Susie gasped.

"I hate to turn up out of the blue uninvited, but I couldn't stay away I couldn't fight it." Everyone except Hannah and Susie was watching Lucy and listening in amazement at how beautifully she was singing.

Susie clocked the man at the bar. "Jesus Christ!" she whispered and moved as if she were about to get up. The man at the end of the bar shook his head almost imperceptibly – a sign to stay where they were. Hannah's controlling hand held Susie back in her seat.

"I had hoped you'd see my face and that you'd be reminded," continued Lucy, "that for me, it isn't over".

"I can't believe he's alive," Hannah said. "I just don't believe it." She was weeping silently.

Will and Hannah stared at each other. Will smiled, gently, and raised his glass just a little, nodding his head.

"You know, how the time flies, only yesterday was the time of our lives..."

Their gaze didn't break for the whole of the song. Lucy finished to rapturous applause. "Thank you very much!" she shouted. "It's someone else's turn now. Where's Tom?"

"Over here," came a shout from the corner of the pub. A pale young man stepped up to the stage with an acoustic guitar. "Evening everybody." There was a muted response. No-one knew who Tom was and pretty much everyone knew who Lucy was, and she was attractive and blonde and he wasn't. "My name's Tom," he started, "and, much like the last tune you heard, this song's about a former relationship. It's called 'Love is Shit'". Susie laughed, as did most of the other punters, but Hannah hadn't heard a word of it.

Lucy walked past the table that Hannah and Susie were sitting at and turned. "Hope you enjoyed that," she said. "He thought it was the most appropriate song he could think of."

Hannah was wary. "Sorry. Who did?" she asked, trying to appear nonchalant.

"My brother. You know, the dead one," Lucy smiled.

The three men she'd identified earlier all appeared to start talking to themselves again, and then got up to leave. Will gave Hannah one last smile. He was sitting in exactly the same place he had been on the first day she met him. He stood up to go. "No," she mouthed. He turned and walked out the door where Billy was waiting for him.

"What? Jesus, that's it!" Susie said. "Come on, let's go. We can find him," Susie pleaded.

Hannah turned to her friend, smiling now, and took her hand again. "No we couldn't. That's not the way it works. It works the other way round."

EPILOGUE

People…

Colonel Charlie York divorced his wife of twenty eight years and bought a smallholding in the Shetland Isles. His three children do not visit him, and that doesn't bother him. He never had a high opinion of them. Perhaps if he had taken more of an interest in their lives they would have achieved what he considered to be achievements and they would all have had a greater affection for each other – but that was not the case. Mrs York died in a car accident shortly after they separated.

* * *

Billy continues to use the underground Whitehall corridors to move from one Government department to the other. He retires next year. He remains one of the best Close Protection drivers for the British Government, and its associated agencies. Billy's proudest moment was when his daughter graduated from Oxford University with a 2:1 in Classics. To this day he is embarrassed that his daughter can quote from, and he cannot pronounce their names, Sophocles, Aeschylus and Aristotle.

* * *

Clement continues in his work as a security guard at the Department of Health. Will Richards was one of the few people who ever showed him kindness and respect. On a Friday night, Clement's wife, Virginia, lets him go to the pub and play dominoes with his friends. He never speaks of Will, but sometimes he looks up at the television news in the pub, which he hates, but sees something, and wonders if Will had anything to do with it. Clement thinks that Will Richards is genuinely immortal.

* * *

Anne Tremaine continues to run MI5. She retains an incisive mind and is unafraid to out-stare the British Director of Special Forces. She has been awarded the title of Commander of the British Empire following recent events. At the age of 56, she remains the fastest swimmer in the Tooting Bec Lido.

* * *

Yu-jin Wong, receptionist at the Chinese Embassy and employee of Chinese State Intelligence, killed herself after learning that the Belgian man she thought was in love with her was homosexual and in involved in a relationship with a Taiwanese government minister. The minister has never been identified.

* * *

"Franco's Sandwich Bar" in Wapping continues to thrive. Franco and his beautiful young wife Victoria work all hours. The original caravan has grown to a purpose built truck, dispensing hot and cold food at all hours.

* * *

Jan, the receptionist at the Daily Herald has had her job title changed to 'Office Manager'. She thinks this is ridiculous because she sits in the same chair and does the same job she always did. She is now six months pregnant and following the ultrasound scan of her baby which confirmed he was a boy has decided to call him William.

* * *

Andrew Telfer, owner of The Daily Herald and reliable conduit for government security and intelligence related information received a knighthood, and was appointed to the House of Lords six months later. After selling his interests in the media he retired to Buckinghamshire and became fascinated by croquet, becoming Secretary of the Croquet Association. He took on this role not so much because of his love of the sport, but because the people he met gave him considerable cause for amusement.

* * *

Susie Jones, Hannah's neighbour, was happy to leave her job in sales in Oxford Street. "Am I going to be a spy?" was the first thing she said when she got off the train in Portsmouth. She was put in the back of a Ford Transit Van, hooded and handcuffed and spent the next five hours on a trip to North Wales. She was smiling when they took the hood off. "Cool," she said, grinning. The interrogator left the room immediately. "I can't deal with that," he said to his boss in the corridor.

"What's the problem?" he asked.

"She makes me want to smile."

The boss walked into the holding cell. "Hi!" said Susie, "what's your name?" The boss walked straight back out of the room.

"Give me a war criminal any day. She's too adorable to be nasty to," he said.

Susie achieved the highest possible range score under time pressure using a 9mm handgun and completed a week-long escape and evasion course only thirteen minutes behind the male record holder. Despite official advice, Susie opened a Facebook account under the name "Wonderwoman".

* * *

Miranda Stevens, the woman who killed so many in the British Museum, was cremated. The British government paid for the service which was attended only by the President of the Mental Health Foundation.

* * *

Dimitry is currently posted in New York, working with the UN. His wife is extremely happy, which makes Dimitry happy too. They have watched the Broadway production of Les Miserables seven times. Dimitry's wife doesn't know it but he has been approached by the CIA and will defect next month. Their lives will never be the same again – Dimitry will be known as David and his wife Natascha will change her name to Natalie. They will never watch another Broadway show. Dimitry and Will meet in a bar in Ohio some years later, not by coincidence, but that is another story.

* * *

Paula, the charming and discreet Spanish manageress of the bar at the Landmark hotel continues to be charming and discreet. "Is he a spy?" she asked, pointing directly at Will's guest on his last visit. Upon hearing that he was, Paula asked, "Well then we should put you on the spy table".

* * *

Susan Smith retired from the CIA with a plaque and a framed certificate thanking her for her service. She lives alone but does not consider herself to be lonely. There are three photographs on her mantelpiece. In the centre is a framed photograph of her and her late husband, laughing while they tried to put up a tent at a literary festival in Canada shortly after they were married. To the left is Sarah's graduation picture. To the right is a picture of Sarah and Will, nothing but desert behind them and hope in their eyes. Susan cannot look at it without crying, which is why she puts it in a drawer whenever she has visitors.

* * *

Margret retired from the Naval Office of the Ministry of Defence as planned, joined shortly afterwards by her husband, the once manager of the tea rooms at Fortnum and Mason. They moved to Dorset, and just under a year later, primarily as a result of boredom, opened a tea-shop in Shaftesbury. Margret has become an accomplished baker.

* * *

Richard and Emma married; she died as a result of complications during childbirth. Richard left the Royal Navy and his daughter, who he named Emma, will have a flourishing career as a concert pianist.

* * *

TWO YEARS LATER

Caroline and Alan looked confused.

"You look confused," said Will.

Caroline looked at her fellow student and he nodded, so she went first. "I am confused Professor Richards. If Milton's God is omniscient and omnipotent, surely he would have known that Satan was going to tempt and seduce Eve to the Tree of Knowledge, and, armed with that knowledge, could have stopped it."

Caroline, like many of the students at Cambridge, was naive and earnest. Having been teaching for only a year, Will still struggled with the complexity of some of the most simple questions his students asked him. And he had originally thought retirement from his previous way of life would make things easier. He sighed, heavily, and stood up. "Right," he said, "it is far too nice a day to be stuck in these stuffy rooms." The

248

summer sun was shining through the leaded windows and the flower beds in the courtyard were dotted with colour. "Outside I think. And refreshments are in order." Will opened the small fridge in the corner of his rooms and took out a bottle of Mosel Riesling. "Alan, grab some glasses," he said, pointing at some open shelves by the window.

Will led the way down the spiralled stone staircase and stepped over the chains guarding the grass covered courtyard in the middle of the chapel cloisters. Caroline and Alan hesitated. The signs instructing all visitors and students to keep off the grass were abundant, and the college porters were known to enforce the regulations rigidly.

Will turned. "Stop buggering about will you? I am not such a tramp as to drink this from the bottle, so I will be needing a glass Alan."

Alan looked at Caroline, who gave him a "what's to lose" expression, and the two of them stepped over the chains and joined Will in the centre of the cloister courtyard.

"Anyone got the point yet?" Will asked, as he pulled a corkscrew from his pocket and started to open the bottle. Caroline and Alan looked confused again. "You two look confused again," he said, pouring the wine.

Caroline nodded. "Yep. Well I am, anyway."

"Me too," agreed Alan.

"Think about it. What have you just done?" There was a silence. Will decided to help his students. "You," he said with emphasis, "have just broken the rules." Will pointed at the multilingual signs stuck in the flower beds on all four sides of the cloisters. "You have broken the rules because I told you to. You know that you shouldn't be here but you have chosen to do so through your own free will. You also know that we are covered on CCTV and that there will be a college porter along any minute now. It is likely that we will be remonstrated with, particularly as we are drinking this rather fine Riesling which Professor Sternekrieg brought me after his last trip back home. I have no time for Anthropology but Sternekrieg, like all good Germans, really does know his wine."

Alan and Caroline were used to Will's occasional eccentricities, but this was new territory. Will was banking on one of the porters to make his point for him. Sure enough, one of them arrived seconds later, barking at them to get off the grass. Will stood up.

"Ah, Mr Davis, how good to see you, would you care to join us?" he asked.

The porter looked a little stunned. "Professor Richards, Sir," he stammered, "that area's off limits. I'm afraid you can't be there."

"Don't be afraid Mr Davis, nothing to be afraid of at all, and I am here. So that's that really."

Porter Davis was beginning to turn red. "Professor Richards!" he exclaimed.

Will turned to his two students. "Getting the point yet?" he asked. Alan and Caroline were clearly uncomfortable. "Right then, I shall explain," he said, sitting back down on the grass, with his back to the college porter. "Alan, make sure he doesn't have a heart attack will you?"

Porter Davis was in a psychological conundrum as to whether he should step over the chain and get close and personal with the Professor, or whether that might constitute breaking College Constitution. He decided to stand still for the moment.

"Eve took fruit from the Tree of Knowledge after being persuaded to do so by Satan, disguised as a serpent. Adam then followed her example. I, disguised as a College Professor," he smiled, "persuaded you to walk onto this grass in the middle of the cloisters, something which is forbidden by the college. You," he pointed at Caroline, "persuaded Alan to follow you."

Alan and Caroline exchanged looks again.

"You asked me about an omniscient and omnipotent God," said Will. "Well you know that the college has CCTV cameras everywhere, and that they're watched in the porters' lodge. You also know that they are the college police. They can see everything, and they enforce the rules. Omniscient? Omnipotent? Not quite. But I bet you they expect students to break the rules, and they have the ability to see when that's happening." Will paused for effect. "Didn't stop us though did it?"

Alan and Caroline were mentally digesting this, and Porter Davis was still trying to figure out what to do next, when the sound of a low flying helicopter prevented anyone from talking. Will recognised the sound of the Agusta 109 immediately. He held his hand to his face. "Bollocks."

He ushered Alan and Caroline off the courtyard, much to Porter Davis's relief. "What's going on?" asked Caroline.

"Air Taxi," said Will, "and this is the runway". The helicopter came down in the middle of the cloisters and a man dressed from head to toe in black ran towards Will. He smiled as they shook hands.

"We need your help Sir."

"Do you now? And I'm not 'Sir' anymore. I'm retired."

"Got a bit of a problem in Cyprus."

"I suggest you fix it then."

"We'd love to Sir, but the general feeling was that you might want to be involved."

"Why?"

"Rebecca Taylor is asking for you."

Half the college had descended on the cloisters after hearing the helicopter land, and so had the Dean. Will turned to him and shrugged his shoulders. "I have to leave," was all he could say.

"We knew this was likely," said the Dean.

"Yes we did."

"I'll keep your rooms for you." The two men shook hands. "And for God's sake don't get killed again this time. You nearly gave your mother a heart attack."

"Thanks Dad."

Porter Davis was very confused. Alan and Caroline were struggling with the concepts of free will and determinism and most of the rest of the college undergraduates were taking photographs of the helicopter with their phones.

Will walked towards the helicopter, his new friend by his side. "So, what's gone wrong in Cyprus?" he asked.

"Long story."

"Shit. I hate those."

Acknowledgements

Many people have been extremely supportive during the writing of this book - they are too numerous to mention but they know who they are. However, some deserve special distinction - somewhat predictably, my family, and in particular my brother for his IT skills.

There was a British Army Officer I will not name who served with an elite infantry unit and who provided vital technical advice on the scenes involving the attack on the Houses of Parliament. For any reader who finds gaping holes in the overall strategy and tactics, it's all his fault.

To the staff and regulars of the Cock and Rabbit Inn, my thanks for your encouragement and constant badgering. This pub served as a refuge and thinktank. I cannot imagine where I could find a more eclectic group of people in such a small village. Italians, Danes, Americans, architects, world famous musicians, actors, artists, bounders, cads and one or two people so stupid they actually become interesting. It was here that I first heard the phrase, "Charlie Big Potatoes". It still amuses me.

Despite the disclaimer, there is a gorgeous Spanish manager of a hotel bar in central London. She has been a good friend. And yes, there actually is a spy table.

It would also be wrong not to recognise the men and women of the Intelligence and Security Agencies, Special Forces and other various military and civilian organisations which are referred to in this book. It is a work of fiction, but it is written with the deepest respect.

Finally, and there is a specific reason for this book's enigmatic dedication, you may be gone, but you will never be forgotten. Eleven and three quarters. And a dot.